WARRIORS

A WARRIOR'S SPIRIT

WARRIORS

NOVELLA COLLECTIONS

The Untold Stories

Tales from the Clans

Shadows of the Clans

Legends of the Clans

Path of a Warrior

A WARRIOR'S SPIRIT

INCLUDES

Pebbleshine's Kits

Tree's Roots

Mothwing's Secret

ERIN HUNTER

HARPER

An Imprint of HarperCollins*Publishers*

A Warrior's Spirit
Pebbleshine's Kits, Tree's Roots, Mothwing's Secret

Series created by Working Partners Limited

For information address HarperCollins Children's Books, a division of HarperCollins Publishers,, 195 Broadway, New York, NY 10007.
www.harpercollinschildrens.com

Library of Congress Control Number: 2019026612
ISBN 978-0-06-285741-5

Typography by Hilary Zarycky
22 PC/BRR 10 9 8 7 6
❖
First Edition

CONTENTS

WARRIORS

PEBBLESHINE'S KITS

Special thanks to Cherith Baldry

ALLEGIANCES

SKYCLAN

LEADER	**LEAFSTAR**—brown-and-cream tabby she-cat with amber eyes
DEPUTY	**WASPWHISKER**—gray-and-white tom
MEDICINE CATS	**ECHOSONG**—silver-gray tabby she-cat with green eyes **APPRENTICE, FIDGETPAW** (black-and-white tom)
WARRIORS	(toms and she-cats without kits) **SPARROWPELT**—dark brown tabby tom **HAWKWING**—dark gray tom **APPRENTICE, CURLYPAW** (long-haired gray she-cat) **MACGYVER**—black-and-white tom **BLOSSOMHEART**—ginger-and-white she-cat **BIRDWING**—black she-cat **TINYCLOUD**—small white she-cat **BELLALEAF**—pale orange she-cat with green eyes **SAGENOSE**—pale gray tom **RILEYPOOL**—pale gray tabby tom with dark gray stripes and blue eyes **RABBITLEAP**—brown tom **PARSLEYSEED**—dark brown tabby tom **FIREFERN**—ginger she-cat **HARRYBROOK**—gray tom

QUEENS (she-cats expecting or nursing kits)

PEBBLESHINE—brown-speckled white she-cat

PLUMWILLOW—dark gray she-cat

ELDERS (former warriors and queens, now retired)

CLOVERTAIL—light brown she-cat with white belly and legs

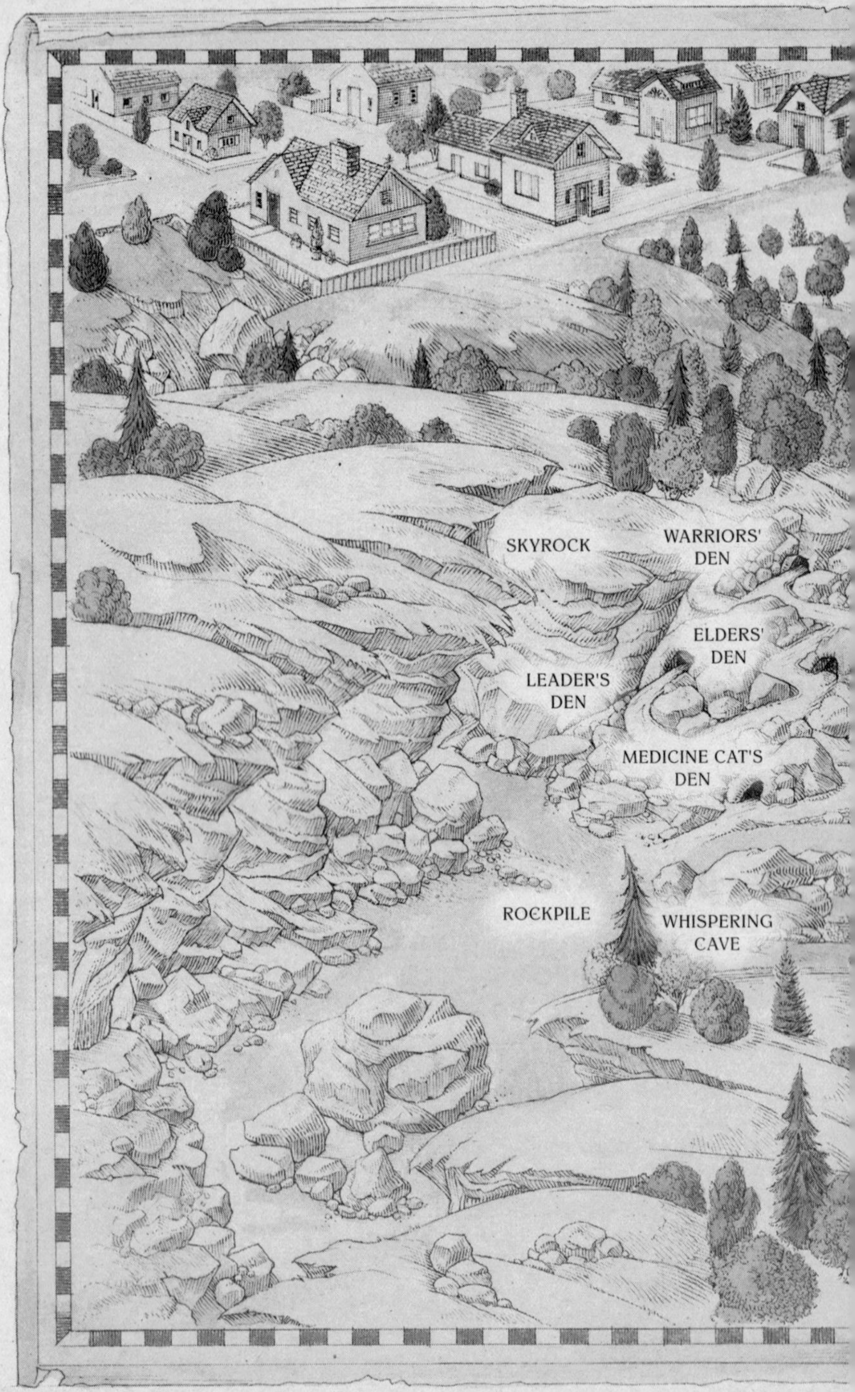

SKYROCK

WARRIORS' DEN

ELDERS' DEN

LEADER'S DEN

MEDICINE CAT'S DEN

ROCKPILE

WHISPERING CAVE

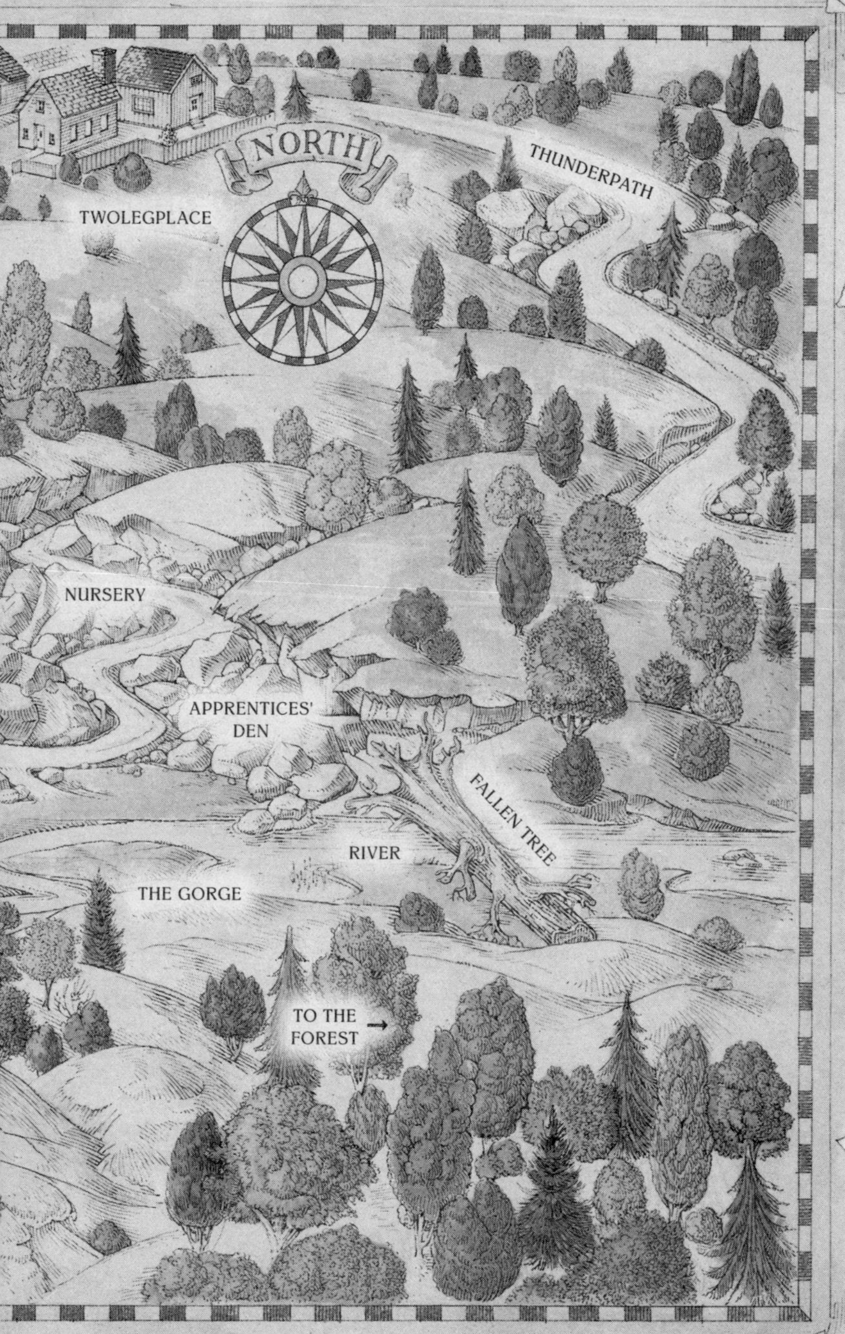
NORTH
TWOLEGPLACE
THUNDERPATH
NURSERY
APPRENTICES' DEN
FALLEN TREE
RIVER
THE GORGE
TO THE FOREST →

ST. ANDREW'S ROAD
BLOFIELD
WAREHOUSE
[disused]
DEEPSANDS
GORGE

NORTH

SOUTH BLOFIELD ROAD

BLOFIELD HEATH

HIGH DENE
WOODS

WARNING, UNSTABLE
CLIFFS IN THIS AREA

DEEPSANDS
POOL

RIVER CHELL

CHAPTER 1

Thorns raked Pebbleshine's back as she pushed through the line of bushes, but the ache of hunger in her belly drove her forward until she emerged on the other side. It had been nearly two moons since SkyClan had left their home at the gorge, and all the warriors were hungry and tired. Pebbleshine felt even more so than the others, since she was heavy with kits. She knew that her Clanmates on the other side of the bushes were nearly ready to give up the hunt. Gazing downward, she froze in shock, digging her claws into the earth.

In front of her lay a wide stretch of ground, covered with the same hard, black stuff as a Thunderpath. Several Twoleg monsters were crouched there, and beyond them rose the gray walls of a Twoleg den. Through a gap in the wall, a narrow Thunderpath led away into the distance.

Pebbleshine began easing herself back into the shelter of the bushes. All her instincts were warning her to get out of sight before the monsters noticed her. But before she had moved more than a couple of paw steps, she became aware of a delicious scent drifting between her jaws. She halted, tasting the air to pinpoint where the smell was coming from. Her eyes widened in surprise as she realized it was rising from one of the Twoleg monsters.

It's prey! There's prey trapped on the back of that monster. Imagine what we could bring back to our Clanmates!

Pebbleshine could see that none of the huge creatures was moving. Maybe they were all asleep. Her heart began beating faster at the thought of the risk she and her Clanmates would have to take, to steal prey out of the very jaws of a monster. Then her belly growled, reminding her of how hungry she was. How long had it been since she and the other cats of SkyClan had been full-fed?

"Let's take our chance!" she muttered to herself.

Pebbleshine let the Clan deputy, Waspwhisker, take the lead as they ventured into the open to investigate the prey-smelling monster. Her mate, Hawkwing, padded along at her side, while Curlypaw and Blossomheart, the remaining members of the patrol, brought up the rear.

As she and her Clanmates drew closer, Pebbleshine began to hear clucking noises coming from the back of the monster, from inside shiny boxes that looked like weird nests.

"There are birds in there!" Hawkwing exclaimed.

"And they're trapped," Pebbleshine added. "They must be some kind of Twoleg prey."

Waspwhisker nodded. "That's exactly what they are. They're called chickens. Some Twolegs near the gorge used to keep them."

Pebbleshine stared up at the shiny nests, close enough now

to see the mass of feathers pressed against the sides, and a few heads poking out with sharp beaks and beady eyes. The tempting smell was even stronger here, and hunger sliced through her belly like a badger's claws.

Pebbleshine twitched her ears impatiently as Hawkwing and Waspwhisker started to debate whether the risk was worth taking. "You know," Pebbleshine meowed, glancing warily around, "the monster is asleep, and there aren't any Twolegs around. Why don't we . . ." She turned her gaze back to the deputy, silently pleading for him to see it her way. *We can do this. I know we can!*

Finally, Waspwhisker nodded. "Let's go for it. Hawkwing, you and Curlypaw keep watch. The rest of you, follow me."

"I can climb up, too," Hawkwing meowed.

"No, I can tell your leg is hurting," Waspwhisker responded. "You're more use here on the ground."

Pebbleshine glanced back at her mate with sympathy. She knew he was frustrated by the lingering effects of the leg injury he'd suffered a moon before, falling out of a tree while hunting a squirrel. Hawkwing looked pointedly at her expanding belly.

"Then Pebbleshine should stay here, too," Hawkwing put in.

"Yes, Pebbleshine, you have to be careful," Blossomheart agreed. Waspwhisker nodded.

Pebbleshine glared at her Clanmates with rising exasperation. She knew they were concerned for her because she was carrying Hawkwing's kits, but they didn't have to treat her as though she were ill. "I'm not big enough yet for it to make any difference," she protested, twitching the tip of her tail. "I can still run just as fast as the rest of you. And it was *my* idea."

Waspwhisker narrowed his eyes at her, then relaxed with a sigh. "Okay. Let's just get on with it before we all die of starvation."

Before she approached the monster, Pebbleshine paused, seeing Hawkwing's worried look, and brushed her tail along his side. Then, alongside Waspwhisker and Blossomheart, she clambered up onto the back of the monster, startled by the unfamiliar sensation of her claws scraping against its hard pelt.

They reached a ledge atop the rear of the monster where they could look down and see the countless tiny dens filled with birds. All three cats leaped down from the monster's back, halted, and stared. *There are so many of these weird nests!* Pebbleshine thought. *And there's a chicken in each of them.* She called down excitedly to Hawkwing and Curlypaw, letting them know what she was seeing.

As Waspwhisker and Blossomheart advanced, the clucking of the chickens rose to panic-stricken squawks. Her hunting instincts kicking in, Pebbleshine followed her Clanmates, prowling toward their nests. Pebbleshine swiped through one of the holes in the shiny lattice, trying to hook a chicken with her claws, but the bird flapped its wings furiously, and she couldn't get a grip. Waspwhisker and Blossomheart were having trouble, too: Blossomheart snatched her paw back with a hiss of frustration as her chicken stabbed at her with its blunt beak, while Waspwhisker only managed to snatch a pawful of feathers.

Water flooded Pebbleshine's mouth as the delicious prey-scent wreathed around her. It was maddening to be so close to the prey they needed so desperately, yet be unable to make a kill.

And even if we do manage to catch one of the stupid creatures, there's no way we can drag it out through these tiny holes, Pebbleshine realized. Doubt flickered through her mind as she wondered if she had been wrong to suggest this patrol in the first place. Determinedly, she thrust it away. *There must be a way to get the nests open.*

Drawing back a pace, Pebbleshine studied the interwoven tendrils that made up the nest. She and her Clanmates wove branches and vines together to make dens all the time, but these tendrils were shiny, hard, and evenly spaced, and they didn't bend to her touch. She tried biting them, but that only hurt her teeth. *What am I supposed to do here?* she wondered. *Surely the Twolegs have a way to open these.* For a few heartbeats she was completely bewildered. Then she noticed a kind of shiny twig that rested in a curly frond at one corner of the nest.

She batted it with her paw and it moved slightly. Pushing it gently from one side, she made it move even more, and suddenly Pebbleshine understood how it was supposed to work. *If I can push that end down,* she thought, *the other end should move up, and the whole side should swing open.*

She slammed down one paw on the twig, but it was stiff and didn't move. Hissing furiously through her teeth, Pebbleshine pressed down even harder, using all her strength. "Move, for

StarClan's sake!" she muttered.

She was so focused on her task that she was only vaguely aware of yowling coming from Hawkwing and Curlypaw, who were keeping watch on the ground below. Then she heard Waspwhisker's voice. "Fox dung!"

Pebbleshine glanced over her shoulder to see Waspwhisker and Blossomheart with their forepaws resting on the ledge they'd jumped down from.

"The Twoleg!" Waspwhisker exclaimed. "Come on!"

He and Blossomheart scrabbled up the wall with their hind paws, stood poised for a heartbeat on the top, then disappeared. "Come *on*, Pebbleshine!" Waspwhisker yowled as he jumped.

"I'm coming!" Pebbleshine responded, but instead of following her Clanmates, she turned back to the nest. *I've almost got it. . . .*

Once again she pushed down on the twig, and this time it gave way, flicking up and out of the curly frond that held it. The side of the nest swung out, just as Pebbleshine had imagined it would. "Yes!" she meowed.

Then the chicken turned to her, its beady eyes mad with fear, and she realized that opening the nest might have been the easy part. This was unfamiliar prey. She crouched and hissed at the creature before diving inside and grabbing at the chicken with teeth and claws.

At the same moment, she heard Hawkwing's voice. "Where's Pebbleshine?"

"I'm still here!" she called back, letting go of a mouthful of feathers to make herself heard. "I've managed to open one of the nests. I've got a chicken!"

"Then get down here, fast!" Hawkwing yowled.

Pebbleshine tried to drag her prey to the side of the platform, but the chicken, squawking frantically, was flailing at her with its wings and swiping at her with taloned feet. It was almost as big as her, and its feathers were so thick and soft they almost choked her. Bits of red flesh sprouted from the top of its head and dangled under its chin; even while she fought with it, Pebbleshine couldn't help thinking how ridiculous it looked. For a few moments she was afraid it was too strong for her. *But I'm not about to give up!* she told herself, struggling to fasten her teeth in the chicken's neck.

Waspwhisker's screech came from below. "Pebbleshine, *now*!"

"I'm coming!" Pebbleshine repeated, letting out all her frustration in her yowl. "But this stupid bird is fighting!"

"Then let it go!" Hawkwing's voice was panicked.

"But the Clan needs it!" Pebbleshine protested.

A deep, throaty growl came from the monster, and beneath Pebbleshine's paws, its back began to vibrate. *Fox dung! It's waking up,* Pebbleshine thought, furious at the thought that the monster might notice her before she could escape with her prey.

With a last desperate effort, she lunged forward and dug her teeth into the chicken's throat. Its squawk was abruptly cut off, and Pebbleshine felt the warm gush of blood over her jaws. The bird's body convulsed once, then lay still.

Forgetting the danger for a moment in her surge of triumph,

Pebbleshine scrambled to her paws and dragged the chicken toward the side of the platform. But before she reached it, the monster began to move, edging backward with a steady, determined purr.

Suddenly afraid, Pebbleshine dropped the chicken and sprang up to rest her paws on the side of the monster's body. "Jump, Pebbleshine! Jump!" Blossomheart shrieked, backing away as the monster bore down on her and their Clanmates.

As it moved closer, the patrol scattered to avoid the monster's huge black paws. Only Hawkwing stood his ground, pushing Curlypaw out of the way and then running *toward* the monster.

Hawkwing, no! Pebbleshine opened her jaws to screech a warning, but just then the monster halted, barely a tail-length away from her mate. He dropped into a crouch, gathering himself to leap up beside her.

"Don't! I'm coming!" Pebbleshine panted, not sure if he heard her, scrabbling frantically to reach the top of the wall and spring off toward the ground below.

But before either cat could leap, the monster lurched into motion again, roaring louder still and belching out a stinking cloud from its hindquarters. It moved forward, heading for the gap in the wall of the monster camp. Beyond the wall, Pebbleshine caught a glimpse of more monsters speeding past along a wider Thunderpath. Her heart pounded. It felt like her whole body was gripped in ice. She tried to jump, but her legs wouldn't move; her mind was filled with a vision of herself flattened under those crushing black paws.

"Pebbleshine!" Hawkwing screeched.

Pebbleshine saw him push off in a massive leap, stretching out his forelegs to grab the back of the monster. But he was too late, falling short and landing with a thump on the hard surface. Pebbleshine winced, knowing how the fall must have jarred his injured leg.

She made one last, despairing effort to clamber over the wall, only to lose her balance as the monster lurched again and picked up speed. By the time she managed to spring back to her paws, it was moving far too fast for her to jump off safely.

Pebbleshine watched the trees begin to blur together as the monster picked up speed. She felt sick, and wasn't sure whether it was the movement or the creeping dread that threatened to overtake her. *What if I never . . . But I can't think that way,* she stopped herself. *Whatever happens next, I have to believe I'll find my Clan again. Because I'm a SkyClan warrior . . . and I will!*

Resting her paws against its side, she stared back at Hawkwing. "I'll find my way back to you!" she yowled.

Hawkwing hurled himself forward, racing after the monster, but Pebbleshine could see that his attempt was hopeless. The monster was giving out a full-throated roar, speeding even faster as it joined the wider Thunderpath.

Pebbleshine was frozen in disbelief. All she could do was keep her gaze fixed on Hawkwing's sturdy gray figure as it dwindled into a tiny dot and was lost to her sight.

When she couldn't see her mate anymore, Pebbleshine dropped down onto the platform. She wanted to wail like an abandoned kit, but she knew that wouldn't do any good. She would have to keep up her strength and stay alert if she was to get back to Hawkwing and the rest of her Clan.

What's going to happen to me when the monster stops? she asked herself. Would it try to make her its prey? *No!* she thought, giving her pelt a determined shake. *My kits and I aren't going to end up as monster food.*

At least she had prey of her own. Crouching beside the chicken she had killed, Pebbleshine tore aside the feathers and began to eat. The flesh was just as delicious as Waspwhisker had promised, but she couldn't enjoy it; she might as well have been eating rotten leaves. To make things even more awkward, the living chickens seemed to watch her from their nests, clucking accusingly. *I'm not sure I like chickens,* she thought.

At the same time, she tried to peer over the wall beside her, watching carefully where the monster was going, searching for landmarks that could help her find her way back. *A dead tree there . . . and three Twoleg dens close together . . . and here the Thunderpath crosses a stream . . .*

But as the monster sped on and on, taking Pebbleshine farther and farther away from her Clan, her brain began to whirl with the effort of observing. Her muscles ached from her struggle with the chicken, and her belly was full of its flesh.

For a little while Pebbleshine fought off exhaustion, but at last she had to give in, letting out a long sigh as the chickens' clucking eased her into a cloud of soft darkness.

Chapter 2

The monster had stopped. Pebbleshine blinked awake and raised her head to look around. A moment later the vibration beneath her paws and belly stilled and the monster's throaty growl was abruptly cut off. Her muscles tensing, Pebbleshine shook off the last vestiges of sleep and braced herself. She glanced at the chickens, looking for signs of panic. *What happens now?* she asked them silently. *Is this where the Twolegs try to eat us? Or do they feed us to the monster?* She flexed her legs, preparing to run.

A bang from the front of the monster made Pebbleshine jump. Crouching low again, not daring even to twitch a whisker, she caught a glimpse of the Twoleg's head, then heard the thump of its huge paws dying away into silence. The monster didn't move at all, and gradually Pebbleshine began to relax as she guessed it must have fallen asleep again. *Thank StarClan! I'll have another chance to escape.*

The chickens were clucking quietly in their shiny nests. Pebbleshine tore a few last bites from the one she had killed. Then she got up and rested her paws on the side of the platform while she looked around.

The monster had come to a halt on a narrow Thunderpath

that cut through wide stretches of tall, rustling grass. Not far away, a big Twoleg den rose up among a cluster of smaller dens. The sun was low in the sky, casting long shadows; Pebbleshine could see that she must have been traveling on the monster's back for most of the day.

With a last cautious glance around, Pebbleshine leaped down from the monster. She almost expected it to rumble to life and pursue her, but it didn't move. She let out a sigh of relief and began to head away from it, stealthily at first but then at a fast lope.

The Thunderpath was made of earth, and the monster's huge black paws had churned the surface up into deep tracks. Hope fluttered in Pebbleshine's chest; maybe all she had to do was follow the tracks backward until she found Hawkwing and her Clan again.

For a while she padded along beside the monster tracks, trying to spot some of the landmarks she had noticed on her outward journey. Then she realized that for the last part she had been asleep; anything she might recognize would be farther away. She began to grow discouraged when she hadn't seen anything familiar by the time the Thunderpath came to an end, melting into a wider one. Glittering monsters whizzed back and forth along the hard, black surface. Where the earth met the edge of this Thunderpath, the chicken-hunting monster's tracks vanished.

Half choking on the acrid stink of the passing monsters, Pebbleshine eased back from the edge of the Thunderpath and sat down to think. There was no hope of following the monster's trail anymore. She could tell the general direction she should travel, from the position of the sun, but she knew that wasn't enough to reunite her with her Clan. The monster had carried her too far away. There weren't even any familiar scents for her to follow.

And once it gets dark, I won't even have the sun to help me.

When she looked around for some kind of guidance, Pebbleshine spotted a Twoleg den in the distance, surrounded by a straggling copse of trees; it reminded her of Barley's barn, where her Clan had stopped about a moon before to rest and feast on the mice that lived among the straw there.

"Maybe there'll be friendly cats in *this* barn," she murmured hopefully to herself.

As she set out toward the distant den, Pebbleshine let herself hope that the cats might be able to point the way to the monster camp where she had lost her Clanmates, or maybe even to the lake where the other Clans lived, the cats SkyClan was looking for.

The thought quickened her paw steps. *How much fun would that be—I'd be there to greet Hawkwing when he and the others arrived!*

Then Pebbleshine realized it wouldn't be fun at all. She shook her head as she thought of how worried Hawkwing would be, through every paw step of the long, weary journey.

No. I have to find SkyClan first.

The sun had disappeared, leaving only a few last streaks of red in the sky, by the time Pebbleshine reached the barn. She hurried through the twilight, her jaws watering as she anticipated sinking her teeth into a juicy mouse, just like the ones in Barley's barn.

Pebbleshine was skirting the trees, bounding across the last stretch of open ground, when a sudden spate of barking burst out behind her. Whirling around, she spotted a huge brown dog charging at her, its tongue lolling and its plumy tail waving.

For a heartbeat, Pebbleshine froze. The dog was between her and the trees. Should she try to dodge around it and hope to scramble to safety in the branches, or should she head for the barn? In the end she did neither, crouching down instead, her fur bristling as she let out a defiant hiss.

"Hey, knock it off, idiot!"

A loud meow sounded from the direction of the barn. To Pebbleshine's surprise, the dog skidded to a halt and sat back on its haunches, panting and twitching its ears in what looked like embarrassment. A small black cat strolled out from behind Pebbleshine, glancing from her to the dog and back again with amused green eyes.

"Hi. My name's Bug," the newcomer announced. "Don't worry about Bunny. He's harmless."

For a moment all Pebbleshine could do was stare in astonishment. *Dogs have names? And this one is called Bunny?*

"I'm Pebbleshine," she choked out at last.

"That's a bit of a mouthful," Bug commented. "Don't your housefolk call you anything for short?"

It's a warrior name! Pebbleshine thought, her fur beginning to bristle. *I'm proud of it!* But then she had a horrible realization. Had she traveled so far from Clan territory that these cats hadn't ever heard a Clan name? *I'd better not act offended,* she thought. *Not when I need her help.*

"I don't have any Twolegs—I mean housefolk," she responded mildly.

Bug blinked in surprise but said nothing more. Instead she padded up to Bunny and gave him a friendly shove with one paw. His tail thumped on the ground, but he stayed sitting.

It looks like Bug and this dog are friends. *I can't imagine any cat wanting that. What's going on here?*

Pebbleshine still didn't trust him, and she kept her gaze fixed on him.

"Do you want to come into the barn?" Bug mewed to Pebbleshine with a welcoming swish of her tail.

Pebbleshine looked away from the dog and dipped her head gratefully. "Thanks."

"Is it okay if I let Bunny get up?" Bug asked. "I promise he won't hurt you."

For a few heartbeats Pebbleshine hesitated. The dog was big enough to swallow her and Bug in one gulp, and she only had the word of a strange cat that he wasn't dangerous. *He doesn't look like he's going to attack . . . ,* she thought warily. She remembered the crazy eyes, drooling jaws, and vicious snarling of dogs she had encountered before. In contrast, Bunny just looked goofy. Even so, all of Pebbleshine's muscles were tense and she was ready to flee at the first sign of a threat.

At last she gave a small, reluctant nod. Bug turned and

looked up into Bunny's liquid brown eyes. "Okay, you can get up," she meowed. "But stay out of the barn for a while, all right?"

Bunny let out a short bark, then heaved himself to his paws and lolloped off toward the trees. Pebbleshine stared after him in amazement. "How does he know what you're saying?" she asked Bug.

The small black cat gave a tiny shrug. "Oh, we've both lived on this farm since we were born," she replied. "We just understand each other. Come on." She turned and headed toward the barn.

Pebbleshine followed, still bemused. *I was right. They are friends. . . . Wait until I tell Hawkwing!* Then a hollow place opened up inside her as she remembered that she couldn't tell Hawkwing, maybe not for a long time.

Her bewilderment faded as she slipped into the barn through the half-open door and breathed in the succulent scent of mouse that surged out from piles of sweet-smelling grass. Pebbleshine almost leaped forward to hunt before she remembered that she didn't have permission. She halted, giving her chest fur a couple of embarrassed licks.

"Help yourself," Bug invited her. "There are plenty of mice here—and they're really fat."

There was little light in the barn as darkness fell outside, but Pebbleshine could make out piles of hay just like the ones in Barley's barn. High-pitched squeaking filled the air. Pebbleshine crept forward until she spotted blades of grass twitching at the edge of the pile and heard the scuffle of tiny claws. She launched herself forward and slammed her paw down on a plump mouse. It was the easiest catch she had ever made.

Bug settled down to keep Pebbleshine company as she ate. "I haven't seen you around here," she remarked.

Pebbleshine shook her head, hastily swallowing a mouthful of prey. "No, I come from a long way away," she told the black she-cat. "I'm looking for my Clan—the cats I live with. I last saw them in a big monster camp in the middle of some Twoleg dens. Do you know anywhere like that?"

Bug was looking at Pebbleshine as if she had no idea what she was meowing about. "A monster camp?" she asked. "What's that?"

Pebbleshine's heart sank. *Not only have you not heard of the Clans . . . you don't even know about* monsters*?* "You know monsters, right?" she asked hopefully. "Big noisy smelly things with round black paws?"

"Oh, them!" Bug nodded. "I know what you mean. But a camp . . . ?"

"A whole lot of them sleeping together," Pebbleshine explained, trying not to let her tail-tip quiver with impatience.

Slowly Bug shook her head. "I've never seen more than one or two monsters together. I don't think this 'camp' of yours can be near here," she added with a doubtful twitch of her whiskers.

Cold dread crept through Pebbleshine. How far had she come since she'd lost Hawkwing and the others? *I felt like I'd traveled a long way in the monster, but it must be even farther than I thought if this cat has hardly ever* seen *monsters.* "Then do you know of any other Clans—I mean groups of cats?" she asked, struggling to keep her voice steady. "They live beside a big stretch of water."

This time Bug's denial was more certain. "I haven't seen any 'Clans' around here," she asserted. "I don't see many other cats, and the ones I have seen have been other farm cats or housecats. And there aren't any big stretches of water nearby."

Pebbleshine dug her claws hard into the earth floor of the barn. "I *must* find my Clan!" she meowed desperately.

Bug brushed her tail-tip down Pebbleshine's side, a comforting gesture. "Finish your prey," she suggested, "and then have a good sleep. You'll feel better in the morning, and you can start fresh."

Pebbleshine let out a long sigh. "Thanks. That's kind of you, Bug."

When she had eaten and groomed herself, Pebbleshine made a nest in the fragrant hay and curled up in it. Bug settled down at her side. Pebbleshine had believed that her anxieties would keep her awake, but she was so exhausted that her eyes closed at once.

I never used to get this tired, before I was expecting kits, she thought muzzily, drifting into a dream where she was searching for Hawkwing in a forest, but finding nothing except a faint trace of his scent, or a glimpse of a whisking tail among the undergrowth.

* * *

The next thing she knew, light was slanting into the barn from the open door and from gaps set high in the walls. Eager yapping from outside had woken her. Pebbleshine sprang to her paws, shaking clinging hayseeds from her pelt as she looked around. There was no sign of Bug. After padding to the door and poking her head outside, Pebbleshine saw the black she-cat wrestling with Bunny. The huge dog had her pinned down beneath one massive paw, while Bug's legs waved helplessly.

Pebbleshine let out a hiss, tensing her muscles to come to her new friend's rescue. *I was right not to trust that dog!* she told herself. *Dogs and cats can't be friends!*

But before Pebbleshine could move, Bug wriggled out from under Bunny's paw. Bunny bent his head, and the two of them nuzzled each other like kits before Bug hurled herself onto the dog's back. Bunny let himself go limp, rolling over, and Bug sprang away before she was squashed.

They're . . . play-fighting? Weird . . ., Pebbleshine thought, shaking her head. Maybe some dogs and cats *could* be friends, but all the same, she had no intention of getting closer to Bunny.

Spotting Pebbleshine, Bug left the dog and raced over to her. "Hi," she mewed. "Are you okay? Do you want to hunt again? We could do it together."

"Thanks. That's a great idea."

With Bug at her side, Pebbleshine plunged back into the hay. At a signal from the black she-cat, Pebbleshine began circling around, moving gradually toward the edge of the pile. Bug circled in the opposite direction. Working together, they steadily drove their prey out of shelter; it wasn't long before frightened squeaks and scurrying told Pebbleshine that their strategy was working. Finally, almost in the same heartbeat, two mice popped out into the open. Pebbleshine pounced on the nearest one, while Bug dispatched the other with one swipe of her paw.

"Great catch!" Bug exclaimed.

A pang of loss pierced Pebbleshine as she crouched down to eat beside the black she-cat; for a moment she had almost felt as if she were hunting with her Clan again.

"I'm really grateful to you for letting me spend the night here," she sighed when she had gulped down the last mouthful of prey. "But I have to go."

"Maybe you should stay," Bug suggested, concern in her green eyes. "You're welcome for as long as you want. I can see you're expecting kits, and it worries me to think of you traveling by yourself."

Pebbleshine felt a jolt of surprise that another cat could tell she was carrying kits just by looking at her. When she had insisted on climbing onto the monster with the chickens, she had thought she wasn't far enough along for it to be obvious. A pang of guilt shook her.

Maybe I did *take a risk that I shouldn't have.*

For a heartbeat she was tempted to stay here, in shelter, with food and Bug's friendship, a place where her kits could be born safely. But she knew how impossible that was. *I can't give birth to our kits without Hawkwing there. Not when I still have enough time and energy to find him, and my Clan!* That was more important than anything.

"No, I have to go," she repeated. "Thanks, Bug, but my kits are the reason I can't delay any longer. I'm determined that my kits will be Clan cats, and come into the world surrounded by their kin. I have a plan," she added. "I have to find my way back to my mate. I'm sure he'll be looking for me."

Bug padded alongside Pebbleshine as they headed back toward the Thunderpath, with Bunny trotting behind them at a distance.

"Good-bye, then," Bug mewed when they stood close to the edge of the black, reeking surface. She touched her nose briefly to Pebbleshine's shoulder. "I hope you find your Clan."

"Good-bye," Pebbleshine responded. "Thanks for everything, Bug. And may StarClan light your path."

Bug looked confused by Pebbleshine's last words, but Pebbleshine didn't wait to explain. *That would take far too long!*

Checking the position of the sun to make sure she would be traveling in the right direction, Pebbleshine set out. She looked back once, waving her tail in farewell, to see Bug's neat black shape sitting beside the Thunderpath, with Bunny's huge figure looming beside her.

A monster zoomed by in the opposite direction, the wind of its passing buffeting Pebbleshine's fur. Flattening her ears, Pebbleshine swallowed in apprehension.

They move so fast, she thought. *And I was on that monster for so long—long enough to sleep and wake up. How far have I come?*

Pebbleshine was beginning to realize what a huge task lay before her. It could take her moons to walk back to the place where she had left her Clan, even if she was moving in the right direction.

That meant there was only one way for her to get back to SkyClan in time for her kits to be born with them.

I'll have to get onto another monster.

Chapter 3

Pebbleshine padded alongside the Thunderpath, her shoulders hunched and her fur fluffed up against a thin, drizzling rain. She was thankful for her SkyClan paws, toughened from leaping up and down the rocks of the gorge. Her muscles were stronger now, she thought happily; in fact, the whole of the Clan had grown stronger. They had lost so much when they were driven out of the gorge, but they had gained, too.

And I've gained more than strength, she told herself, thinking of the kits she carried. *So has Plumwillow. She must be close to kitting by now.* Pebbleshine was sure that their kits were StarClan's promise that SkyClan would survive.

The realization made Pebbleshine more determined than ever to return to her Clan before her kits were born. *I have to climb onto another monster. But how can I?*

Monsters raced past her on the Thunderpath, some of them going in the right direction, but they were all moving too fast for her to jump onto. All around her was open territory, with no more monster camps or dens where they might go to sleep.

Pebbleshine was beginning to despair when she made out a cluster of Twoleg dens in the distance. New energy flowed into her paws, and she picked up her pace until she reached the outskirts of the Twolegplace.

Padding alongside the dens, Pebbleshine passed several monsters, but they were all asleep, some tucked away in little nests beside their Twolegs' dens. Every one of them was closed up, with no way that she could see of climbing inside.

"Mouse dung," she muttered. "These monsters are a lazy bunch. They do nothing but sleep!"

Finally, Pebbleshine spotted a monster sitting beside the Thunderpath, pointing in the direction she wanted to go. It looked nothing like the one she had traveled on, with the chickens, but its back was open to the air.

When Pebbleshine glanced around, she couldn't see any Twolegs inside the monster or near the den. Warily, she stalked toward it. Hoping the monster was asleep, Pebbleshine sneaked closer and, with a last cautious glance around, leaped lightly into its belly.

Inside, the monster was full of weird shapes and scents: huge, odd-shaped rocks and brightly colored scraps of Twoleg debris. Pebbleshine squeezed into a space under one of the rocks and curled up, grooming her wet pelt with rapid strokes of her tongue. She hoped that when the monster's Twolegs came, they wouldn't notice her.

Her whole body tingled with apprehension, but at the same time she felt a trace of the same thrill she had felt when she'd leaped onto the other monster to hunt chickens.

We're on our way, kits! she thought, then added, *I really hope this works.*

Pebbleshine's muscles tensed as she heard the thump of Twoleg paw steps outside the monster. Suddenly a shadow loomed up at its back and the opening slammed shut. She almost gave herself away with a screech of alarm, but managed to choke down the sound.

I'm trapped inside a monster!

Her fear spiked into panic as two adult Twolegs and a Twoleg kit clambered into the monster, meowing to one another. The kit sat on top of the rock where Pebbleshine was hiding, so close that if Pebbleshine had stretched out a paw, she could have touched it.

The monster woke up with a cough and a rumble and began to move off. Pebbleshine pressed herself as low as she could and kept still, not even twitching a whisker. At least, as far as she could tell, they were moving in the right direction.

But after a few moments, the Twoleg kit let out a loud noise. Pebbleshine started, but forced herself to stay quiet. For a moment she couldn't work out what the sound was, until the kit did it again, and she realized that it was sneezing. *Poor thing, it must be sick,* Pebbleshine thought. *Maybe it needs to see a medicine Twoleg.*

A heartbeat later she slid, her claws scrabbling at the hard floor as the monster suddenly swerved and began speeding off in a different direction. *No! Let me out!* Pebbleshine wanted to yowl the words aloud, but she knew the Twolegs wouldn't understand her. *I'll only be in more trouble if they find me here. I just have to figure out a way of escaping.*

But the monster sped on and on. There was no opening for

Pebbleshine to squeeze through, and even if she had found one, it would have been too dangerous to leap out.

The kit kept sneezing, and the male Twoleg turned around to speak to it. Pebbleshine didn't understand what he was saying, but he sounded puzzled. The kit's only reply was another sneeze, and now it seemed as if it couldn't stop.

The adult Twolegs began speaking to each other, their voices agitated. Then the monster shuddered and drew to a halt. The Twolegs pushed out openings on the monster's flank and scrambled out. The female Twoleg peered under Pebbleshine's rock; the Twoleg was blocking her escape path, so Pebbleshine tried to hunch herself up into an even smaller space, but it was no use. The female let out a squawk of surprise, pointing at her. Pebbleshine glanced toward the other opening the Twoleg kit had escaped from, but it was just swinging closed.

Oh, StarClan, no! They've spotted me . . . and I'm trapped!

The male Twoleg walked around to the back of the monster. Pebbleshine guessed he was going to open it up. She felt every hair on her pelt bristling with fear, but she bunched her muscles, ready to leap out. She had no idea what the Twolegs would do to her if they caught her, but she was sure it couldn't be good.

The back section of the monster swung up; the male Twoleg reached for Pebbleshine, but she was too fast for him. She leaped past him, feeling his outstretched paw brush her pelt, and fled.

Pebbleshine's legs were cramped from spending so long

tightly curled up, but she forced herself into a run, heading away from the Thunderpath and into the scatter of unfamiliar Twoleg dens that bordered it. She was certain that the Twoleg was chasing her, but when she finally had to halt, panting for breath, there was no sign of him.

Trembling with relief, Pebbleshine tried to work out where she was. Then, somehow, she would find her way to where she wanted to be. She stood on a stretch of grass outside a Twoleg nest, with other Twoleg nests all around her, as far as she could see. None of the sights or scents were familiar to her.

What is this place?

Pebbleshine realized that she wasn't even sure how to get back to the Thunderpath, much less discover the direction she needed to take to rejoin her Clan. The rain had stopped, but clouds still covered the sky, so she couldn't work out a route from the position of the sun. For a moment despair threatened to overwhelm her. She didn't recognize anything here.

What if I've only made things worse? What if that monster carried me even farther away? She felt herself sinking. It seemed clear now that she'd never be able to get back to SkyClan by riding a monster, because there was no way to predict where they would go. *But then how will I ever get back all that way?*

Pebbleshine summoned her courage, determined not to give in to these dark fears. *It's all right. I can make it. I'm a warrior!* Her chest still heaving after her frantic dash for safety, she sat down on the grass to think.

It had already been a couple of days since she had been carried away from Hawkwing and her Clanmates. Pebbleshine knew that they would be waiting for her to come back, but she knew too that they couldn't wait forever. They had to go on searching for the place beside the water where the other Clans lived. It was SkyClan's only hope of survival.

My kits have *to be born in a Clan,* Pebbleshine thought with a growl of frustration.

At that moment, an angry hiss broke out from the nearest Twoleg nest. Pebbleshine whipped her head around to see a fluffy gray she-cat burst out of a small opening near the ground and head toward her, stiff-legged and snarling.

"This is my place," she hissed. She was a big cat, and her bristling fur made her look bigger still. "You don't belong here. Keep moving—or else."

Pebbleshine rose to her paws. Normally, she fought alongside her Clanmates, but she knew she could handle a kittypet alone, no matter how fierce. Still, as tired and worried as she was, a fight was the last thing she needed.

"I'm just passing through," she mewed, turning and beginning to pad away.

"Yeah, keep moving, coward!" the gray kittypet spat.

Pebbleshine spun around, her decision not to fight flying out of her head. *I'm a warrior of SkyClan! No kittypet is going to talk to me like that!*

Letting out a growl from deep in her throat, Pebbleshine stalked toward the kittypet. She slid out her claws and let her neck fur bush up defiantly. *I'll show her what a warrior is—and how a warrior fights!*

The kittypet's eyes suddenly widened in alarm, and she

took a pace back, as if she hadn't expected Pebbleshine to stand up for herself. Pebbleshine was almost close enough to take a swipe at her when another voice broke in.

"Leave her alone, Coco! Can't you see she's expecting kits?"

Pebbleshine glanced over her shoulder to see two young kittypets—a thin black-and-white she-cat and an orange tom—come racing across the grass and thrust themselves between Pebbleshine and Coco, scolding the gray she-cat as they approached.

"What's wrong with you?"

"Can't you be friendly for a change?"

Coco let out a furious hiss. "Like I'd want to be friends with you flea-pelts!" she exclaimed. She backed away a few paces, then turned and flounced off toward her Twoleg den, disappearing again inside the small door.

The black-and-white she-cat ducked her head to Pebbleshine. "Sorry about that," she meowed.

"Yeah," the orange tom added. "We hope Coco didn't scare you. I'm Milo, by the way, and she's Olive."

Pebbleshine stifled amusement at the thought that the two kittypets were trying to protect *her,* a fully trained Clan warrior. But she thought they were quite cute—hardly more than kits—and she didn't want to hurt their feelings.

"I'm Pebbleshine," she responded, dipping her head politely. "Thanks for your help, but I'm fine, really. What is that cat's problem?"

"Oh, Coco!" Olive twitched her ears dismissively. "She always has her tail in a twist. Are you sure you're okay?" she added, brushing her tail along Pebbleshine's side. "Are you hungry? You could come and eat with us."

"Our housefolk have plenty," Milo agreed. "Water, too. And it's not far."

Pebbleshine shook her head. "Thank you, but no. I really don't want to go into a Twoleg nest."

Olive and Milo exchanged a bewildered glance, as if they couldn't imagine why Pebbleshine would object to entering their den. "Twoleg?" Olive sounded puzzled. "Do you mean housefolk? Don't you have a den of your own?"

I had one once . . . a beautiful den, in the gorge. Pebbleshine thrust the pang of homesickness aside and forced herself not to think about the past. In any case, that wasn't what Olive had meant. "No," she replied. "I'm a Clan cat. We don't live with Twolegs."

The two kittypets looked at each other again, still clearly confused. Pebbleshine felt the same dread return: *How far must I be, if no cat seems to know what a Clan is?*

Eventually Milo shrugged. "Okay," he mewed, "would you at least like us to show you where you can get water out here?"

At his question, Pebbleshine suddenly realized how thirsty she was, as if her mouth were full of sand. *If I must be surrounded by kittypets who don't even know about the Clans,* she thought, *at least they can be helpful!* "Oh, yes, please!"

"Follow us," Olive told her.

The two kittypets set off across the grass, strolled down the Thunderpath a little way, and then wriggled under a Twoleg fence. Squeezing through after them, Pebbleshine found herself on the edge of a wilder area, where the grass was longer and rougher, and narrow paths wound among clumps of bushes. The clouds were breaking up; weak sunlight glittered on the wet foliage. In the distance Pebbleshine could hear the shouts of playing Twoleg kits.

"This way." Milo took the lead down a slope to where a small stream trickled between stones. With a gasp of relief Pebbleshine crouched down beside it and gratefully lapped at the cool water.

"Thanks," she meowed at last, sitting up and shaking drops of water from her whiskers. "That was exactly what I needed."

"Is there anything else we can do to help you?" Olive asked, her blue eyes wide with anxiety.

"No, I—" Pebbleshine broke off. She had been feeling hopeless, realizing how far she had traveled from her Clan—so far that she wasn't sure of the direction anymore. But these kittypets clearly knew their way around. *They probably don't ever wander that far from their nests.* She remembered Bug's reaction when she'd asked about the monster camp. *These kittypets probably won't know, either. But it has to be worth asking.* "I'm looking for a monster camp," she began. "A big space covered with that black Thunderpath stuff. There are Twoleg dens around part of it, and bushes along one side. Is there anywhere like that around here?"

"Hey, we know a place like that!" Milo exclaimed.

Olive nodded vigorously. "It's not far from the Cutter's—that's where our housefolk take us when we're sick," she explained to Pebbleshine. "And for . . . well, other stuff."

Shock jolted through Pebbleshine as if a rock had fallen on her head out of a clear sky. "Really?" she responded, her heart lifting. *Maybe soon I'll see Hawkwing again.* "Can you tell me how to get there?"

The two young cats exchanged a doubtful glance. "It might be easier to show you," Olive mewed. "But it's a long way. We'd have to be gone overnight."

Milo scrabbled in the grass with his forepaws. "Our housefolk will be really scared if we're missing."

"Please," Pebbleshine begged. "It's so important for me to get back there. My Clanmates—my friends, I mean—will be waiting for me."

"Well . . . our housefolk could probably survive one night without us," Olive responded, looking hopefully at Milo. "I mean, at least we have housefolk to keep us safe. You don't have *anyone*—and you're expecting kits!"

Thank . . . you? Pebbleshine thought, not sure what to make of that. *I'd rather have Clanmates than* housefolk *any day.* But the kittypet seemed determined to help her, so Pebbleshine tried to look encouraging.

"Come on, Milo," Olive mewed to her friend. "We have so much . . . helping Pebbleshine is the least we can do! Besides, it'll be an adventure!"

The orange tom hesitated for a moment longer. Then his eyes widened and he let out an excited purr. "Okay. We'll go with you," he promised.

CHAPTER 4

"We ought to eat first," Olive meowed. "As much as we can, so we don't get too hungry on the way."

"I'm always up for that!" Milo purred, swiping his tongue around his jaws. "And we ought to say good-bye to our housefolk, too."

"Are you sure you won't eat with us?" Olive asked Pebbleshine, twitching her whiskers anxiously. "How will you manage overnight, if you don't?"

Pebbleshine hid her amusement at the younger cat's attempt to care for her. "No, thanks. I'll hunt on the way," she replied.

"Really?" Milo sounded impressed, but there was a doubtful look in his eyes. "Are you sure?"

"Quite sure."

Though they still looked reluctant to accept Pebbleshine's decision, the two kittypets bounded back up the slope and wriggled under the fence. Pebbleshine followed more slowly, in time to see them vanish into the nearest den, through a small opening like Coco's.

She settled herself under a bush to wait, but she was so excited that she couldn't stay still for more than a couple of heartbeats. She paced back and forth along the edge of the grass, wondering if she was really about to find her Clanmates again.

At last I've got an idea where to go. I just hope these kittypets really do know where to find the monster camp.

The sun was slipping down the sky by the time the two kittypets returned. Pebbleshine felt as if she had been waiting forever; she had begun to wonder if they had changed their minds. Finally the main door of the Twoleg den opened; Milo and Olive appeared with a female Twoleg. Pebbleshine quickly ducked back into the shelter of the bush and watched while the Twoleg crossed the garden and began to pick some of the brightly colored flowers that grew around the edge of the grass.

Maybe those are Twoleg herbs, Pebbleshine thought, interested. *Could she be a medicine Twoleg?*

Milo and Olive twined themselves affectionately around the legs of the Twoleg until she bent down and gave each of them a stroke. Cold shudders crept through Pebbleshine at the sight of them. *I'd never want to get that close to a Twoleg! Not if I could help it!*

Finally the Twoleg went back inside the den. The two kittypets waited until she was gone, then raced across the garden and joined Pebbleshine under the bushes. "Okay, we're ready to go now," Milo mewed. He looked around thoughtfully, then pointed with his tail. "It's this way."

He started to weave a path through the bushes, but Olive

didn't follow. "Are you sure?" she asked, with a doubtful glance in the other direction.

Milo halted and let out an exaggerated sigh. "It's the way we go to the Cutter, fur-for-brains!"

Olive hesitated for a moment, then twitched her ears. "Okay. Have it your way."

Pebbleshine felt her heart sink. *Do they really know where to go, if they can't even agree between themselves?* But following the kittypets was the only choice she had, so she tried to crush down her doubts. *It has to be worth a try.*

Once they decided on a direction, the kittypets led the way confidently through the long grass on the edge of the Thunderpath that wound through the Twolegplace. Pebbleshine's nose wrinkled at the acrid scent of monsters.

"Do we have to follow Thunderpaths all the way?" she asked.

"Sorry, we do," Milo replied. "Almost, at least. This is the only way we know, because our Twolegs take us this way to the Cutter."

Pebbleshine nodded, accepting his explanation. At least, she thought, the kittypets were young and strong, keeping a steady pace without getting scared about being away from their nest, or demanding a rest because they were tired.

Not all kittypets are weak, she reminded herself, thinking of the daylight warriors of SkyClan. But she was still surprised that cats with no Clan training had so much stamina. They even relaxed enough to chase butterflies and have a friendly scuffle along the way, Olive rolling with Milo among the roots of a tree. Pebbleshine's spirits lifted as she watched their teasing and fun.

"So do you live in the . . . monster camp, was it?" Olive asked Pebbleshine after a while, shaking debris from her pelt. "It sounds a little scary."

"Monsters can be scary, but I don't live in their camp." Pebbleshine sighed, struggling with another pang of homesickness for her den among the rocks. "My Clanmates and I are traveling. I used to live in a gorge, beside a stream, with the rest of my Clan."

"What's a Clan?" Milo asked.

Pebbleshine explained how she and her Clanmates lived together, how they trained to fight and hunt, and took care of one another. "My Clan is called SkyClan," she finished.

"That sounds great!" Milo exclaimed.

"And what about your kits' father?" Olive asked. "Is he part of your Clan, too?"

Pebbleshine nodded. "Yes, and that's partly why it's so important that I get back to them."

"What's his name? What is he like?" Olive's questions were tumbling out of her.

"He's called Hawkwing," Pebbleshine replied. Her voice grew warm with memory, even though the pain of missing her mate felt like thorns piercing her heart. "He's the best cat in the Clan."

"Is he your leader?" Milo asked.

"Not yet," Pebbleshine told him. "Maybe one day . . ."

Olive blinked, looking a bit wistful. "I wish *we* could be part of a Clan."

"It's not always easy. In fact, recently, SkyClan has had a very hard time." Pebbleshine paused, feeling a prick in her heart as she remembered the troubles with Darktail, and leaving the gorge.

"I'm sorry to hear that. What happened?" Milo asked, his ears tipped curiously toward her.

"A very bad cat came along pretending to be our friend, but he stole our home," Pebbleshine began slowly. She didn't want to get into details these kittypets wouldn't understand . . . and she didn't want to think too hard about it herself. Memories of life at the gorge still hurt too much. "It was difficult, and we had to leave some Clanmates behind. Now we're looking for a new home."

Olive's eyes filled with sympathy. "Don't you have anywhere to go? Maybe you could come live by us. There's a lady a few houses down who has lots of cats! I bet she'd take you in. . . ."

Pebbleshine looked at her warmly. "That's kind, Olive, but Clan cats don't usually live with Twolegs. We like to be in charge of ourselves. Sometimes it can be a hard life," Pebbleshine warned her. "But I think you and Milo would make fine warriors."

"But we couldn't leave our housefolk," Milo insisted. "What would they do without us?"

"When we lived in the gorge," Pebbleshine meowed, "some of our Clan members were daylight warriors. They lived in the gorge in the daytime, and hunted and trained with the rest of us, but at night they went back to their Twolegs."

Milo gave an enthusiastic swish of his tail. "That would be perfect!"

"Where is SkyClan going now?" Olive asked. "I mean, if you can't go back to the gorge."

"Well, we're headed to a lake," Pebbleshine explained, struggling to think of a way to explain Echosong's vision in a way these kittypets would understand. "We have cats in the Clan who are very wise, who communicate with our ancestors. One of those cats had a vision that told her we should live by a lake."

She had been expecting more questions, but Olive and Milo looked satisfied. Olive gave her an earnest look. "I hope you find it," she said softly.

"Thank you." Pebbleshine nodded. "I do too." *More than you know.*

While they'd been talking, the cats had continued to travel, and Pebbleshine realized that the sun had sunk below the horizon, casting long shadows over their route. "Is it much farther?" she asked.

At the same moment, Milo exclaimed. "We're almost there!"

A narrow path led upward between two Twoleg dens. Milo bounded along it, while Pebbleshine and Olive followed. "It's just over this hill," Olive panted.

Leaving the Twoleg nests behind them, the cats burst out onto an open, grassy slope, leading to a ridge outlined against the sky. Pebbleshine's heart was pounding so hard she thought it would break out of her chest. *Maybe my Clan will still be waiting for me! Maybe I'll see Hawkwing again, right now!*

Pebbleshine raced up the slope, outstripping the two kittypets. Cresting the hill, she halted as if she had slammed into a wall of rock.

She was looking down at the monster camp—but it wasn't the right one. It was bigger than the one where she had lost her Clan, the walls that surrounded it were red, not gray, and where the line of bushes should have been was a tangle of brambles and a few stunted trees. She felt farther from her Clan than ever.

"Are they here?" Olive gasped as she climbed the hill to stand beside Pebbleshine. "Are your friends here?"

Pebbleshine shook her head. She wanted to wail her desolation, but she made her voice remain steady as she replied, "No. This isn't the right place after all."

"Are you serious?" Milo exclaimed, reaching the top in time to hear Pebbleshine's words. "But it sounded so much like what you described! Take a good look. Are you sure?"

Pebbleshine looked downhill again, then looked him in the eye. "I'm sure, Milo. It *is* what I described to you. It's just not the one where I left my friends."

Milo looked at the ground, but Olive bounded up to Pebbleshine, leaning in to nuzzle her cheek sympathetically.

"I'm so sorry, Pebbleshine!

"I can't blame you," Pebbleshine responded. "I asked you to show me a monster camp, and that's what you've done. It's not your fault that it isn't the right one."

Milo stepped forward, and the two young cats pressed themselves against Pebbleshine, one on each side, trying to comfort her. Pebbleshine just felt empty. She had no idea what she should do next.

"Maybe we should sleep," Olive suggested after a few heartbeats. "It's going to be dark soon. Probably things will look brighter in the morning."

Pebbleshine murmured agreement. *I could sleep for moons and nothing would look brighter, but I don't want to upset Olive.*

"I wish my housefolk were here to give us some food right now," Milo meowed. "My belly's growling so hard!"

"I'll hunt for you," Pebbleshine offered immediately.

"Oh, no, you don't have to," Olive objected. "You've had an awful shock, and you need to rest."

"Hunting will take my mind off my worries," Pebbleshine insisted. She wasn't sure that was true, but she knew that she had to get away by herself for a while, to come to terms with how all this effort had been for nothing. She was in danger of breaking down completely in front of two kittypets.

And that's the last thing I want, when they've gone to all this trouble to help me. They can't possibly understand how hopeless I feel right now.

The slope leading down to the monster camp was shallower than the one they had already climbed, dotted with bushes and the occasional outcrop of rock. Pebbleshine left the kittypets in a sheltered spot beside a gorse thicket and prowled off to look for prey.

The sun had set and twilight was gathering. At first all Pebbleshine could scent was the acrid tang of monsters, but as she worked her way around toward the brambles and trees that edged the camp, she began to pick up definite traces of mouse and squirrel.

She realized too that the discipline of hunting was helping to dispel the fog of misery that surrounded her. She felt the familiar tingle in her paws as she spotted a plump squirrel scuffling around in the debris at the edge of a bramble thicket and dropped into the hunter's crouch, focusing on her prey as she crept up on it.

A breeze sprang up as Pebbleshine was almost within pouncing distance, carrying her scent toward the squirrel. It sat up, then leaped away; Pebbleshine hurled herself toward it, but her outstretched forepaws slammed down on empty ground.

The squirrel raced away toward the nearest of the stunted trees. Pebbleshine pelted after it, but she couldn't catch it before it swarmed up the trunk and crouched on a low branch, chittering angrily at her as if challenging her to a fight.

Good luck with that! Pebbleshine thought. *I'm a SkyClan cat!*

Launching herself upward in a tremendous leap, she snagged her claws into the squirrel's tail and dragged it down off the branch. The squirrel struggled briefly, until Pebbleshine killed it with a swift bite to the neck.

Breathing hard, she stood over the limp body. "Thank you, StarClan, for this prey," she mewed. But then the thought struck her: *Can they even hear me?* She was so far from home, so far from SkyClan; she didn't even know where she was. *Does StarClan?*

She shuddered. For a few heartbeats she had forgotten her troubles, but now they returned in full force. Back in the gorge she would have carried the squirrel to the fresh-kill pile, but there was no more camp in the gorge now, and she would eat her prey alone, not even knowing how far she was from her Clanmates.

I wish Hawkwing had seen that catch, and I could share it with him.

Forcing her grief to the back of her mind, Pebbleshine headed back to where she had left the kittypets. Their eyes gleamed in the gathering darkness as they spotted the prey she was carrying.

"Wow, that's huge!" Milo exclaimed. "You really just caught that?"

"You must be a brilliant hunter," Olive added.

Not bad, Pebbleshine thought, a bit ashamed of herself for enjoying the kittypets' praise. "Let's share it," she meowed, dropping her prey at her friends' paws.

Both Olive and Milo sniffed dubiously at the squirrel; Pebbleshine had to encourage them by tearing off a mouthful of the flesh. "Try it; it's really good," she mumbled as she gulped the prey down. *Imagine, not wanting to eat fresh-kill!*

First Milo, then Olive, tasted the squirrel and took a few tiny bites. "It's . . . er . . . very nice," Olive murmured politely.

"I don't think you like it," Pebbleshine responded, hiding her surprise. *I've never met a cat who didn't like a nice, juicy squirrel!*

She suddenly felt very alone again . . . just as she'd felt while hunting. She was the only Clan cat here. Possibly she was the only Clan cat anywhere around here. "I'm sorry."

"We're sorry, too," Milo told her. "Especially after you went to all the trouble of catching it. But we really prefer the food pellets our housefolk give us. They're not quite so . . . furry."

When they had eaten what they could, the two kittypets curled up together in the shelter of the bushes and went to sleep. Pebbleshine stayed awake for a long time, staring up at the warriors of StarClan glittering above her. *If I can see them, they can see me,* she decided. They were the same stars that she had always known, ever since she was a kit in the gorge.

As long as they're there, I'm not alone. Surely StarClan will help me and my kits find SkyClan again.

Pebbleshine slept at last, and woke at sunrise to find Olive and Milo grooming themselves beside her.

"We have to head home now," Milo meowed. "You can come with us if you like."

"I'm sure our housefolk would welcome you," Olive added.

Pebbleshine shook her head. "Thank you, but no. I have to go on looking for my Clan."

"Then just come for a little while," Olive urged her, reaching out to touch the tip of her tail to Pebbleshine's shoulder. "So that your kits will be born somewhere safe."

For a heartbeat Pebbleshine was tempted. Olive and Milo would make good daylight warriors someday. Perhaps she could stay with them, only until her kits were born, like they said, and then she could seek out SkyClan. . . . *They could even come with me.* But then she realized how impossible that would be. She was so far from the Clans—Milo and Olive would never leave their housefolk to travel that far. And her kits, if they were born as kittypets, might not want to leave. If she was even allowed to stay with her kits. She remembered tales the daylight warriors had told, of Twolegs taking kits away from their mothers, who never saw them again. *No. My kits will be Clan cats,* she vowed.

"I can't," she mewed firmly. "It's kind of you, but I need my kits to be born in a Clan. I'm more grateful than I can say for everything you've done."

The two young cats were clearly reluctant to leave her, but finally they said good-bye, inviting her to visit them if she ever returned this way. Pebbleshine stood at the crest of the hill, watching them race down the slope. At the edge of the Twolegplace they turned back, waving their tails in a last farewell, then vanished among the Twoleg dens. Pebbleshine let out a little sigh as she saw them go.

When they were gone, Pebbleshine finished up the remains of the squirrel and sat for a while as the sun rose above the Twolegplace. She knew she would have to move on, but first she had to decide where to go. While she sat there, she felt a strange stirring in her belly, and drew in a wondering breath as she realized her kits were moving for the first time.

From out of nowhere, a strong feeling swept over her: the certainty that her kits would be all right. *They are the future of*

SkyClan. They have a destiny, and StarClan will make sure they will find their way to their Clan.

But Pebbleshine realized that her chances of finding SkyClan now were next to none. Even if she could somehow find her way back to the place where she had lost them, they wouldn't still be there. Leafstar would have made the decision to move on, for the good of the entire Clan.

Pebbleshine knew that she had only one choice. She didn't know where SkyClan was now, but she knew where they were going to be.

I have to find the water—the place where the other Clans live.

Exhaustion overwhelmed her at the thought. But as she drew to her feet, she glanced up at the sky, knowing that her ancestors were still there, watching her from behind the brightness of daylight.

I've made it this far on my own, she thought. *I'm stronger than I ever knew. And I will find them!*

CHAPTER 5

Pebbleshine halted and opened her jaws to taste the air. She stood in a copse of thin trees, on the edge of another Twolegplace, and though her senses were almost swamped by the scents of Twolegs and monsters, she could just make out the smell of nearby birds.

Almost a moon had passed since Pebbleshine had said good-bye to Olive and Milo, and her belly was heavy with her kits. Their weight made hunting harder, but at the same time she had gotten more practiced at hunting alone.

Determined now, she dropped into the hunter's crouch and began to slink in the direction of the scent. Soon she spotted a plump pigeon sitting at the end of a branch, seemingly unaware that Pebbleshine was creeping up on it. Pebbleshine paused to test the breeze and realized it was blowing in the right direction, keeping her downwind of the pigeon.

If I time this just right, and keep quiet, my kits and I should have a good meal.

The squirrel she had caught near the second monster camp had been the last time Pebbleshine had felt full-fed. Since then she had kept going on mice and shrews, but she desperately needed something more substantial.

If I were still with SkyClan, Hawkwing and the other warriors would make sure I had enough to eat. But they aren't here, so I have to depend on myself. I can do this!

Pebbleshine reached the foot of the tree without alerting the pigeon. She knew that her days of amazing leaps were over until after her kits were born. Instead she began to climb up the trunk of the tree, careful to stay on the opposite side from the pigeon. When she reached the level of the branch where the pigeon was sitting, she realized that it might be too thin. If she landed on it, weighed down as she was by her kits, the branch could easily break before she had the chance to pounce.

Glancing upward, Pebbleshine spotted a branch above that was sturdier. She clambered up and ventured out onto it, planning to leap down to strike at her prey. But just as she reached the spot above her quarry, the branch dipped under her weight, and the shadows of the leaves swept across the pigeon.

With a cry of alarm, the pigeon unfolded its wings. Pebbleshine instinctively leaped after it as it took off, sailing over the roof of a small Twoleg den nearby. Her claws brushed the pigeon's wing feathers, but before she could get a grip she and the bird thumped down together onto the roof. The impact drove the breath out of Pebbleshine. She rolled over, grasping for her prey, only to feel the roof give way under her weight. She let out a yowl of dismay, paws flailing, as she crashed through the flimsy covering and fell.

For a few heartbeats, Pebbleshine was too stunned to be

sure of what had happened or where she had ended up. She crouched where she had fallen, her eyes tight shut and her breath coming in shallow gasps.

Eventually, still trembling with shock, she opened her eyes to see that she had fallen onto a pile of straw and some kind of soft Twoleg pelts. Her heart pounded with fear for her kits, and she curled herself around her swollen belly until she felt them shifting inside her. Letting out a long sigh of relief, she whispered, "Thank you, StarClan."

Determined to pull herself together, Pebbleshine scrambled to her paws and looked around. The pigeon was long gone. Light pouring through the hole in the roof showed her walls made of rough strips of wood with one small window. Unfamiliar shapes were stacked around the walls—some kind of Twoleg stuff stored there, Pebbleshine supposed.

Right . . . How do I get out of here?

Pebbleshine padded over to the door and reared up to press on it with her forepaws, but it didn't give way. The hole in the roof was too high for her to leap up and escape that way. She tried two or three times to jump up at the window, but her heavy belly made her clumsy, and there was less power behind her leaps than she was used to. She couldn't break the clear-stone even though there was a crack in it. And there was no other way out, not even a mouse hole.

The little den was full of dust and cobwebs, telling Pebble-shine that the Twolegs didn't visit it very often. By the time anyone came to let her out, it would be too late. A shud-der passed through Pebbleshine from ears to tail-tip at the thought that she might give birth to her kits while she was trapped here, and all of them would starve together.

She was alone. She couldn't even see StarClan from here, or feel their guidance. Suddenly she felt more hopeless than she ever had.

If Hawkwing or any of my Clanmates were here, they would know I was missing and come to look for me, Pebbleshine thought, utterly miserable. *I wouldn't be in this mess. But as long as I'm alone, there's no chance for me, or for my kits.*

Tired and discouraged, Pebbleshine curled up in the straw and fell asleep. It didn't seem long before she felt a warm sensation rousing her: some cat was licking her ears. Startled, she opened her eyes to see Hawkwing standing over her.

But he can't . . . he can't be real, can he?

"You have to get up," he mewed, nudging her to help her stand.

If I can feel him, he must be . . . Pebbleshine pressed herself against her mate, twining her tail with his and purring so hard she thought she would never stop. For a few heartbeats Hawkwing leaned closer and his scent wreathed around her, so that she felt it was soaking into her pelt, carrying a flood of strength with it. *Is he dead, and communicating with me from StarClan?* The terrible thought squeezed her chest. *But he's not sparkling with starlight . . . he looks just like when I left him! What's happening?*

Hawkwing stood back. "Pebbleshine, there are things you must do," he told her. Pebbleshine looked around and was relieved to see that others of her Clan were there, too: the deputy, Waspwhisker; Echosong the medicine cat; Tinycloud and Macgyver; and more behind them, vanishing into a blur. At their head stood the Clan leader, Leafstar, gazing at Pebbleshine with joy and affection in her amber eyes. A weird light surrounded them, flowing from the cats until it filled every cranny of the den.

"I'm dreaming, aren't I?" Pebbleshine asked, her voice cracking with disappointment. Even Hawkwing's touch and scent—they must have been part of the dream! For a few moments she had believed that Hawkwing and her Clan had really come to rescue her.

Hawkwing nodded, curling his tail around her shoulders. "I'm sorry," he meowed. "I wish I could really be with you."

"I've been trying to get back to you, ever since I was carried off on the back of that monster!" The words burst out of Pebbleshine, filled with all her fears and bitter regret for her useless striving. "But I can't do it alone—I can't!"

"You can." Hawkwing's voice was strong and encouraging. "Pebbleshine, you must. Our kits have important destinies, and right now they're in your paws. You can do what needs to be done."

"But how?" Pebbleshine wailed.

"You must keep calm," Hawkwing meowed. "Think the problem through, and remember that StarClan is always with you." Bending his head, he gave her ears another lick. "Walk toward the setting sun," he murmured. "Come back to me."

Then the light began to fade. "No, don't leave me!" Pebbleshine gasped. "Not yet!"

But it was no use. The dream slipped from Pebbleshine as if she were trying to catch mist in her paws. Hawkwing and the rest of the Clan were gone. Pebbleshine woke and found herself still alone in the dusty little den.

Her heart ached with renewed loss. *What* was *that?*

A communication? A vision? Pebbleshine knew she didn't have those powers; she wasn't a medicine cat. Besides, she thought darkly, something *truly* terrible would have to have happened if all the cats she'd seen were now in StarClan.

It was just a dream.

Still, Hawkwing's words about their kits' destinies echoed in her mind. *I want to believe my kits will be important to the Clan. . . . Is that why I dreamed Hawkwing saying it?*

It didn't matter, she decided. What mattered was that before her dream, she'd felt sure she was going to die . . . but now she believed she could find her way out on her own. *I have to. For my kits . . . and for me. There has to be a way of escaping.* I have *to escape. And I can figure it out all by myself.*

Looking more carefully around the den, Pebbleshine spotted a long stick leaning against the wall. A second stick with lots of protruding teeth was fixed across it at one end. Pebbleshine had no idea what Twolegs might use it for, but it looked like it might be just what she needed. She began pushing it carefully along the wall until the upper end was propped against the cracked window.

Pebbleshine crouched, staring at the stick for a long time while she worked out what to do. She tried pouncing on the bottom of the stick, where the teeth were; when she did that, the other end lifted a little way from the window, and when she let go, it fell back, hitting the hard clearstone.

Yes!

At first, Pebbleshine could only make the stick tap lightly, but as she tried with stronger and stronger pounces, the taps became harder. Finally, one tap made a tiny crack. And when she pounced again and again, wearing herself out, the crack got bigger and bigger, spreading in all directions. Finally, when she was sure she couldn't keep going much longer, a tiny shard of transparent stuff fell out. She pounced one more time, and this time, when the stick struck the window, some of the transparent stuff fell out to make a hole big enough for her to fit through.

"I did it!" she yowled aloud.

Even better, the long stick remained leaning against the window, so Pebbleshine could run up it as if it were a tree branch. When she reached the window, she squeezed herself carefully through the gap, avoiding the sharp shards that still clung to the sides. More of the glittering fragments lay on the ground outside; Pebbleshine had to brace her muscles and push off in a strong leap that carried her beyond them.

As she landed safely on the soft grass, confidence flowed through her like a drink of cool, clear water. "My kits and I are going to make it," she meowed. "I can do this alone. I'm strong enough!"

Thank you, Dream Hawkwing, for reminding me to believe in myself, she added silently. *Now I know that I'll find my Clan again.*

Chapter 6

Pebbleshine hauled herself to the top of a hill and flopped down in the long grass to rest. Several days had passed since she'd escaped from the little Twoleg den, and she had been traveling ever since.

Relaxing in a patch of sunlight, Pebbleshine let her thoughts drift back to the day before, when she had met a strange yellow tom named Tree.

Because she was expecting kits, Tree had stayed close to her during the night, helping her keep watch for predators. And it was a good thing he did—a hunting fox had disturbed them, and it had taken all their strength and fighting skill to drive it off.

That morning, Pebbleshine had invited Tree to come with her and search for SkyClan, assuring him that he would be welcome. But Tree had refused. He had insisted that he was a loner, and however hard Pebbleshine had tried to convince him that it was good to have other cats to rely on, Tree wouldn't change his mind.

Regretfully, Pebbleshine had said good-bye to Tree, but she couldn't shake off the feeling that somehow their destinies were intertwined. "Maybe I will see him again," she mewed softly to herself. "But that's in the paws of StarClan."

Ever since the dream, Pebbleshine had been following the setting sun, just as Hawkwing had told her in her dream. She still wasn't sure where exactly his message had come from, but it had gotten her out of that tiny den, and so she trusted it. She had made good progress since that day, but now that her belly was heavier, it made her awkward and slow, and she grew tired quickly.

It can't be long before my kits come, she thought.

Not for the first time, Pebbleshine wished that Echosong and Frecklewish could be with her, to tell her whether she was headed in the right direction and how close she was to kitting. A cold claw of fear touched her when she thought of giving birth without a medicine cat. All she could do was have faith that seeing Hawkwing and the others hadn't been just a dream, and that StarClan really was helping her.

Ready to go on, Pebbleshine raised her head and looked around. From her vantage point on the hill, the landscape ahead stretched out in front of her. Pebbleshine drew in a gasp of excitement as, far in the distance, she spotted a gleam of water. She felt an odd flutter in her belly, but she tried not to get too optimistic. This wasn't the first time she had seen water in her journeying, but she still hadn't found any Clans.

Then a breeze picked up, blowing toward Pebbleshine from the direction of the water. Tasting the air, she could discern the faint scent of a cat. She blinked, puzzled. It wasn't Sky-Clan scent, and she was much too far away from the water to pick up any cat's scent from there.

Besides, this scent was different. It was icy, the scent of cats who walked with the night wind and the stars. *Stars! Yes!*

"StarClan, is that you?" Pebbleshine asked, her voice quivering. She was so far from her Clan, and she knew she wasn't a medicine cat. But perhaps—now and with her dream—StarClan was finding new ways to send her messages? "Are you really here?"

There was no reply, no vision of a starry warrior. The strange scent wreathed around her for a moment longer and then faded. But Pebbleshine wasn't in any doubt about what she should do now.

Pebbleshine rose to her paws and set off down the hill, heading toward the water. Although she soon lost sight of it, she kept the direction fixed in her mind. Her paws urged her on, as quickly as she could with the weight of her kits, but finally she had to make herself stop and hunt.

I have to keep my strength up for my kits, she thought, even though she felt restless. She wanted to reach the water as fast as possible.

She had halted beside one of the gorse bushes that dotted the hillside. Angling her ears toward it, Pebbleshine picked up the faint sound of scuffling, along with a strong scent of mouse. She swiped her tongue around her jaws in anticipation of the juicy prey.

Creeping forward cautiously, remembering that a mouse would feel the vibration of her paw steps before it heard or smelled her, Pebbleshine ducked under the outer branches of the bush and spotted her prey nibbling on a seed. She pushed off with her hind paws in a long, low pounce and brought both forepaws down hard on the mouse. It didn't even have time to squeal.

"Thank you, StarClan, for this prey," Pebbleshine mewed aloud before bending her head to take a bite. *And thank you for guiding me on my way,* she added silently.

Setting out again after she had eaten, Pebbleshine felt a sudden pain shoot through her belly. She had to halt and catch her breath before walking on again, more slowly. But the pain came again, and again, and finally Pebbleshine realized what it meant.

My kits are coming!

Everything in Pebbleshine fought against the knowledge. She had been so desperate to reach home and Hawkwing before their kits were born. And now that StarClan had sent her a sign and directed her toward the place where she would find the other Clans, all she wanted was to keep moving until she reached the water.

But it seems my kits have other ideas, she thought dryly.

Pebbleshine padded onward for as long as she could, but the pains were coming closer and closer together, and at last she had to accept that she couldn't go any farther. She had to find somewhere safe for her kitting.

She was heading toward a Thunderpath, and for a few moments the roaring and the harsh tang of the monsters, their speed and their glittering colors, bewildered her so that she couldn't think what to do next.

Oh, StarClan, this can't be what you meant!

Then Pebbleshine noticed that the Thunderpath was raised on a steeply sloping bank, a few tail-lengths above its surroundings, and that not far away from where she was standing a dark hole gaped at the foot of the slope. A dip in the grass led down to it. As she padded cautiously nearer, Pebbleshine could see that it was the mouth of some kind of tunnel. A damp, musty smell flowed out of it to meet her, but there was no scent of other creatures inside. Bars of harsh Twoleg stuff covered the opening, though they were set wide enough apart that she could slip between them.

"Do I really want to go in there?" Pebbleshine asked herself.

At the same moment another wave of pain came, so overwhelming that Pebbleshine realized she didn't have any choice. There was no time left to look for somewhere else. At least she could hope that the tunnel would be sheltered and safe.

Pebbleshine padded down to the bottom of the bank and slipped between the bars at the entrance to the tunnel. The musty scent was all around her, and the stones of the tunnel floor were slick with water. Damp cold struck up through Pebbleshine's paws as she splashed her way farther into the tunnel.

She was beginning to despair of finding anywhere safe for her kits when in the dim light she made out a raised area at one side of the tunnel, and managed to drag herself onto it.

The stones were uneven and covered with debris, but at least they were dry.

"That's it!" she gasped as she flopped onto one side. "Kits, this is as far as we go."

Pain after pain rippled through Pebbleshine's belly. She could feel her muscles bunching and stretching as her body tried to push the kits out into the world, but nothing happened. She lost count of how long she had been lying in the tunnel, but the dim light that filtered in from the entrance eventually faded, leaving her in the dark. And still her kits didn't come.

"Oh, StarClan, give me strength!" she choked out through gritted teeth.

"Here." Pebbleshine felt a paw on her shoulder, and looked up to see a pale yellow tom standing over her, pushing a stick toward her. "Bite down on the stick when the pain comes," he meowed.

"But who—" Pebbleshine began, but then the pain swept her up again and overwhelmed her, and she bit down hard on the stick until the agony ebbed away.

"Who are you?" she asked when she could speak again. She blinked up at the yellow tom, who was stroking her flank with the tip of his long tail. "You can't be a medicine cat, not here."

"That doesn't matter," the tom replied. His voice was warm and gentle. "Come on now, push hard, and you'll soon have your kits here with you."

"I'm trying my best . . ." Pebbleshine's voice trailed off as she wondered for the first time how she could see the yellow tom when the tunnel was so dark. Then she noticed the frosty glimmer on the tom's paws and the ends of his whiskers. "Oh . . ."

The pain came again, so intense that Pebbleshine thought her belly would burst open. She gripped the stick in her jaws, and through the chaos she heard the tom's voice again. "Well done, Pebbleshine! A little she-cat."

Pride and love flooded through Pebbleshine as the tom nudged the wriggling bundle toward her. She bent her head to lick the kit's wet fur, when pain pulsed through her once again, and she felt a second kit slip from her onto the gritty floor of the tunnel.

"Another she-cat," the tom announced. "And that's all. You've done it, Pebbleshine."

"They're so beautiful . . . ," Pebbleshine whispered.

She pulled both kits into the curve of her belly and licked them vigorously until their fur was soft and fluffy. One of them was black-and-white, while the other had a gray pelt just like Hawkwing's.

"Thank you for—" she began, raising her head to speak to the tom, only to realize that the mysterious cat had left her. *Maybe I imagined him,* she thought, even though she knew deep inside that he had been too real, and she had needed him too much, for that.

But Pebbleshine was too absorbed in her kits to think for long about the StarClan cat who had come to help her. She was exhausted, and still in pain, but she was so full of joy and love that she felt it would spill out of her like a pool flooding in newleaf.

The kits squirmed closer to Pebbleshine's belly and began sucking strongly. Tiny squeaking noises came from them as they pummeled her with soft paws. Pebbleshine felt that her heart would burst, it was so full of love. She knew that she would willingly give her life for these two precious little creatures.

"I wish your father could be here, little kits," Pebbleshine murmured. "But I know that when Hawkwing sees you, he'll love you just as much as I do."

CHAPTER 7

Pebbleshine bent her head and gently licked her two daughters as they suckled at her belly. Almost a day had passed since she gave birth; they were still in the tunnel, but she had ventured out while her kits were sleeping and collected enough moss and leaves to make a cozy nest.

They are so beautiful. . . . Pebbleshine marveled that after all the danger and heartache she had suffered, her kits had been born strong and healthy. *I promise I'll get you to SkyClan,* she told herself silently. *You will grow up to be Clan cats. I don't know how I'll do it, but somehow, I will make it happen.*

Pebbleshine couldn't remember when she had last eaten, and her belly was rumbling with hunger. She knew that she had to keep her strength up now to care for her kits and provide enough milk for them. So when the kits were full-fed and had fallen asleep, curled around each other in a furry bundle, she rose to her paws, careful not to disturb them. She hated to leave them, glancing back over her shoulder as she padded reluctantly toward the tunnel entrance.

"That's another problem with being a loner," she muttered

to herself. "You have to catch your own prey, even when you have tiny kits."

When Pebbleshine emerged from the tunnel, she saw the sky still streaked with scarlet where the sun had just set. Dusk was already gathering in the hollows beneath the Thunderpath. Now and then the glaring light from the eyes of a monster swept over Pebbleshine as she stood at the foot of the bank and tasted the air.

Soon Pebbleshine picked up the scent of shrew. She tasted the air and pinpointed it in a clump of long grass a few tail-lengths away. She stalked forward until she spotted the small creature; then, with a bound and a swipe from one forepaw, she killed it and devoured it in two massive gulps.

The shrew was too small to have satisfied her hunger, but Pebbleshine didn't want to spend any longer away from her kits. She would hope for more filling prey later.

But as she was making her way back to the tunnel, Pebbleshine picked up another scent, strong enough to swamp even the harsh tang of the Thunderpath.

Badger!

Pebbleshine froze, only her head moving as she tried to spot the intruder. The scent was fresh; the creature must be close by. Eventually she made out the clumsy dark body, the white stripe on the badger's head seeming to glimmer in the twilight.

The badger was lumbering toward her, alongside the bank, thrusting its snout into clumps of grass as it approached. Pebbleshine guessed that it was hunting for slugs or beetles, but it wouldn't turn its snout up at larger prey. She crouched down, trying to make herself as small as possible, while still keeping her gaze fixed on the fierce creature.

At first she thought that the badger would ignore the tunnel entrance and go harmlessly on its way. But as the badger was passing the tunnel, one of the kits inside sent up a thin wail.

Pebbleshine felt her heart begin to pound with terror. *Oh, no! My precious kits! Why did you have to wake up now?* She knew how strong and vicious badgers were—if it got in and found the nest, it would attack her kits and probably eat them.

The badger halted and turned back, its head raised alertly to sniff the air. It was too big to slip between the bars over the tunnel entrance. Pebbleshine waited for a moment, hoping they would be strong enough to keep it out. But as the wailing broke out again, louder now, the badger hurled itself forward, thumping against the bars. Pebbleshine heard a crack, as if the barrier was about to give way.

"No!" she screeched.

She raced toward the badger and flung herself at it, raking her claws down its side, then darting away. The badger turned toward her, startled, and Pebbleshine leaped at it again and clawed its shoulder.

The badger let out an angry growl. Seeming to forget the kit crying in the tunnel, it lumbered toward Pebbleshine. She let it get almost close enough to strike at her with its blunt, powerful claws, then turned and dashed away, up the bank to the edge of the Thunderpath.

Her heart pounded in a mixture of fear and exhilaration as she waited for the badger to follow her. She exulted in her own strength and speed, the warrior skills that gave her the power to save her daughters.

It's so keen to catch me, it won't think any more about my kits!

Pebbleshine glanced over her shoulder as she raced out onto the Thunderpath. The huge beast was hard on her paws, its jaws open to show a mouthful of strong teeth. "Come on, slow mole!" she taunted it. "You can't—"

Pebbleshine broke off as a flash of light swept over her. Roaring filled her ears. A hard blow landed on her side, and she felt herself flying through the air. She barely had time to let out a choking cry before the whole world turned black.

CHAPTER 8

Pebbleshine opened her eyes to find herself lying on the hard surface of the Thunderpath. Harsh light surrounded her, and she could hear the sound of a monster, its roaring diminished to a throaty purr. When she tried to raise her head, every muscle in her body shrieked in agony.

Twoleg voices sounded somewhere close by; Pebbleshine wanted to get up and run away, but her legs wouldn't obey her. The next moment a Twoleg was standing over her. Pebbleshine renewed her weak struggles, but she couldn't fight back when the Twoleg stooped and gently picked her up, then wrapped her in something soft and carried her toward the nearby monster.

"No!" Pebbleshine yowled desperately. "I have to get back to my kits! Put me down! I have to get back to my kits!"

But the Twoleg didn't understand a word.

Pebbleshine wanted to claw at the Twoleg's restraining paws, but she was caught up in the soft wrapping, and she couldn't control her legs. The Twoleg carried her into the monster's belly; Pebbleshine made a last massive effort to struggle, but pain washed over her again and she had to give way to the darkness. *This whole adventure started with a monster carrying me away,* she realized. *Then, it pulled me away from Hawkwing and my Clan; now, it's my kits.*

Her last sensation was of the monster beginning to move off.

Pebbleshine felt the warmth of sun on her fur. Her nose twitched at the scents of fresh growing things all around her. She wasn't in pain anymore. It should have been a relief, but she couldn't help feeling alarmed.

This isn't right. . . . What happened to me?

Blinking her eyes open, Pebbleshine was dazzled by sunlight. When her vision cleared, she found that she was lying in lush meadow grass. A cat was bending over her; Pebbleshine let out a gasp as she recognized the pale yellow tom who had helped her give birth to her kits.

"It's you!" she exclaimed. "I thought I'd imagined you."

Amusement glimmered in the tom's eyes. "No, I'm real," he responded. "My name is Micah. I was the first SkyClan medicine cat. I'm glad I was able to help you when you needed it."

The first . . . Pebbleshine caught her breath in wonder. *He came from so long ago . . . for me?*

"There are some friends waiting to greet you," Micah told her.

He moved aside. Sitting up, Pebbleshine saw a group of cats standing a few tail-lengths away from her. A handsome ginger-and-white tom stepped forward and dipped his head. "Welcome, Pebbleshine," he mewed.

"Billystorm!" Pebbleshine gasped out his name as she sprang to her paws. Her former mentor looked strong and healthy, not ripped apart by a badger's claws as she had last seen him. "But you're—"

"Dead, yes." Billystorm let out an affectionate purr. "This is the territory of StarClan."

For the first time Pebbleshine noticed the frosty glitter on Billystorm's pelt, and the pelts of the other cats who still waited to greet her.

"Then am I dead too?" she asked. Glancing down at her paws, she couldn't see any trace of the glimmer of starshine there.

"Yes," a tom with a dark ginger pelt replied, his sharp green eyes focused on Pebbleshine. "But you haven't yet entered StarClan. We've come to welcome you."

"Sharpclaw!" Pebbleshine whispered as she recognized the SkyClan deputy who had died fighting against Darktail and his rogues in the gorge. "And Duskpaw, you're here too," she added, turning to a young ginger tabby tom. "Oh, Duskpaw, you look great! I'm so sorry we couldn't rescue you from the fire. And Bouncefire, and Snipkit . . . I thought I'd lost you all forever!"

For a few heartbeats, Pebbleshine felt nothing but joy at seeing her dead Clanmates, safe and happy now in StarClan. But then the terrible sights and sounds crowded back into her mind: the badger's blunt, destructive claws; the harsh light and acrid scents of the monsters on the Thunderpath; worst of all, the heartbreaking wails of her abandoned kits. Anxiety gnawed at her belly, sharp as a fox's fangs.

She turned back to Micah. "My kits!" she exclaimed. "I have to get back to my kits. They're not safe alone."

"Your kits will be well," Micah reassured her. "Come here, and I'll show you."

"But—"

Micah interrupted her with a wave of his tail. "Come."

Not sure if she believed the medicine cat's reassurance, Pebbleshine followed Micah across the grass until they came to a dip with a pool at the bottom of it. Micah bounded down to the water's edge and waved his tail once again, beckoning Pebbleshine to join him.

"Look into the water," he instructed Pebbleshine when she had reached his side.

Pebbleshine gazed into the depths of the pool. At first all she could see was waterweed, and the silver flashes of tiny minnows darting to and fro among the fronds. Then her vision blurred, and when she could see clearly again, she found that she was gazing at the Thunderpath and the entrance to the tunnel where she had left her kits.

The sun was shining. Every hair on Pebbleshine's pelt bristled with apprehension at the thought that her kits had been alone for at least one night, and maybe more.

For a moment she felt that she could leap into the pool and get back to her kits that way, but Micah extended his tail across her chest, blocking her.

"No," he mewed gently. "Watch."

As Pebbleshine gazed into the water, she spotted movement

on the grassy slope that led down to the Thunderpath. Two young cats were padding slowly downward: one of them was a dark ginger tom, and the other a she-cat with a silver-gray pelt. Pebbleshine caught her breath in a gasp of relief as she recognized the thin, muscular bodies and familiar patrolling movements of Clan cats. She guessed from their age that they must be apprentices.

"Who are they?" she asked. "They're not SkyClan, but they are Clan cats, aren't they?"

Micah nodded. "Yes, they are. They will find your kits and take them to the Clans. One day, your daughters will be able to rejoin SkyClan, and they will meet their father, Hawkwing."

Pebbleshine was glad to hear that, though she felt that her heart would break as she realized for the first time that she would never make it back to Hawkwing.

She tried to comfort herself with the thought that her kits would know their father, but she still wasn't sure that she believed Micah was right. "I still have to watch over them," she protested. "They have a special destiny, I was told in a dream. And they're *my* kits. I'm not ready to trust strange cats to look after them."

Micah looked down at her, his eyes deep pools of understanding. "There is a way to go back," he told her at last.

"How?" Pebbleshine felt her fur bristling with eagerness. For a few heartbeats the medicine cat seemed reluctant to speak. "Tell me what I have to do! I'll risk anything!"

Micah blinked, still looking indecisive. "You'll only be

an observer," he meowed at last. "Your kits won't be able to see you, or know that you're near them. And neither will any other cat you care about. It's a lonely way to be. Are you sure that's what you want?"

Pebbleshine felt a sudden pang of desolation at the thought that she would never be able to nurse her kits again, never lick their soft fur or teach them the warrior code. And she shuddered at the thought that even if she saw her kits in danger, she wouldn't be able to help them. But that wasn't enough to make her change her mind.

"Of course I'm sure!" she insisted, digging her claws into the ground with impatience. *Maybe I* will *be able to help them somehow, like Micah when he brought me that stick.* "Let's get on with it!"

"If you leave now, you might not be able to get back to StarClan for a long time," Micah warned her. "Perhaps you should do what all your warrior ancestors have done, and watch over your kits from StarClan."

"I'm *sure,*" Pebbleshine repeated. "I've lived as a loner for many days now. I can stand it for as long as I need to, to take care of my daughters. And I don't need to be in StarClan to watch over them. Besides," she added, "my warrior ancestors knew that their loved ones would be safe in their Clan—in SkyClan. But the other Clans drove SkyClan from the forest. Why should I trust those Clans now? I hope they'll treat my kits fairly, but there's no way I can *know* that. I want to stay at least until SkyClan finds them—until they reach the end of their journey to the lake."

Micah sighed, then nodded, accepting her decision at last.

"You're a brave cat, Pebbleshine," he meowed.

Pebbleshine dipped her head in thanks for his praise. She remembered watching Milo and Olive walk away, and then striking out on her own . . . she remembered hitting the window over and over in the tiny den, and the satisfaction she felt when her paws touched grass again. "If I've learned anything on this journey, it's that I can rely on myself to do what has to be done. I hope my daughters can learn that lesson too—either on their own or because I'll be watching over them. Being part of a Clan is a wonderful thing, but so is knowing that you can depend on yourself."

She straightened, head and tail erect. "So, Micah, what do I have to do?"

CHAPTER 9

Micah brushed his cheek against Pebbleshine's. From behind him, Billystorm called out, "Good luck!" The rest of Pebbleshine's former Clanmates echoed his good wishes, while Duskpaw bounded forward to twine his tail briefly with hers and give her ear an affectionate lick.

"You'll make it back here in the end," he assured her. "I know you will."

Her friend's promise warmed Pebbleshine's heart, convincing her that she wasn't doomed to loneliness between life and death forever. "Thanks, Duskpaw," she murmured.

As Duskpaw retreated to join his Clanmates, Micah gestured with his tail. "Step forward into the pool," he meowed.

Determinedly Pebbleshine slid from the grassy bank. For a heartbeat she shivered at the touch of cool water splashing around her paws, and then she began swimming through a whirl of green and silver. The colors faded before Pebbleshine could lose consciousness, and she spotted an exit and began swimming toward it. She left behind a blue sky covered by a thin drift of cloud. At the next moment she reached dry ground and climbed onto it. When she got out, she realized her paws weren't even wet.

Blinking, Pebbleshine looked around. She was standing on a grassy slope close to the Thunderpath, and not many fox-lengths away she could see the bank that held the dark gap of the tunnel entrance.

Her paws itched to carry her down the slope and into the tunnel to find her kits, but before she could move, she began to hear the voices of two cats somewhere behind her, farther up the slope. They were too far away for Pebbleshine to make out the words, but they sounded as if they were having an argument.

If only one of them were Hawkwing! she thought. *Maybe my Clanmates have found me after all.*

Pebbleshine turned and swallowed a cry of disappointment as she recognized the ginger tom and the silver-gray she-cat Micah had shown her in the pool. They were coming down the slope toward her. She began to duck down behind a thick tussock of grass before she remembered that the living cats couldn't see her. The two unfamiliar apprentices halted so close to her that if she had stretched out her tail she could have touched them. Pebbleshine found it hard to believe that she was so close to them and yet they had no idea that she was there.

"Mouse-brain," she muttered to herself, and pricked her ears to listen to what the cats were saying.

"I don't think Sandstorm meant a *literal* different path," the ginger tom was meowing. "Just . . ."

Excitement welled up inside Pebbleshine at hearing the name Sandstorm. *That's a warrior name! They really* are *Clan cats!*

Preoccupied by the discovery, she missed the ginger tom's next few words, though she realized that the two cats still seemed to be in the middle of some kind of squabble. Pebbleshine could tell that the argument wasn't serious. They looked like friends, so surely they would act together to rescue her kits.

Pebbleshine let out a purr at the thought that help for her daughters was so close. A heartbeat later, every hair on her pelt tingled with shock as the gray she-cat turned toward her, a puzzled look on her face. *Can she hear me?* Pebbleshine asked herself. *That's not what Micah said!*

Pebbleshine padded closer to the silver-gray cat. "This way," she whispered into her ear. "Down into the grassy dip, where you can see that dark hole."

At first the she-cat didn't react. *I have to get her attention!* Pebbleshine thought, agonized. *Somehow I have to lead her to my kits. Maybe if I just* think *hard enough . . .*

She concentrated on the tunnel, imagining herself slipping through the bars and padding along in the dim light until she found the nest. She called up an image in her mind of the two tiny kits, gray and black-and-white, huddled together and wailing for help.

Come on! Pebbleshine directed her thoughts toward the gray she-cat. *They need you!*

The she-cat gave her pelt a shake, looking as uncomfortable

as if she felt ants crawling through her fur. She couldn't see Pebbleshine, but clearly she was picking up *something*. Her paws shifted and she glanced down the slope.

"Look!" she yowled. Without waiting for her companion to respond, she pelted downward to where the tunnel entrance gaped in the bank.

"What are you doing?" the ginger tom called after her, fluffing up his pelt in irritation as he trailed along in her paw steps. "That looks dangerous."

Pebbleshine watched as the gray she-cat turned back, rolling her eyes at her friend. "Have you got bees in your brain, or what?" she demanded. "Look, we came *over* the Thunderpath, and now here's a 'different path' that leads *under* it. Plus it's all in shadow! We can go this way!"

The ginger tom still looked reluctant. Pebbleshine wanted to give him a shove, but she knew that he wouldn't feel anything if she tried. Fear cramped her belly as she wondered whether he would be able to persuade his friend not to enter the tunnel.

But though the tom still argued, the she-cat wasn't listening. Hope sprang up inside Pebbleshine as with a flip of her tail the silver-gray cat wriggled through the bars at the tunnel entrance and disappeared. The ginger tom hesitated, letting out a sigh, then followed.

Pebbleshine raced down the slope and entered the tunnel after them. At first she couldn't hear anything except for the voices of the two Clan cats, and renewed fear gripped her.

Does time pass differently in StarClan? How long have I been away?

Pebbleshine knew that her kits were too young to survive for long without their mother. They could be lying dead in the nest at this very moment, and all her struggles would have been for nothing.

Then a vast relief swamped her as from somewhere up ahead Pebbleshine heard the soft cry of a kit. The she-cat had hurried past without noticing the nest, and it was the tom who heard the cry; he halted with his ears pricked. Then he set off again, padding forward until he reached the kits.

"Oh, my darlings! You're alive!" Pebbleshine whispered. But as she gazed over the tom's shoulder, she saw how thin and frail her two daughters looked. Though their eyes still weren't open, they seemed to sense the tom's presence, and they stretched their necks toward him, letting out tiny wails of distress.

The she-cat came bounding back down the tunnel to join her friend. "What's the matter?" she asked. "Why are you—" She broke off, skidding to a halt as she spotted the nest. "They're *kits*!" she exclaimed. "Where's their mother?"

Pebbleshine shivered. "I'm right here," she mewed. "I wouldn't leave them."

The gray she-cat glanced around, and for a heartbeat Pebbleshine thought she might have heard. But the she-cat's gaze swept right over her. "Their eyes aren't even open yet," she continued. "They can only be a few days old."

"And they're so thin," the tom added. "I can tell they haven't eaten in a while."

"I'll go and look for their mother." The gray she-cat

bounded off along the tunnel and out the entrance at the far end. Pebbleshine could hear her calling outside.

Once she was gone, the ginger tom bent over the two kits and examined them more closely, letting his paws run over their tiny bodies and bending his head to give them a thorough sniff. His paws were gentle and seemed to move with sure knowledge.

He's too young to be a medicine cat, Pebbleshine thought. *But he seems experienced. . . . Maybe he's a medicine-cat apprentice.*

Eventually the tom straightened up. "Hey, Needlepaw!" he yowled. "Forget their mother for now. These kits need to eat. Catch something, right away!"

Thank StarClan! Pebbleshine was relieved that the young cat was intelligent enough to see what her kits needed and take care of them at once. There had been authority in his voice as he called out to his friend. *My kits need another she-cat to nurse them, but they can't have that until they reach the Clans. Some chewed-up prey will keep them going until then. Maybe everything will be all right.*

Pebbleshine padded past the tom and curled herself around her kits in their nest. Though she knew they couldn't feel or scent her, they seemed to sense her presence in some way, because they stopped wailing and settled down. Pebbleshine bent her head and nuzzled them gently.

If only Hawkwing were here to keep you warm . . .

Beneath her anxiety about her kits, Puddleshine's heart ached at the thought that she would never return to him, never be close to him again, never share tongues with him or feel the warmth of his fur.

Even now she could picture Hawkwing still near the monster camp, vainly waiting for her to return with their kits, or frantically searching wide stretches of territory, through Twolegplaces and along Thunderpaths, still hoping that he might find her.

She had always believed that she and Hawkwing would grow old together, proudly watching their kits grow up and raise kits of their own. Now she had to let go of that dream, or part of it, anyway. She would never again be with Hawkwing in the way that she wanted to, but nothing would stop her from watching over her newborns. She remembered what Micah had said, that she wasn't following the path of her warrior ancestors . . . no, she was striking out on her own path, just as she had on the journey that began with the chicken monster. But now, as then, she knew she was on the right path: close to her kits, and close to these two young cats who must be deeply connected to her destiny and the destiny of her Clan.

I may never see my former home again. I'll never live at the gorge, and I'll never sleep surrounded by my Clanmates, she thought. *And yet . . . I am home. This is my home now—wherever they are.*

"I'm right here," she whispered again to her kits. "I promise, I'll stay with you."

WARRIORS

TREE'S ROOTS

Special thanks to Clarissa Hutton

ALLEGIANCES

THE SISTERS

LEADER

MOONLIGHT—big, long-haired gray she-cat

SISTERS

SNOW—large white she-cat with blue eyes

FURZE—big ginger she-cat

HAWK—large ginger brown she-cat with golden eyes

ICE—green-eyed she-cat

PETAL—mother of Stream

SPARROW—young ginger-and-white she-cat

SUNRISE—big yellow she-cat

TEMPEST—big tabby she-cat

HAZE—pale gray she-cat

TOMS

EARTH—yellow tom

SNAIL—gray tom

MUD—brown tabby tom

STREAM—tabby tom with blue eyes

CHAPTER 1

Earth squeezed his eyes shut and attempted to become one with the grass. Breathing slowly, he tried to center himself in just the way his mother, Moonlight, had told him, so he would be able to sense the world around him clearly. *This shouldn't be so hard,* he thought.

His ear itched. Earth scratched at it impatiently with his six-toed paw. His stomach growled, and he pushed away thoughts about how long it had been since dawn, when he'd last eaten prey. *Focus,* he told himself sternly, remembering Moonlight's instructions. *Be one with the grass, with the land beneath your paws.* Could he feel what it was like to have tiny roots stretching through the soil? He concentrated. *Can I hear the grass speaking to me?*

No, I can't. His ear was still itchy, and now his nose itched, too. Earth sneezed and opened his eyes.

Next to him, his friend Stream was shifting around restlessly, his eyes half closed.

"I can't concentrate," Earth complained. "I'm hungry."

Stream flicked his tabby tail, opening his eyes wider to look at Earth. "I can't concentrate either," he confessed, then added, "It's probably because your fur's as bright yellow as the sun. . . . I can't see!" He squinted exaggeratedly at Earth until, with a purr of laughter, Earth leaped onto his back, knocking him over.

The two kits rolled in the grass, aiming playful swipes at each other. At last, Stream wrestled Earth onto his back and Earth kicked up with his hind legs, pushing the tabby kit off and ending the play fight.

"You're pretty strong for your size," Stream observed, getting to his feet and shaking the dirt from his fur.

Earth scowled at him. "I'm not *small*," he meowed. "I'm just . . . smaller than most of the Sisters."

He was uncomfortably aware that, even though he was four moons old, just like Stream, he was significantly smaller than both the long-legged tabby tom and Earth's own littermates. *My father, whoever he was, must have been small,* Earth thought. He looked down at his bright-furred paws. *And yellow.*

"You're right," Stream meowed apologetically. "You were much bigger than those everkits at the Twopawplace a moon ago, and they said they were already six moons old."

"I guess," Earth said. He smoothed his fur with his tongue and sat down beside Stream, gazing out over the valley below them. It was sunny and warm, with dandelions and buttercups growing here and there among the grass. He could scent prey, and the familiar smell of the Sisters. Further downhill, near the low, thick bush that was the nursery, he saw his mother, Moonlight, talking seriously with two of the other Sisters. One of them—Stream's mother, Petal—nodded obediently in response to something Moonlight said, then trotted away.

Earth sighed. He wished that Moonlight would take more time to instruct him and Stream on how they were supposed to use meditation to speak to the grass and the soil below them. Maybe if she'd told them exactly what those things sounded like, he'd know how to hear them. But she was always so busy. *It's a big responsibility, leading the Sisters,* he reminded himself.

A soft breeze ruffled his fur, and he took a deep breath, scenting cedar and pine from the woods beyond the valley and the fresh smell of the river nearby.

"I like it here," he told Stream. "It's better than that garden by the Twopawplace." He and Stream had both been born and lived their first two moons in an overgrown Twopaw garden by a crumbling old stone barn. There had been plenty of shelter there, but the rosebush protecting the nursery had pricked his paws. And every cat had kept scolding the kits to keep quiet and avoid attracting the attention of Twopaws. This wide valley surrounded by grassy hills was better.

"I like it, too," Stream said. "There's no point in getting attached, though. In two moons, we'll go on our wander. And the Sisters will move on, too."

Earth shivered a little, the breeze suddenly feeling colder. Toms born to the Sisters only stayed with their mothers and sisters for the first six moons of their lives. Toms were meant to wander the world and find their own paths while the she-cats stayed together. It was just the way things were. Two of the other young toms would be sent on their wander tonight. Earth couldn't stop thinking about it, how someday he'd be the one leaving everything he knew behind.

The world seemed like a big place to wander. Earth knew it went past the garden where he'd been born, over Thunderpaths and rivers, farther than any cat could see, even from the top of the tallest hill.

"Maybe we could come back here," he suggested to Stream. "After the Sisters move on. We could live here." He looked around again, at the blue sky and the open grasses and flowers. "This would be a good home."

Stream's blue eyes opened wide. "Earth!" he yowled. "That's the *opposite* of wandering. That's not what toms *do*!"

"I guess." Earth tucked his tail closer to his body. "But it's a good territory. What if when we travel, we end up somewhere worse? I like it here."

"That's because we haven't been many other places," Stream said. "Just wait. Once we're on our own, we're going to travel everywhere. It'll be fun."

"You're probably right," Earth agreed, feeling a little happier. At least he wasn't going to be alone on his wander. Stream would be with him. Maybe it *would* be fun, as long as they were together. "Let's try meditating again," he suggested. "Moonlight wants us to really try to talk to the land."

"Okay," Stream agreed, settling more comfortably on his haunches. "I'm not sure what that means, though."

"Me either," Earth said. "Maybe if we focus hard enough, it'll just happen?"

"Let's try." Stream took a deep breath and shut his eyes. Earth shut his own eyes and reminded himself again what

Moonlight had told them.

Concentrate. Be one with the soil and the grass, the rocks and the trees. Toms were the guardians of the earth, while she-cats spoke to the skies. It was very important to get this right. Earth dug his claws into the dirt beneath him and listened hard, his ears trembling as he strained them.

Nothing.

Focus.

Wait. He pricked up his ears, a thrill of excitement running down his spine. Was that a voice he heard? Distant, but there. Was he hearing the voice of the growing grass? He strained, his ears aching with the desire to just *hear* . . .

"—a chipmunk, but it was the size of—"

Earth sighed, slumping with disappointment. It was the voice of his sister Ice. Without opening his eyes, he knew the breeze had carried her voice faintly to him from the valley below. He hadn't heard the grass after all.

This is pointless, he thought, and opened his eyes again. Turning toward Stream to meow his annoyance, he stopped with his mouth half open.

Stream was sitting perfectly still, his face calm but his mouth moving. He was muttering softly to himself, a low purr of words that Earth couldn't quite make out. He paused now and again as if to listen for an answer. *No,* thought Earth, amazed. *He's not muttering to himself. It's to the grass and the soil. He's talking to the* land, *just like we're supposed to.*

Earth closed his eyes once more, tense and determined. He strained his ears, but, other than the rustle of the wind in the trees and the meows of the Sisters in the distance, he couldn't hear a thing.

What's wrong with me, that he can do it and I can't?

He opened his eyes and waited, his tail twitching restlessly, until Stream finally looked at him, his eyes wide and peaceful. "I'm ready now," the other kit said.

Walking back down to camp, Earth peeked at Stream out of the corner of his eye. The other kit didn't *look* any different. Earth badly wanted to ask Stream what had happened. Had he really spoken to the grass? *How? And how did it* feel*? What did the grass say?*

Earth hesitated. He didn't want to sound stupid. Stream had meditated the right way, had spoken with the ground and plants beneath their paws . . . and Earth hadn't. Even though he'd really tried, he'd gotten it wrong. Did he want to tell Stream that?

He'll think there's something wrong with me. But he's my best friend. . . .

Earth was still worrying about whether to tell Stream the truth as they reached camp. The Sisters were busy but peaceful: Tempest and Furze were just back from a hunting patrol, fat voles dangling from their mouths as they strode toward the prey-hole. Petal and Hawk were sharing tongues in the sunshine while Snow, Moonlight, and Haze talked quietly by the bush that was Moonlight's den.

"Earth! Stream!" His littermate Sunrise burst out of the nursery and raced toward him, their sister Ice behind her. "Did you do it?" she panted as she halted beside them. "Did you talk to the land? What did it sound like?"

"Um." Earth gave a quick, embarrassed lick to the fur on his chest. "It went fine."

"Mm-hmm." Ice's green eyes narrowed as she sauntered up behind Sunrise. "You didn't hear anything, did you?"

"Well, it's hard!" Earth said defensively.

"It *is* hard," Stream agreed. "You should try it yourself before you start teasing Earth."

Sunrise flicked her tail. "Sisters don't talk to the land," she said. "We sing to the stars."

Ice sat down and tucked her paws neatly beneath her. "It's really important that you get this right, Earth," she said, mock seriously. "Did you do something to offend the land? Is that why it won't talk to you?" She lowered her voice and glanced around. "Did you . . . make dirt in the wrong place, maybe?"

"You'd better get the land back on your side before you go on your wander!" Sunrise added, joining in on the teasing. "What if you fall asleep in a mud puddle and it just swallows you up?"

"Oh, ha-ha," Earth replied with as much dignity as he could muster, while the two she-cats purred with laughter. He wasn't going to let his sisters bother him. *It'll be okay,* he told himself. *The land isn't angry at me.* Is *it?* He shook his pelt, feeling as if he were shaking away his worries. "I'm hungry."

The prey-hole was full. His mouth watered as he caught the scent of rabbit, and he began to head across the camp toward it.

"Wait," Sunrise meowed, serious for once, and blocked his path. "Chestnut and Snail get first choice today."

That's right. Earth's appetite disappeared, his stomach dropping. Chestnut and Snail would start their wander tonight. They were only a couple of moons older than he was, and they were going to leave the Sisters and find their own path. *Soon it'll be my turn. Will I be ready by then?*

Stars hung low in the sky, the Claw Stars pointing to the setting sun. The stars would guide the young toms on their first journey. The shadows deepened, and the full moon rose, cold and pale. At last, Moonlight got to her feet and padded silently across the camp toward the hills. The other she-cats, the mothers and sisters of the Sisters, followed. Chestnut and Snail walked close beside their mother, Hawk, but their tails were high and their steps light, as if they were excited to begin their wander. Earth and Stream glanced at each other, then trailed after the other cats.

At the top of the hill, Chestnut and Snail stopped, their dark fur shadowy in the moonlight. The Sisters gathered around them, and Moonlight stepped forward to touch her nose gently first to Snail's ear, then to Chestnut's. "I wish you happiness," she told them softly, then stepped away to let another Sister brush her muzzle against theirs.

One by one, the cats of the Sisters said their good-byes to Snail and Chestnut. "We won't forget you," one murmured. "Take care of each other," another mewed. Hawk pressed her face to each of theirs, hard, and closed her eyes as if she was memorizing her sons' scents.

At last, it was Earth's turn. His chest was tight with anxiety. Chestnut and Snail had always been part of their group, only a little older than Earth and Stream and their littermates. They had organized the best games of moss-ball when they were all younger and had led daring, sneaky raids on the prey-hole. How could they be leaving the Sisters forever?

"Good luck," Earth said awkwardly, touching his cheek to Snail's as the larger tom bent down to him. He turned to Chestnut and touched his cheek as well. "Maybe we'll see each other on our wanders someday."

"Maybe," said Chestnut lightly. His eyes were bright, and he was already looking past Earth, down the hill. Earth watched as he exchanged an excited glance with Snail. It was as if they couldn't wait to begin their wander.

Earth wondered what that felt like.

At last, the good-byes said, Moonlight dipped her head to the two toms. "This is the beginning of your adventure," she meowed, her voice warm. "Our love goes with you as you set off on your endless wander. You are guardians of the land now. You must listen to what it tells you. Be honorable cats, and the land will guide your paws."

Snail and Chestnut both nodded earnestly. "We will listen."

Moonlight blinked at them approvingly. "Walk through the night without looking back," she told them. "At dawn, you will have left your kithood behind you and become true toms. May the ancestors who walk the land find you and give you guidance."

Chestnut dipped his head again. "Thank you," he replied, and Snail echoed him.

Earth shuddered, his tail lowering, then looked around to see if anyone had noticed. The Sisters regularly spoke to their ancestors—*ghosts*—and every cat believed that these same ancestors would find toms on their wander. The spirits were supposed to guide them, to give them advice. But Earth had never seen a ghost, and he didn't want to. It sounded *creepy*. What would a ghost look like?

Chestnut and Snail probably already knew. No doubt they could see spirits and talk to the land. They were ready for this.

Earth watched as Snail and Chestnut walked down the hill and out of sight. They didn't look back. They were hurrying, eager for whatever came next.

A cold, sudden wind blew through Earth's fur and flattened his ears. He shivered again and looked up. Dark clouds were racing across the sky, blotting out the Claw Stars. The branches of the trees farther along the hill thrashed wildly.

"Let's get to shelter," Moonlight called, waving her tail for the Sisters to follow her.

Earth looked in the direction where Chestnut and Snail had gone. There was no sign of them now. They had disappeared into the night.

Stream shivered beside him. "Let's go," he mewed.

"I hope Snail and Chestnut find somewhere dry to sleep," Earth told him. "It's going to rain."

"They have to look after themselves now," Stream answered. "Come on!"

With one last glance after the older toms, Earth followed Stream back to their camp and into the nursery, where he curled up, grateful for Stream's warmth on one side and Sunrise's on the other. He let his eyes close. *Chestnut and Snail will be all right,* he thought. *They'll look after each other.*

Earth didn't know how long he slept, but he woke with a start. The nursery was dark, not even a hint of moonlight shining through the branches. Cold water was dripping through the thornbush and trickling through his fur. It was raining hard.

"Mrrrrooooooooooow!"

Earth sat straight up, every hair on his pelt trembling. The frightened yowl had come from outside, cutting through the steady beat of the rain.

It was his mother.

CHAPTER 2

"Moonlight!" Earth jumped to his paws. He'd never heard his mother sound like that before.

"What's going on?"

"It's not morning yet."

The other kits were stirring and meowing complaints, but Earth ignored them and pushed his way out of the nursery.

"Moonlight! Where are you?" The rain was coming down so hard, it felt like claws slashing through Earth's fur. Cold wind whipped water into his eyes and blew back his ears and whiskers. He could hear cats calling to one another throughout the camp, but he couldn't see any of them.

Stream came out of the nursery behind him, his cold fur brushing Earth's briefly. "I'll look this way," he yowled, waving his tail toward the hill from which they had watched Chestnut and Snail leave.

"Wait!" Earth told him. "We should—" *Stick together,* he began to say, but a crack of lightning, quickly followed by a rumble of thunder, drowned out his words. When he blinked the lightning dazzle from his eyes, Stream was gone.

"To me! Sisters, to me!" Moonlight was suddenly there,

calling through the rain. She was almost on top of him before she saw him. "Earth," she meowed, "why are you out of the nursery? Where are the other kits?" Before he could answer, she had stepped past him and poked her head into the nursery. "Ice! Sunrise! Haze! Come with me!"

The three she-kits tumbled out of the nursery after her, huddling together and hunching their shoulders against the rain.

"Where's Stream?" Moonlight asked briskly.

"I don't know," Earth answered. "He went . . ." He gestured with his tail toward the hill. "I tried to stop him."

"Okay," Moonlight mewed. As another bolt of lightning lit the clearing, she looked past Earth, her worried gaze searching the camp. "This way." She brushed her tail across the kits' backs, guiding them toward the far end of the clearing.

The rain beat against Earth's face as he followed his mother. Other voices were calling across the camp, panicked. He narrowed his eyes to slits as lightning lit up the sky again. Beside him, Sunrise jumped as another crack of thunder sounded.

Moonlight led them to a large stone on the side of the clearing. "Stay here," she ordered firmly. "I have to help the others."

"We can help!" Earth volunteered. The she-kits yowled their agreement.

"You can help by staying put," Moonlight replied, already turning away. "I need to gather the Sisters together." She disappeared into the darkness.

The stone provided a little shelter from the rain. Earth pressed against it, the cold of the rock seeping into his wet skin. His heart was beating so wildly it felt as if there were a frantic bird trapped in his chest.

He could hear Moonlight calling to the Sisters, marshaling them into position to survive the storm. His tail lashed with irritation: *Why* was he too small to be of any use?

"Help! Help me!" A faint yowl came to them on the wind.

"That's Stream!" Earth stepped out from the stone's shelter, his ears pricked to catch his friend's cry.

Sunrise followed him out into the rain. "I don't think Moonlight can hear him," she mewed worriedly. "She's still gathering the Sisters."

"Help!" Stream sounded even more frantic this time. Without pausing to think, Earth began to run toward his friend's voice. He slipped in the mud and scrambled up again and kept running.

"Earth! Moonlight said to *stay here*!" Sunrise wailed behind him, but Earth didn't turn back. Water streamed down his sides as he tried to get his bearings: in the dark and rain, the familiar camp was suddenly full of unidentifiable shapes and impossible to navigate. He took a few more tentative steps, his paws sinking into mud. Blundering against a bush—*the den where Furze and Tempest were sleeping, maybe*—he hissed as thorns scratched his pelt.

"Help!" Stream yowled again, and Earth changed course to head straight toward him.

Earth was moving uphill now, and it slowed him down. He tried to run faster. "I'm coming!" he yowled, but the wind whipped the words away so that he could barely hear his own voice. His paws slipped in the mud, making him slide backward. Thick mud splattered across his fur. He fell again and struggled to get up, the mud sticking to him and pulling him back.

The land is stopping me from getting to Stream, he thought. *I couldn't speak with it, and now it hates me.* How had he managed to upset the land so badly?

Clenching his jaw, Earth felt carefully through the mud in front of him. There were rocks beneath the surface of the hill, and he extended his claws to grip their edges, slowly pulling himself up.

He slipped again, and again, mud now sticking to his fur and weighing him down. His claws ached, but he was making slow progress. The climb seemed like a nightmare: mud and darkness, sore muscles, and the rocks pulling at his claws.

As he finally came over the top of the hill, the wind caught Earth again, blowing rain into his face. He hunched automatically, blinking, as a dazzling bolt of lightning, accompanied by a crash of thunder, lit up the hilltop.

Stream was right in front of him, fur plastered to his sides, his eyes wide with panic. His mouth was half open in a yowl.

Everything went dark again, and Stream pressed his cold, shivering side against Earth's. "I shouldn't have run up here," Stream panted. "I couldn't get down, it was so dark. I didn't know which way to go." His meow was shaky. Earth had never heard his friend sound so frightened.

"It's okay," Earth told him. He was scared, too, but one of them had to be brave. "We'll go downhill together."

Another flash of lightning lit up the camp in the valley below them. Muddy streams of water were flowing through the clearing and flooding through the dens. The Sisters were wading through mud, running to save themselves and one another, the clearing more chaotic than anything Earth had ever seen.

As the world went dark, Stream pressed more closely to Earth. "This is bad."

"Yeah." Earth took a deep breath. "We can go down and help. There are rocks under the mud. If we dig our claws in, we can get down without falling." *I hope.*

He went first, feeling carefully with one paw, then the other. He slipped several tail-lengths before he was able to stop himself, legs and claws aching. He could hear Stream behind him, thrashing through the mud.

He turned to call encouragement. "It's not too—"

The world lit up bright white, with a simultaneous *boom* of thunder. His fur stood on end, and he could smell the sharp scent of lightning.

Then the world was dark again. Earth's ears were ringing. Something fell past him in the darkness, sliding and rolling. *Just a rock,* Earth told himself, but his stomach twisted into a knot. Some tiny part of him knew it wasn't a rock. *It was . . .*

"Stream!" he yowled, and tried to run. Losing his footing, he slithered and slipped down the hill, finally rolling, then landing in a heap in the valley, his fur clumped together with wet mud. "Stream," he called again, but the rain was pounding down, drowning him out.

Blundering forward, his paws struck something soft and warm. "Stream?" Earth asked, bending to nose at the huddled shape. It *was* Stream, but with something strange beneath his scent. His body was hot as fire. His soft fur was standing on end. Earth stiffened, his stomach heavy with dread.

Stream smelled like burning. He smelled like fire and pain.

Earth gasped and staggered back a step, mud squelching beneath his paws.

Stream was dead.

Two days later, there was still evidence of the storm's destruction everywhere. Earth and the remaining Sisters were huddled between the roots of a beech tree. Furze was scratched and cut all over from being washed through a thornbush as the river flooded their camp. Tempest had a sprained leg from pulling Ice out of a stream of mud, keeping her from being swept away. All the Sisters had scrapes and bruises, and their gazes were bleak.

Stream was not the only cat who had died. Haze, half a moon younger than they were, a close friend of Earth's sister Sunrise, had drowned right in front of the Sisters as they struggled to reach her. Grief for the two lost kits battered the Sisters like another storm, Earth thought, drenching them in sorrow.

Sunrise was huddled close to Haze's mother, Snow, her tail entwined with the white she-cat's. They seemed to be taking comfort in each other. A little way from them, Stream's mother, Petal, sat alone, her face somber.

Moonlight stood and brushed her tail comfortingly across Snow's back. "We will sing for her," she meowed softly. "Our sisters are never really lost."

Snow nodded, her eyes closing for a moment. Moonlight headed toward the clearing, brushing her tail across Petal's back too as she passed, but saying only, "I'm going to gather more herbs to treat injuries. We lost everything." Petal said nothing.

Earth watched his mother walk away; then, with a sudden surge of anger, he jumped to his paws and followed her. "Mother," he called, when they had walked out of earshot of the other cats.

Moonlight turned to him. "Are you going to help me find herbs?" she asked. "We can look for tansy and chervil farther from the river."

Earth flexed his sore claws angrily. "Why are we singing for Haze and not Stream?" he asked angrily. "Stream was a kit of the Sisters, too."

"Stream was a tom," Moonlight answered gently.

"So?" Earth snapped. "That's not fair."

Moonlight sighed. "It's not a matter of fairness," she told him. "As a tom, Stream was always destined to return to the earth. We do not need to sing for him. Maybe we will see his spirit before he steps into his own afterlife; maybe we will not. The earth takes care of its own." Her gaze grew stern. "Although, when I went back to the stone and you were gone, I was full of grief. You are far too young for me to accept the land's taking you. Stream's youth is the cause of Petal's sorrow. You must *not* disobey me like that."

Fur prickled uncomfortably along Earth's spine. "You mean you won't grieve for me if I die when I'm full-grown?" He couldn't imagine his mother not loving him.

Moonlight's gaze softened, and she bent to brush her muzzle against his. "Of course I would," she told him. "I will never stop caring what happens to you. But before long, you'll leave the Sisters for your wander. We might never see each other again. If the land takes you, I may never know." She sighed again. "Mothers of toms have to take comfort in knowing that those toms will be taken by the land they guard during their lives. There is honor in a tom's death."

Earth stood silent, not knowing what to say. His mother touched her nose to his once more, then turned away. "I am going to look for herbs. I will be back soon."

Earth watched her go, her pace steady and purposeful. He knew that Moonlight had had other litters, older sons who had gone on their wanders before he was born. But he had never thought about the fact that they had left and she had never seen them again. Was believing that a tom's death was an honorable one, that he would die guarding the land, something a mother cat *needed*? He sat back and scratched thoughtfully at his ear. It was too big a question for him, he decided. How could he know how a mother felt?

Another thought occurred to him, and he dropped his paw, his chest tightening. Stream was gone, but Earth was still four moons old. In two moons, would he still be sent on his wander?

Alone?

As the sun set and the stars rose, the Sisters gathered once more, this time in the remains of their camp. Looking around, Earth saw that the bushes that had been the nursery and the Sisters' dens had been torn apart and flattened by the streams of mud and water that had raced through camp. One bush—Moonlight's den, he thought—had been entirely uprooted and washed to the edge of the woods.

His tail drooped at the devastation around the camp. *We won't stay here,* he thought. It had been such a good camp. Stream's bones would lie here, held safe by the land, but Earth and the Sisters would be gone.

The she-cats gathered around Moonlight, and Earth hung back at the fringes of the group. Being a tom hadn't felt as *separate* from the Sisters when there had been four of them. It was weird to be the only tom now.

"Tonight we sing our sister Haze into the sky," Moonlight began. "She was a good Sister, and we lost her far too young. She should have grown to have her own kits and to travel the Sisters' path for many leafrises. We will show her the way to her afterlife. If she would like to speak to any of us first, we would welcome her." She glanced briefly at Earth and added, "And if Stream, or any of our ancestors, wishes to visit us, we would be glad to speak to them again."

Then she raised her head and looked to the sky. Moonlight

sang first, a high, mournful note, and the Sisters chimed in, their voices blending with hers as they rose to the sky.

Good-bye, Haze, Earth thought. He hoped the younger kit would find happiness in the afterlife. Would she come and visit them first? Would Stream? His fur prickled uneasily. He had never seen a spirit, hadn't really wanted to. But he wanted to see *Stream*, didn't he? And he couldn't imagine his best friend didn't want to see him.

He glanced around, a nervous hope rising inside him. *I do want to see him.*

Gradually, the singing trailed off, and the Sisters waited, their gazes turned expectantly toward the stars. Earth waited, too, glancing around eagerly, his eyes on the trees lower down the hill. *He'll come from the land, won't he?*

Sunrise gave a squeal of delight and leaped to her feet. "Haze! Are you okay?" She paused, her head cocked as if she was listening, then went on. "I'm glad. I was so scared when the water took you away."

One after another, the other she-cats rose, their welcoming faces turned toward cats Earth couldn't see.

"It's been so long . . ."

"A few moons ago, we went past that Twopawplace where we lost you. . . ."

"New kits in your family since we spoke last . . ."

Finally, Petal gave a warm purr. "Stream, my kit, are you well?" Then she listened, her eyes bright for the first time since dawn had risen over Stream's broken body two days before. Earth stared, blinked hard, stared again. He strained his eyes and ears, hoping to see even the slightest outline of a cat, to hear the faintest whisper of Stream's meow.

He saw nothing.

The sky was beginning to lighten by the time the Sisters called their good-byes to the dead. Sunrise ran to Moonlight and pressed her face against her mother's fur. "She's gone," she wailed.

Earth watched, feeling cold and empty, as Moonlight comforted his littermate. He was hovering just outside the group: when he'd realized that he was the only cat who couldn't see the dead walking among them, he'd backed away, ashamed.

When Sunrise was calmer, she and Ice began to talk quietly, their heads close together, and Moonlight walked toward Earth.

"So," she meowed when she reached him. "Stream was here. How was that for you?" Her eyes were sharp, and fixed on him.

Does she know I couldn't see him? Earth wondered. For a heartbeat, he thought of lying, but what good would that do? He was a cat of the Sisters—a *tom* of the Sisters—and he would need the spirits of his ancestors to help him on his path.

"I didn't see him," he said dully. "I didn't see any of them."

Concern flickered across Moonlight's face, and then she purred soothingly, "It takes some cats longer than others. You'll get there, I'm sure."

"Really? You don't think there's something wrong with me?" Earth asked.

"Of course not." Moonlight dipped her head to lick his shoulder.

Earth wanted to believe her, and to be comforted. But he remembered two other young toms who had been sent away before they ever saw spirits. "What about Mud and Spider? Do you think they ever saw spirits? Did our ancestors come to them?"

Moonlight sighed. "I have to believe that they did," she told him. "But they wandered, so we can never know for sure."

Earth's mouth went dry with dread. *I'm never going to see my ancestors,* he knew suddenly. If he had been going to, he would have seen Stream.

If Stream had lived, *he* would have been able to speak to the dead. If he and Earth had gone on their wander together, as they'd planned, Stream would have listened to their ancestors' guidance for both of them. But Stream was gone now. Once Earth left the Sisters, no spirits would come to him. Once he left, he would be alone.

Chapter 3

Glumly, Earth sniffed at the roots of a pine tree and wrinkled his nose at its sharp scent. *I hate it here.* He was supposed to be practicing hunting, but he didn't smell any of the shrews or mice that Hawk, his teacher for the day, had told him to search for. *I miss Stream.* Learning to hunt had been more fun with his friend beside him.

It was full leafshine now, sun warming the beds of pine needles and glinting off a little pond nearby. Part of Earth had to admit that this—their second new territory in the last two moons—was a good place for the Sisters.

It's not like it matters for me. I won't be here long. Giving up his halfhearted effort at hunting, Earth batted a twig out of his way as he meandered beneath the trees.

Since they had left the camp where Stream and Haze had died, it had felt to Earth like the Sisters were always traveling. And he was always trailing after them, alone, the only tom now except for one of Furze's newborn kits, who was too young to count.

The Claw Stars would align to send him on his wander in just a few days. He'd been watching them, full of dread, as they moved closer and closer to where they'd be when he had to go. Earth's stomach clenched anxiously at the thought.

If Stream had still been alive, they'd have been leaving together. They'd have looked out for each other, given each other courage. The ancestors would have come to them and guided their paw steps. If Earth saw the ancestor spirits on his own, he might run for his life like a hunted mouse, he thought glumly.

And what would happen if the ancestor spirits tried to speak to him, but he couldn't see them? Would they be angry? Earth swallowed hard and swiped another twig out of his way.

"You call this hunting?" Earth jumped at Hawk's sharp meow. He'd been thinking so hard he hadn't even heard her come up behind him.

"Hawk!" he said. "Sorry, I was . . ." He found it hard to meet the stern gaze of the tall brown she-cat, so he stared at the ground instead. "I got distracted."

Hawk sighed. "Earth, you haven't been paying attention when I try to teach you, or when Furze does, or Snow, or any of us. We're trying to show you skills you need to know."

Earth felt his shoulders slump even further. He knew he wasn't doing well. Nothing the Sisters had taught him since the storm had stuck. *Stream was better at all of this.* "Sorry," he repeated, his pelt prickling with misery and embarrassment.

Hawk's golden eyes seemed to soften. "I know you are, Earth," she meowed. "But you need to learn to stay alert. In just a few days, you'll begin your wander. You'll have to take care of yourself."

Panic stirred in Earth's chest. "But I'm not *ready*," he protested. "One of Furze's kits is a tom, too. Maybe I should wait until he's old enough to wander, and then we could go together. We'll take care of each other."

Hawk's tail twitched dismissively. "Don't be silly," she told him. "Furze's kit won't be ready to wander for moons. His eyes only opened yesterday." Nudging him with her shoulder, she added, "You're six moons old now and you're a smart cat, Earth. You'll be fine."

"I guess." Earth shifted his paws uneasily. Maybe Hawk was right, but he doubted it.

"Come on," Hawk meowed, looking around. "Let's go out to the long grass. We can hunt together."

A little way beyond the pine forest was a long stretch of open land where grass rippled in the breeze. Earth scented the air, his heart lightening a little.

Hawk tasted the air, too, her mouth open. "This clearing is full of voles and mice. I'll go that way," she decided, gesturing with her tail, "and you pick a scent trail to follow. If you spot a vole, try to drive it toward me."

As she disappeared through the grass, Earth crouched low, his belly to the ground. Dutifully, he sniffed around. *I probably won't catch anything.* There was a strong smell of vole and he tracked it, listening to see if he could hear a tiny heartbeat. There was a tangle of dry, dead grass near the roots of the growing plants, the perfect place for prey to hide. He crept forward, one slow paw step after another.

His nose twitched. There was another scent, getting stronger.

Cats, he realized. *Strangers.*

Earth jerked his head up. *Rogues!*

A thin gray tom was prowling toward him. Earth tensed, then caught another scent. A brown tabby she-cat was crouched on Earth's other side, her tail slashing furiously.

"This is our territory," the tom snarled. "Get out."

Earth froze. What was he supposed to do now? Moonlight always said that cats who claimed territory were foolish—the land belonged to every cat. But Moonlight wasn't here.

"We're just passing through," he mumbled, tucking his tail tightly around his legs.

The tom prowled forward, growling. "We don't want strangers on our territory."

"We'll teach you to stay away," the she-cat added, drawing close to his other side.

Earth turned his head to look at her and a sharp hot pain slashed across his ears. The tom had clawed him. Earth's legs trembled. He couldn't run; he couldn't fight. The she-cat hissed and swiped at his shoulder, a stinging blow. Earth wailed in terror.

"Hey!" Hawk ran through the grass and leaped at the she-cat, knocking her away. "Leave him alone!"

Earth gave a gasp of relief. Hawk would save him. Hawk and the tabby she-cat grappled on the ground, rolling over and over. With a howl of fury, the gray tom threw himself into the fight. Horrified, Earth watched him dig his claws into Hawk's side as the brown tabby kicked and slashed at her from below. Hawk was bigger than either of them, and she was a good fighter, but so were both these cats, and she was outnumbered.

Earth tried to remember what he'd learned about fighting. Since Stream and Haze had died, the Sisters had been so busy, but Tempest and Snow had both trained him on techniques for battling another cat. *Do I leap? Or is it better to go low?* He couldn't remember anything. He couldn't move.

With a heave, the brown she-cat rolled out from beneath Hawk, and Hawk fell heavily onto her side, yowling in pain.

Earth made a huge effort and broke free from his stillness. Squeezing his eyes shut, he barreled forward. He had to help her.

His head bashed into the gray rogue's side, and he heard a grunt and the other cat falling backward. Earth opened his eyes as Hawk leaped to her paws.

"Run!" she shouted, and Earth ran. He could hear Hawk behind him, and then she was beside him, slowing her long stride so that they ran together. The rogues were snarling threats and warnings behind them.

"Don't come back here!" the tom yowled, and the tabby added, "There's more of us! Stay off our territory!"

As they came in sight of the Sisters' current camp, Earth was gasping for breath. Hawk slowed to a walk. "Are you okay?" she asked.

"I'm fine." Earth noticed a stream of blood running down

Hawk's hind leg. "Are you hurt?"

Hawk grimaced and bent to give the leg a quick lick. "That tabby had sharp claws," she meowed.

Earth cringed. "I'm sorry, I should have helped sooner. I just . . . froze."

"Don't worry about it," Hawk told him. Leading the way into camp, she headed straight for the hollow where they had stored some healing herbs. Earth's belly felt hot with guilt as he noticed she was limping.

He trailed after her. "Can I help?"

"No, I think I can get it myself." Hawk sat and began to chew some chervil to put on her wound. Earth watched, feeling useless.

Moonlight came over, her gaze worried. "What happened?" she asked. Hawk, her mouth full of chervil, shrugged, and Moonlight turned to Earth.

Earth stared at his paws, his whole body burning with guilt now. "We were hunting, and two rogues attacked us," he mewed softly. "I froze, I couldn't fight, and Hawk had to fight them alone. She protected me."

Bristling, Moonlight looked stern. "You're six moons old; you should be able to protect yourself. A good Sister could have died looking after you."

"I'm *sorry*," Earth whispered.

When he met Moonlight's eyes, he felt like she was looking straight into his thoughts. "You'll be going on your wander in just a few days," she told him. "You will have to take care of yourself. You *will* take care of yourself."

Do you really *think I'm ready?* Earth dug his claws into the ground. How could the Sisters believe he was prepared to wander?

He wanted to hiss at her, to make her see how *not* prepared he was. But his mouth was too dry to speak. Instead he watched her walk away.

"She's working to protect every cat," Hawk mewed gently, looking up from licking the chervil onto her leg wound. "She doesn't mean to be cruel."

Moonlight wants to protect every cat, Earth thought. *I couldn't even protect myself.* At least he wouldn't be a danger to the Sisters anymore, once he was gone.

As the sun rose on the morning of the day when Earth would set out on his wander, Ice was whimpering in the sick den. From outside the den, Earth listened to his sister's pained little whine, his heart clenching.

"Is she going to be okay?" he asked Moonlight as she stepped out of the den.

"I hope so," Moonlight told him, her face tight with worry. "I think she's just eaten some bad prey. But if she doesn't feel better soon, I might take her to a Twopaw den to see if we can have them help her."

Earth shifted his paws nervously. "Twopaws? Really?"

"Some of them are softhearted, and they have their uses," Moonlight mewed crisply. "Never forget that the Sisters' ancestors once lived with Twopaws." She shook her pelt slightly, as if shaking away the idea. "But I hope it won't be necessary. Fetch some fresh moss for Ice's nest? What she really needs is sleep."

"Of course," Earth replied. He knew where the softest moss grew, down on the banks of the little stream at the edge of camp.

As he carefully scraped moss off the rocks by the stream, choosing the freshest and thickest-looking pieces, his fur tingled with anxiety. He'd been trying not to think about it, but *today* was the day.

Today he would leave the Sisters forever.

Ice had been so sick lately that concern for her had pushed the thought of leaving to the very back of Earth's mind. Since she had first begun retching miserably in the nursery, she'd been feverish and nauseous, confused and glassy-eyed and calling out for their mother. Moonlight had stayed by her side, and the other Sisters had taken over Moonlight's duties, doing all the things Moonlight usually did to keep their camp running smoothly.

With Moonlight preoccupied with Ice, and Hawk resting her injured leg, no cat had taken over Earth's training. *I'm not ready,* he thought. He knew he'd freeze again if he had to fight. His hunting was okay, he supposed, if he could concentrate—but he didn't feel confident about that, either.

He couldn't see spirits. *How can I travel without spirits to guide my steps?*

And he kept trying to meditate, to speak to the land the way the Sisters had told him, but there was no connection. He heard nothing. *How can I protect the land without a connection to it?*

Picking up the moss to carry back to Moonlight, Earth made up his mind. He would talk, calmly and reasonably, to Moonlight about it. She'd see that he couldn't leave yet.

"Thank you, Earth," Moonlight meowed when he reached her. "That'll make Ice's bed nice and comfortable."

Earth dropped the moss in front of her and, as she bent to pick it up, cleared his throat.

"What is it?" Moonlight asked, looking up.

Earth swallowed hard. "I don't think I'm ready to wander," he blurted out. "I can't—"

"You *are* ready," his mother interrupted. "You have to be."

"I'm not a good fighter," Earth argued. "I haven't seen the spirits." He hesitated. "Maybe I shouldn't be sent away yet? If I could stay with the Sisters just one more moon . . ."

Moonlight sat down, looking serious. "That's not the way things are," she told him. "We've learned that it's bad luck for a tom to stay past his sixth moon, bad for the Sisters and bad for the tom."

"But—" Earth began to object.

"Once, when I was young, a tom who was afraid to leave the Sisters was allowed to stay a few moons longer," Moonlight went on, her eyes shining with sorrow. "Cloud, who led us then, thought it would do no harm. But that icetime was the hardest the Sisters had ever faced. Fierce snow drenched our fur. Frozen earth broke our claws. There was no prey, and Sisters died. And in the leafrise, when the tom left, he was weak and vulnerable, too used to the Sisters protecting him. He ended up choosing to go to Twopaws to be their everkit."

A cold shudder went down Earth's spine. "I don't want that to happen to me," he meowed. He knew toms sometimes did choose to live in the nests of the Twopaws—long ago, all the ancestors of the Sisters had—but it just felt *wrong* to him. He didn't want them touching him with their long furless paws.

"No," Moonlight agreed with a comforting purr. She bent to press her cheek against his. "It won't happen to you. You're a smart and resourceful cat. But you *must* go out into the world and become the tom you're meant to be."

"I guess," Earth conceded, as Moonlight pulled away again. "But I don't like the idea of being on my own. Look what happened when Hawk and I ran into those rogues. What if I go onto another cat's territory again? When I'm alone?"

Moonlight's tail twitched. "You have to give yourself more credit," she told him. "You're going to be a strong, capable cat, I can see it. You're a lot like your father, you know, and he was a cat well suited to the world."

Earth felt a stab of interest. Moonlight had never said much about his father. But right now he needed to make her see how he felt. "I don't feel like I'm going to be that kind of cat," he admitted.

A faint, fretful mew came from the sick den behind them, and Moonlight got to her paws. "Earth, it's going to be fine. But I don't have time to talk about what kind of cat you *might* be in the future. Not when I have a sick cat to take care of *right now.*"

"Okay," Earth muttered. He watched her head back into the sick den, a terrible ache in his chest. *I wish she loved me like she loves my sisters,* he thought bitterly. Moonlight seemed all too ready for him to leave.

Strong and capable, he thought, staring down at his small yellow paws. No matter what Moonlight said, he didn't feel strong and capable at all.

CHAPTER 4

The Claw Stars were pointing toward the setting sun. It was time.

Earth followed Moonlight toward a low hill at the edge of the pine forest, where they could see the sky. His paws felt heavy and stiff, and there was an anxious ache in his belly. *I don't want to do this.*

When they stopped, the she-cats gathered around Earth, just as they'd done for Chestnut and Snail two moons before. All except Ice, who was still in the sick den.

Earth glanced longingly back over his shoulder toward the camp. *I should have said good-bye.* Was he ever going to see his sister again? What if she died of this illness, and he never knew? Shivering at the thought, Earth wanted to run back to camp, to share tongues with Ice one last time. But it was too late now.

Moonlight pressed her nose gently against Earth's cheek. "I will miss you, my son," she meowed softly. "I wish you happiness."

Earth shut his eyes and breathed in the familiar scent of his mother. *Don't make me go.* He wanted to yowl it, but who would listen?

Sunrise nudged her nose against his cheek, and her meow was rough with sorrow. "I don't want you to leave," she whispered, and Earth pressed his face to hers, unable to speak for a moment.

"Tell Ice good-bye for me," he whispered back at last.

His sister stepped away and, one by one, each of the Sisters approached him, touched her nose or cheek to his, and murmured a few last words.

"You'll be fine," Hawk murmured reassuringly. "Follow the scents and you'll find plenty of prey."

Petal nosed his ear gently. "I believe that Stream will go with you," she whispered, her voice shaking.

Pain shot through Earth's chest; he couldn't answer her. *Everything would be different if Stream were with me.*

When every cat had said her good-bye, Moonlight came forward again and bowed her head to Earth. "This is the beginning of your adventure," she meowed. "Our love goes with you as you set off on your endless wander. Be an honorable cat, and the land will guide your paws. You are a guardian of the land now. You must listen to what it tells you."

Earth knew what he was supposed to say—*I will*—but the words seemed to be stuck. He opened his mouth, but he couldn't meow. *How can I listen to what the land tells me? I can't* hear *it!*

There was a long pause. All the cats were watching him. Furze and Snow glanced at each other, looking worried.

Moonlight stepped closer to murmur into his ear, "Be strong. Don't worry—if your courage wavers, an ancestor will help you to safety."

Not me. They won't help me. Earth's mouth was dry. He'd still never seen a spirit. And, despite everything Moonlight had told him, the idea of a dead cat watching him seemed scary.

Finally, he cleared his throat. "I'm ready," he croaked, his voice small and dry. He sounded completely unconvincing to his own ears, but Moonlight purred in approval.

"Walk through the night without looking back," she continued. "At dawn, you will have left your kithood behind you and become a true tom. May the ancestors who walk the land find you and give you guidance."

Earth jerked his head into a nod, turned toward where the Claw Stars hung in the sky, and began to walk. His paws felt heavy at first, but he made an effort and walked faster, feeling the eyes of the Sisters on his back.

Remembering how excited and proud Chestnut and Snail had seemed as they left, he raised his tail high, trying to look unafraid. He didn't want them to remember him as a coward. Would they watch him until he was out of sight? He desperately wanted to turn and look back, to see if the mothers and sisters were still watching, to see if they looked sorry to see him go. He steeled himself and kept walking.

But it was so dark. The sun had set now. Underbrush crackled nearby, and Earth glanced around, his pelt prickling with apprehension. *A spirit?* He didn't see anything.

He must be out of sight of the Sisters by now. Earth stopped for a moment. Crickets chirped steadily in the bushes around him, and he heard the deep croak of a frog in the distance. A breeze ruffled his fur. He sensed nothing threatening nearby, but suddenly Earth's heart was pounding as hard as a rabbit's, and he crouched low to the ground, as if to hide.

It's just that I've never been out alone at night before, he reassured himself. *Everything's okay.*

The world seemed bigger and emptier than anything ever had, and Earth was alone. He began to walk again, one paw after another. Where was he supposed to stop to make camp? How was he going to know if it was a good spot? Moonlight had always chosen the Sisters' camps. *This is so stupid,* he thought. *Why do toms have to start their wander at night? Who thought up* that *dumb rule? Night makes everything more difficult.*

Earth thought of turning back—things would be better closer to camp, wouldn't they?—but remembered what Moonlight had said. *Walk through the night without looking back.* Gritting his teeth, he kept going.

A sudden rumble made him jump; then bright light flashed in his eyes. *Lightning!*

Earth yowled in terror. But the light swung past and something huge and dark growled as it rushed away.

A monster. Earth tried to catch his breath and calm his pounding heart. *I must be right by a Thunderpath.*

He stood stock-still, his paws sinking into mud. There could be anything out here, and he didn't know what he was supposed to do.

After a few deep breaths, he made up his mind and scrambled under a bush. *I'll stay here tonight.* So what if he was still close to the Sisters' camp? No Sister could say he was wandering wrong, because which of them really knew what a tom did on his wander? He might not have walked through the *whole* night, but he hadn't turned back.

Earth curled into a tight ball and squeezed his eyes shut. He missed the warmth of his sisters beside him. He missed the sounds of the Sisters.

"Ancestor spirits, if you're out there, watch over me," he whispered. "I'm sorry I can't see you, but I hope I'm not alone."

He listened, straining his ears, but there was no response.

When dawn broke over the forest, Earth stretched and shook his pelt, cold and stiff from sleeping by himself. He could see the Thunderpath through the trees now, so he turned his back on it and walked into the forest.

I guess the first thing I should do is hunt, he thought. If he was going to wander alone, he needed to take care of himself. He sniffed carefully at the ground: a trace of vole, a light scent of shrew . . . and his own scent from last night, leading straight back to the Sisters' camp.

He hesitated for a moment. Did he really have to be *all* alone? Surely, he could take care of himself closer to all the cats he knew. The land he wandered could be near the Sisters, he supposed, just as easily as it could be far from them. Making up his mind, he followed his own scent, his paws feeling lighter. He had walked farther than he'd thought last night; the sun was high in the sky by the time he could hear the voices of the Sisters.

"Petal, don't forget to cover up the dirtplace!"

"I'm just going to spread out the old bedding."

They're leaving, Earth realized. He recognized what they were doing—destroying the signs that they'd lived there so that no predator would track them to a new camp.

Scrambling up a nearby pine tree, he looked down through its thick needles onto the clearing. He'd been right—the Sisters were hurrying around, burying the remains of the prey-hole and making sure the dens where they'd slept held no sign of them.

It's like they couldn't wait to get rid of me, Earth thought. He knew that wasn't true, but his belly felt hollow with grief. Couldn't they have waited, just a few days, to make sure he was okay?

Finished with their tasks, the Sisters gathered around Moonlight. With a wave of relief, Earth saw Ice among them. She looked thin and frail, leaning against their mother, but she was standing on her own paws. He wanted to run to her, to speak to her one last time, but he could imagine the look of disapproval on Moonlight's face, and he stayed where he was. *Good-bye, Ice,* he thought. *I hope you'll be okay.*

Moonlight bent to nuzzle Ice gently, then straightened up and led the Sisters out of the camp and into the forest, heading away from Earth. He watched until they were out of sight.

Good-bye, he thought again. *Good-bye, every cat.* He felt as if something with sharp claws were tearing its way out of his chest. *I guess now I'm really alone.*

Chapter 5

Evening was falling as Earth padded back to his new den, a shrew dangling from his mouth. His current home was within view of the Sisters' old camp. *I haven't left my kithood behind at all,* he thought, guiltily hunching his shoulders. He'd done the opposite of what a tom was supposed to do.

At least I'm managing all right as a hunter, he thought, crouching down at the entrance to his den. Remembering Hawk's lessons had been easier than he'd imagined. When he hunted alone, every sound his prey made was practically deafening. He bit into the shrew, trying to enjoy the crunch of its bones.

Without company, though, his meal seemed tasteless. And he wasn't used to eating a whole piece of prey by himself. With the Sisters, he'd always had some cat to share it with. As he took one more reluctant bite, he looked toward the camp, imagining Sunrise and Ice play-fighting by the nursery. Snow pacing the edges of the camp, keeping a sharp eye out for predators. Hawk and Petal, carrying in prey. Moonlight building a new nest for her den. Stream napping in the sunlight . . .

Stream. His appetite left all at once. Earth let the shrew drop into the dirt and batted it away.

The sky was getting darker, pale stars beginning to appear. A gust of wind made the pine branches above Earth's head creak, and he shivered. He still wasn't sleeping well. At night he lay awake in his den, listening tensely to every snap of a branch or hoot of a low-flying owl.

He hadn't met any rogues, and no ancestor spirits had come to guide him. At this point, he was so tired of being lonely that he almost would have welcomed either one.

I should be able to see spirits, Earth thought, shifting on his haunches. A ball of resentment burned hotter and hotter inside him. If the Sisters hadn't sent him away so early, he *would* be able to see them. And he wouldn't be afraid, not if he were *ready* to see spirits, ready to be on his own.

Why did Moonlight have to stick so closely to tradition? She'd told him of *one* tom she knew who had been unlucky. What proof was that? She wouldn't have sent Ice or Sunrise away because of one thing that had happened in the distant past. Why did the rules have to be different for toms?

Earth huffed and glared at the darkening forest around him. Everything had changed because Stream had died. And now he couldn't even see his friend's spirit, because Moonlight had made him wander before he had learned to see ghosts.

There was another crackle in the branches above him, and Earth flinched. *If only Stream were with me . . .*

Maybe he should try again. Maybe he hadn't wanted to see Stream's spirit badly enough back in camp, because he'd been too scared. But now . . .

Earth looked around at the empty forest. "Stream," he

called. What had Moonlight said, when she'd called to the spirits? He thought back, then cleared his throat and tried again. "Stream, if you'd like to visit me, I'd be glad to speak to you again." That didn't seem like enough. "Stream," he went on, "I'm so sorry. I didn't want you to die. That was such a terrible storm, but I thought we would make it through together. But I lived and you died. I wish that hadn't happened."

The wind blew through the branches again. A pinecone, caught by the sudden gust, rolled past Earth's den. It reminded him of batting pinecones all over camp with Stream, Sunrise, Ice, and Haze. "I miss you," he added, his meow hoarse. "I'm so sorry you're dead, and if you want to come and keep me company, or just say hello, I'd really like that."

Earth waited, eyes wide and ears pricked for any sign of Stream. But silence spread through his little section of woods. He couldn't even hear the wind blowing anymore. He listened tensely, expecting something to happen any moment.

Something moved in the tree over his head and Earth looked up, his heart pounding hard.

Only a squirrel. Too high to chase, the squirrel ran across its branch and leaped to another tree, farther away from Earth.

Earth dropped his head onto his paws. He couldn't do it. He would never meet an ancestor spirit, never see Stream again.

Or . . .

What if the wind crackling through the pines or the cone rolling past his den had been *sent* by Stream? Signs from his friend that he *wasn't* really gone?

Earth's pelt prickled with excitement as he pushed away his feelings of failure. *Maybe I just communicate with the spirits differently than the Sisters do,* he thought. After all, who said ghosts appeared the same way to all cats?

He listened again, harder, and squinted his eyes to peer into the darkness, hoping to see that pinecone again. "Stream, send me a sign," he whispered.

But nothing happened.

His hope dwindling, Earth sighed and, ducking his head, crawled into the makeshift den he'd made beneath the bracken. He needed to sleep if he was going to be able to hunt again tomorrow. Maybe he'd be able to reach Stream another day. If the Sisters were right, he would.

Maybe.

The next morning, Earth padded through the undergrowth on the other side of the Sisters' old camp, his mouth open to taste the air. There was a rustling in the bushes, and he caught the scent of a vole. Tensing, he lowered his belly close to the ground and began to slink forward, listening for the quick beat of the vole's heart.

Wait. Catching a new scent, Earth straightened up abruptly, no longer interested in the vole. *Those are cats.* He glanced around warily, thinking of rogues, before he realized how familiar the scents were and sniffed harder.

Sunrise. Furze. Hawk. Tempest. Moonlight. Ice. Earth's chest ached. He'd found the scents the Sisters had left as they'd moved camp. It had been several days, but it hadn't rained in that time, and their trail was still clear.

They headed toward the hill, Earth thought, nose to the ground. He'd known that, of course; he'd seen them leave. Following the trail, Earth headed uphill. At the top, he could tell they'd stopped for a little while. *They must have been letting Ice rest,* he thought. Yes, there was a spot where her scent was stronger. She had probably lain down here, he thought, sniffing. But then they'd continued downhill, Ice walking near the center of the group. *At least she was strong enough to keep going.* He went on, tracking the scent.

The sun had passed its midpoint when Earth finally admitted to himself: *I'm following them, and I'm going to find them.*

He *knew* it was a terrible idea. If he caught up with the Sisters, they might be angry. They might even attack him. *They sent me away on my wander. Toms aren't supposed to be with the Sisters once they're grown-up.*

But he wasn't grown-up, was he? Moonlight had been so *stubborn,* she hadn't been able to admit that he wasn't ready to be on his own.

Now he'd tried living alone for a while, and it had been awful. He was scared all the time, and cold, and he hadn't been able to bring himself to go far from familiar territory. He was so lonely. Maybe if he talked to Moonlight now, she'd see the truth. He couldn't see any spirits, so he had no cat to guide him—he must need more training. Maybe he'd be able to convince them to take him back, just for a little while. Surely, they'd missed him. They were his kin.

And he really, really wanted to see them all again.

He kept walking, following the Sisters' scent.

There was growling in the distance and, as Earth got closer, the sharp smell of monsters. *A Thunderpath.* The Sisters' scent trail was leading straight toward it.

As he came out of the undergrowth onto the short grass at the side of the Thunderpath, Earth's stomach sank in dismay. Monsters sped by as if they were chasing one another, growling steadily, their blank eyes passing over him as they went around a curve. He'd never seen so many monsters at once before. Their foul smell was chokingly thick, and Earth crouched closer to the ground, breathing hard, hoping the monsters were too focused on one another to notice him.

He sniffed the ground carefully. Maybe Moonlight had turned and led the Sisters away from this terrible place. It was hard to make out the Sisters' scent among the thick, foul smells. But when he finally found the trail, it headed straight toward the Thunderpath. His heart sank.

I can do this. Earth gritted his teeth and glared at the monsters. He'd crossed Thunderpaths before, a few times, with the rest of the Sisters. He could do it again.

He had never crossed one so crowded with monsters. But the general idea must be the same. Earth waited for a space between the monsters, trying to remember exactly what Moonlight had done when they'd crossed.

At last there was a moment with no monsters in sight, although he could still hear them growling, not far away.

"Straight ahead, as fast as you can," Earth muttered. "Don't stop for anything." That was what Moonlight had told them.

Ears flattened, body low to the ground, Earth began to run.

He was halfway across when the growling got louder and louder, closer and closer. He glanced up and caught his breath, his paws skidding on the rough black surface of the Thunderpath. A monster was bearing down on him.

It howled, a loud, deep noise rising above its steady growl, and Earth yowled back, panicked, and ran faster than he'd ever realized he could. The world was blurry around him, and he couldn't think, couldn't feel anything but the thumping of his heart and the pounding of his paws.

His paws hit the short grass, so much softer than the Thunderpath, and he staggered a few steps before collapsing. The monster howled again, once, and for a heartbeat Earth saw the strange hairless form of a Twopaw inside as the monster dashed past him. A rush of air ruffled his fur.

Earth tried not to think about how close he'd been to being squashed under the monster's fat black paws. He lay on the grass, exhausted, and panted.

After a little while, he slowly got to his paws again and began to search for the Sisters' scent. Finally, he found it—heading in a straight line away from the Thunderpath. Earth breathed a sigh of relief.

He was going to find them. And maybe, just maybe, they wouldn't send him away again. He hoped not. Not when he'd been through so much already.

Chapter 6

By the next morning, the scents that Earth was following had changed. The signs of the Sisters were fresher, and as he sniffed his way past a large oak tree, Earth smelled that here the trails of scent led in all directions, crossing and recrossing. Just as he realized that, he came out of the trees onto a wide-open moor. Long grass blew across level ground, broken here and there only by scrubby, low-growing bushes. The scent of the Sisters was even stronger out here. He wasn't following the Sisters' journey anymore; he had found their new camp.

Instinctively, Earth's ears flattened and he crouched lower. *I don't want them to see me.* It would have been better if their camp were among trees, so that he could hide in the branches and watch them unobserved before he decided whether to approach. *What if they think I'm attacking them? What if they attack me?* He had never heard of a tom returning from his wander.

Sliding out his claws, Earth ripped at the ground in frustration. He'd come all this way, and now he was afraid to face the Sisters again. *Why* didn't they want him? Just because he was a tom? They were his kin!

With a lash of his tail, Earth turned away from the moor

and took a few steps back under the trees. What was the point of looking for his kin, if they were just going to send him away again, or maybe even drive him away with their claws and teeth? He would leave on his own before they had a chance to tell him to go.

He took another step, then turned back toward the moor. *I've come too far to leave now.* They might turn him away, but he couldn't be so close and not try to talk to them. Maybe they wouldn't let him stay, maybe they'd be angry—but at least, for a little while, he wouldn't be alone.

Holding his head high, Earth strode out onto the moor. He knew the kind of camp Moonlight always picked, and he was sure that the Sisters must have made their dens beneath some of the small thornbushes growing here and there among the grass. Spotting a likely group of bushes—several growing close together—he headed toward them.

"Hey!" A fierce yowl came from behind him, and Earth spun around.

Ice was glaring at him, fur bristling along her back. When she saw his face, though, her expression changed from anger to shock. "Earth?" she asked, her eyes wide. "What are you doing here?"

Earth sucked in his breath. Ice looked healthy, her fur shiny and her eyes bright. Whatever was about to happen now, he was glad to see her well. "You're all right," he purred.

Ice looked pleased. "I was so sick when you left that we didn't get to say good-bye," she meowed. "Is that why you're here? To see me again?"

"Sort of." Earth sat down on the grass with a sigh. "I wanted to see you. I wanted to see every cat." There was a tug of hope in his chest. It was good that he'd run into Ice, alone, first. At least she would listen to him. She might even talk to Moonlight for him.

"What's going on?" Ice glanced around as if checking that they were alone, then sat beside him. She curled her tail neatly over her paws, her face serious. "You know you're supposed to be off wandering. Mother told me that if we ever saw you again, it would be by chance and probably not for a long, long time. It hasn't even been a moon yet!"

"I can't do it." The words burst out of Earth as if he'd been saving them up the whole time he'd been on his wander. "I tried, but I'm so lonely. It's scary on my own, and nothing feels right." He hung his head.

Ice's eyes were full of sympathy. "I'm so sorry, Earth," she told him. "Maybe you should try wandering in a different direction? You might meet other toms. They all must be out there somewhere."

"How do you know?" Earth mewed sharply. "The Sisters don't know what happens to the toms when they leave. They could all be dead, or everkits. And the Sisters don't *care*."

"We do care," Ice protested, dropping her gaze to the ground. "But this is the way it is."

"I don't understand why." Earth hunched his shoulders and his voice came out as a whisper. "I want to come back to the Sisters." His whole body was tense. Maybe Ice would help him. Maybe he *could* come back.

But Ice was shaking her head sadly. "Earth, you know the rules. No tom can live with the Sisters. You have to wander and guard the land."

"I know." Earth felt small and miserable. He *had* known, hadn't he? If even his own littermate felt this way, none of the Sisters would want him to stay. The Sisters would never let him be one of them again.

"Is it really so awful?" Ice asked tentatively. "Maybe I could . . ." She hesitated.

"You can't do anything," Earth told her. Part of him wanted to beg her to talk to Moonlight, but he knew nothing was going to change. If Ice spent her time trying to fix things for him, she wouldn't be working for the Sisters. They needed her to hunt and patrol and teach the younger kits, like all the Sisters did. If she was worrying about him instead, it would hurt every Sister.

He swallowed hard and went on. "It's fine. You're right—I don't belong here anymore. But I wanted to see you."

"I'm glad you did." Ice leaned forward as if to nuzzle his cheek, then pulled back. *She doesn't want the other Sisters to scent me on her,* Earth realized, his tail drooping. "You will be all right, really, won't you?" she asked hopefully.

"Of course I will." Earth knew he was lying. He stood up, lifting his head high. "I guess we won't see each other again," he meowed.

He started to turn away as Ice answered, "I hope that's not true." Her voice trembled.

Earth couldn't bring himself to reply. He looked straight

ahead and walked quickly away. As he got farther from Ice, he began to run.

I can never go back.

By the time the sun set, Earth was far away from the Sisters' camp. He'd run and run after leaving Ice, run until he was breathless and sore-pawed. When he'd finally come to a stop, there hadn't been time to find a good den for the night. Instead he twisted and turned, roots jabbing into his sides as he tried to sleep in a narrow hollow at the foot of an alder tree.

What will I do tomorrow? And for the rest of my life?

His stomach growled. He hadn't had the heart to look for prey after seeing Ice. *Maybe this is what happens to toms who leave the Sisters,* he thought. *They starve because they're too lonely to hunt.*

He couldn't imagine going on like this. Earth rolled over to try to find a more comfortable spot, grunting as he hit another root, and stared at the lights of a Twopawplace in the distance.

Maybe he should go there tomorrow. That was what happened to cats who couldn't take care of themselves, wasn't it? They became some Twopaw's everkit? Something in him shuddered at the thought—he'd never wanted that.

But what else was he good for? He couldn't just wander alone forever.

A sudden rough sound, not far away, jerked Earth out of his thoughts. *Was that a bark?* He could smell something now on the breeze: a thick, meaty scent that made his fur prickle along his spine.

A dog? He'd heard of dogs, and had seen them in the

distance, but he'd never gotten close to one. Moonlight had told him how dangerous they were. Getting to his paws, Earth peered into the darkness, trying to see where the scent was coming from.

There was a rustling to his right, and Earth began to back quietly away around the tree trunk, placing his paws carefully so they didn't make a sound. But then another noise—a strange jingling—came on his other side, followed by a growl just behind him.

Not a dog. Dogs! Earth froze, his heart pounding. They had him surrounded. Three dogs, coming toward him.

He could see them now: a big black dog with golden eyes, its tongue hanging out as it panted. A smaller brown one, its teeth bared. And one with long black-and-white fur, eyeing him as if he were prey. They were padding toward him slowly, like they were sure he couldn't get away.

Earth couldn't move. He could barely breathe. *This is the end.*

Suddenly a sharp yowl rang out, and a cat shot past him in the darkness, heading *toward* the dogs. With a flash of claws in the moonlight, the stranger slashed the black dog across the nose as he meowed back to Earth.

"Run!"

CHAPTER 7

Earth ran only a few tail-lengths away, into a tangle of bracken. Then he turned and watched, awestruck. In the moonlight, he could see that the strange cat was pale-furred and not very big, but moved quickly and smoothly, dodging the dogs' teeth with ease. He drew his claws across the brown dog's shoulder, then leaped with a yowl to land on the long-furred dog's back, his tail bristling.

The dog yelped and bolted into the darkness, the other dogs on its heels. The strange cat was still on its back, his tail waving back and forth for balance as he clawed at the dog. Earth's mouth dropped open as he watched them vanish into the woods. Should he run? Or should he go after the dogs to help the stranger? The other cat was amazingly brave, but eventually the dogs would stop running.

Before Earth could make up his mind, the strange tom came sauntering back into sight, his head high. His eyes were gleaming with what looked like enjoyment. "You hurt, kit?" he asked. Now that they were closer, Earth could see that his fur was as yellow as Earth's own. His green eyes were shining with excitement.

"I—I'm fine," Earth replied. He felt suddenly shy—he'd never spoken to an adult tom without one of the Sisters at his side. And this one was so brave, and had saved him. "That was amazing. You chased off all three of them."

"You just have to keep a steady mind," the tom meowed. He eyed Earth. "You're a little young to be on your own, aren't you?"

"No, I'm not!" protested Earth indignantly, drawing himself up to his full height. "I'm almost seven moons old." *Well, six and a bit, anyway.*

The tom's whiskers twitched. "I'm not trying to insult you," he meowed. "I'm Root. I'm glad I could help out."

"Yes. Thank you," Earth told him, feeling a little wrong-pawed. This cat had *saved* him; he should be polite. "I'm Earth."

There was a glint of amusement in Root's eye. "That's a big name. I'm sure you'll grow into it." He gave Earth a friendly nod. "Well, take care. Watch out for strange dogs. You might be alone next time."

"I will," Earth promised, but he was confused. Was Root just going to leave now? What if those dogs came back?

With a flick of his tail, Root turned and began to walk away. Earth watched him, then looked around at the dark, empty underbrush. *I don't want to stay here alone.* Quietly, he followed the other cat.

After a few steps, Root stopped, his ears cocked back toward Earth. "Are you lost?" he asked. "Do you need some help?"

"Well." Earth's tail drooped. "I'm not really *lost,* but I don't know this place. I'm not sure where to go that's safe." He hesitated, thinking of Root's second question. *Do I need help?*

Root turned around and looked Earth up and down. He hesitated, as if he was making up his mind about something. "Come on," he meowed at last. "I know a place where we can sleep tonight."

"Really?" Delighted, Earth hurried to Root's side, their fur brushing. "I can stay with you?"

Root flicked his tail dismissively. "For one night," he answered. "Tomorrow I'll walk around here with you and help find a good place to make your own camp. I'm only passing through."

"Me too," Earth assured him. They began to walk side by side, Earth's paws light with happiness. Of course, it would be even better if Root wanted to stay together—*maybe he will once he gets to know me,* Earth thought—but it was so *good* to be with another cat for a while, even if it was only for one night.

He stuck close to Root, matching his pace to the older tom's. Root kept looking around and scenting the air, his ears pointing this way and that. "You have to be alert all the time," he told Earth. "The forest is full of danger for a loner."

Nodding, Earth walked even closer to him, his fur bristling at the thought of the forest's dangers.

At last, Root stopped by a tall oak tree. "This looks like a good one," he meowed cheerfully.

"A good what?" Earth followed Root's gaze up to the spreading branches above them. "Wait," he mewed, blinking. "You want to sleep in a tree?"

"A tree is the best place," Root told him confidently. "Nothing will be able to get at us. And when we wake up, it's easy to get the lay of the land."

"Yes, but . . . ," Earth began. *What if we fall out?* He'd climbed trees to look around, or chase squirrels, but the idea of being asleep that high up made his pelt tingle uncomfortably.

But Root was already clambering up the tree trunk. "Come on!" he called in a cheerful meow. Unwilling to be left behind, Earth followed.

Up in the tree, Root nodded to the space where a wide branch met the trunk. "That's a good, safe place," he meowed. Sprawling along the next branch, he let his tail dangle and shut his eyes.

Earth turned around cautiously, then curled up on the branch, pressed close against the trunk. A breeze ruffled his fur, but the branch felt sturdy and roomy beneath him.

He looked up at the stars, feeling more comfortable than he had since he'd left the Sisters. Root was right: nothing could get him up here. And if anything tried, Root was with him. The leaves of the tree made a soft whispering sound as the wind went through its branches.

Suddenly sleepy, Earth shut his eyes. Listening to Root's steady breathing, reminded that he was not alone, he fell fast asleep.

The rising sun woke Earth early the next morning, and he yawned and stretched, feeling more rested than he had in a moon.

The branch beside his was empty. Earth looked around, first in the tree and then on the ground below, but there was no sign of Root. *He wouldn't have left without saying good-bye, would he?* Earth wasn't sure: the older tom had been friendly, but he'd made it very clear he wasn't looking for a companion. Maybe he'd decided not to help Earth make a camp. *After all, the Sisters left me,* Earth thought. *And they're my kin.*

He scrambled down the tree, and, after sniffing around to see if Root was nearby—he wasn't—carefully washed his paws and ears. *Should I stay or go?* he wondered. If Root wasn't coming back, there was no reason to stay here; he could continue his wander, looking for a better territory. But he wanted to see the other cat again. Earth decided he would wait until at least sunhigh.

A cool breeze ruffled his fur, and Earth hunched his shoulders, feeling cold with no cat to huddle together with. Having had another cat beside him, even for one night, would make it even harder to go back to being alone.

Earth sighed and thought of Stream. Had he really made contact with his friend that one evening in the forest? Was it Stream who had sent the pinecone rolling past his den?

Closing his eyes, he tried to focus on Stream, just as he'd done then. "Stream," he meowed. "If you want to come to me, I'd be glad to see you and speak to you again." He strained his senses, his ears and whiskers twitching, hoping to catch any hint of his friend. *Nothing.*

"Please come," he went on, his voice shaky. "I am trying, I've *been* trying. I hate being on my own. I even went back to the

Sisters," he confessed, lowering his voice. "I know I shouldn't have, but I was so lonely. They'll never let me be one of them again." A hot jolt of anger shot through him. "It's not *fair*," he meowed. "Stream, they wanted to send us away when we were too young, just because we were toms. I don't know how to look after myself, and they don't care. Sometimes I wish I'd never been born, if the Sisters were just going to throw me away." Earth squeezed his eyes shut even tighter and added, bitterly. "I'll *never* forgive them."

Pausing for a breath, he heard a small noise, like a paw step nearby. *Stream?* With a surge of hope, Earth opened his eyes.

Stream's spirit wasn't there. But Root was, a fat squirrel dangling from his mouth as he stared at Earth. Hot with embarrassment, Earth stared back, not knowing what to say. How long had Root been standing there, watching Earth talk to himself with his eyes closed?

Root dropped the rabbit. Cringing, Earth waited for him to comment, but when Root spoke, it wasn't what Earth had expected at all.

Instead Root said, in a rather hesitant voice, "Do you know a group that's all she-cats? Big, long-haired she-cats?"

"You know the Sisters?" Earth asked, amazed. But Root's expression darkened.

"I know them all right," he answered angrily. "I spent a lot of time with them for a little while."

Earth's eyes widened. Was Root a wandering tom, an older kit of the Sisters? "What do you mean?" he asked. "When?"

"I was mated to one of the Sisters," Root told him. "I was

with her for a while, and I thought they were great, strong and fierce. My mate was expecting my kits. But then Moonlight and the others moved on without me. She said that toms don't travel with them and that they don't stay in one place, so she'd have to leave me behind." He slashed his tail angrily. "She left me without a second thought."

Earth stared at Root, feeling numb with shock. *Moonlight?* Root's fur was as yellow as Earth's, and one of his paws, Earth suddenly noticed, had six toes, just like Earth's. *Could this be my father?*

He licked nervously at the fur on his chest, then said, softly, "They left me, too. I'm one of their kits, but toms can't stay with the Sisters after they're six moons old."

"See?" Root meowed furiously. "They're cold, the Sisters. They follow their rules, not their hearts." His voice was so low that it almost seemed like he was talking to himself.

Earth took a step closer to him, his heart pounding wildly. "Moonlight was my mother," he meowed, hoping that Root would understand what he was saying.

Root stared at him, his green eyes wide. "You said you're six moons old." He circled Earth, his gaze raking over him as if he was categorizing all the things Earth had noticed they had in common—his size, his paws, his yellow fur.

"Almost seven," Earth reminded him.

Root was still staring. "You're my son," he realized, sounding shocked. "You must be."

"I guess so," Earth whispered, looking away. Suddenly, he felt too shy to meet Root's eyes.

After a second of silence, Root snarled. Earth's heart sank: *My father hates me, too.*

"They threw you out?" Root raged. "You're not old enough to take care of yourself! Look what happened. Those dogs could have killed you!"

Earth's eyes widened. Despite Root's anger, a warm feeling grew in Earth's chest. Root was *angry* at the Sisters for making Earth leave. He agreed that Earth was too young!

"They're so *cold*," Root growled again. "Her own kit, and she left you, just like she left me."

"But now we've found each other," Earth said eagerly, hurrying a few paw steps closer, until he was right in front of Root. "Moonlight and the sisters left both of us behind, but now we can take care of each other. It's perfect!"

Root paused, his eyes narrowing, and Earth gulped. "Isn't it?"

Root looked away. "I told you I was a loner," he meowed quietly.

"But . . . but you're so angry that Moonlight left me," Earth argued. "You're going to leave me, too?"

"It's not the same," Root muttered.

"It is," Earth insisted. He let his claws out and ripped at the dirt beneath him. He'd been so *happy*, just for a heartbeat.

"Look," Root told him, sounding guilty, "we'll stick together for a moon or two. I'll teach you to look after yourself properly. I promise, I'll help you until you're ready, not just throw you out like the Sisters did."

"You will?" Earth asked, thin tendrils of hope beginning to spread through him.

"Yes," Root promised. "I'll teach you everything you need to know. But I'm used to being alone. Running with a friend, or kin, leads to being responsible for them. It's too hard to rely on another cat. If you lose them, it'll rip you apart. It's better not to count on any cat. Moonlight showed me that," he added bitterly.

"Okay," Earth agreed. This was better than nothing: he'd have Root for a moon, maybe two. He'd learn how to take care of himself—Root was smart and tough and could teach him a lot. And who knew? A couple of moons was a long time. *Maybe Root will change his mind and want to stick together.* "Okay," he repeated, more cheerfully. "What's my first lesson?"

"Well," Root meowed, his tone warmer in response to Earth's, "there's your name."

"My name?" Earth asked, bewildered.

A teasing light began to shine in Root's eyes. "Like I said, it's a big name for a kit your size. And it's the name the Sisters gave you. You're not one of them anymore, are you? You can choose who you want to be."

Earth thought. Did he still want the name Moonlight gave him? Did he want anything from her? He looked around.

Above him, the oak where he and Root had slept spread its branches. It was solid and comforting. It had taken care of them through the night. It wasn't going anywhere.

"You're right," he told Root. "I don't want to be Earth anymore. From now on, call me Tree."

CHAPTER 8

"I'm telling you, it's the best way," Root meowed, shaking leaves off his pelt as he got to his paws. He bent down and used his mouth to pick up the mouse he had just killed.

"I'm not convinced that lying around until prey decides you're a bush instead of a cat is really the *best* way to hunt," Tree replied dubiously. Root cocked his head and waggled the mouse back and forth—as if saying, *And yet, see this mouse?*—until Tree purred with laughter.

"Okay, I get your point," Tree admitted. "Here, I'll take it back to camp unless you're hungry now."

"Great," Root meowed, dropping the mouse at Tree's paws. "I'll keep hunting." He lay down again, placing a few leaves on his own back for effect.

Shaking his head in amusement, Tree carried the mouse back to the foot of the tree where they'd been sleeping and scraped up a few pawfuls of dirt to bury it for safekeeping.

In the two moons that he and his father had spent together, Tree had learned a lot. Root didn't always hunt the way the Sisters did: he believed in taking care of himself while expending as little energy as possible. So not only did he have unique hunting techniques, but he had also taught Tree to find food in Twopaw trash and in the unattended bowls of everkits. He'd shown Tree how to pick the safest spots to rest. And he'd shown him fighting techniques, but also what he said was more useful: how to arch his back and snarl and frighten off rogues and dogs so that they might not have to fight at all.

I would have had such a hard time without Root, Tree thought as he brushed some dry leaves across where he'd buried the mouse.

Another leaf drifted down from the oak tree, and Tree's tail drooped. Icetime was coming. Root had always said that they wouldn't stay together for more than a moon or two, and it had been two moons.

Tree knew how much he owed Root. But still . . . he would be adrift and lonely when they went their separate ways.

If he couldn't stay with his father forever, Tree wished he could be like the rest of the Sisters. If he could talk to the land, and if he could see spirits, he'd never be alone. Would he *ever* be able to? Moonlight had told him he would, someday, but he had tried so hard, and nothing had come of it. . . .

He straightened, struck by a new idea. Maybe—just *maybe*—something had changed since he was a kit. He was bigger and smarter and more capable now; was it possible that the land would speak to him in a way it had refused to when he was younger?

Tree glanced around half guiltily, making sure that Root wasn't in sight. Root didn't like to be reminded of Moonlight and the rest of the Sisters. He didn't like to see Tree acting like them. The older cat wasn't nearby, though, so Tree settled comfortably among the soft, dry leaves and tried to remember what Moonlight had taught him.

Oh, yes. He was supposed to try to become one with the grass. Shutting his eyes tightly, Tree listened hard. If he could just do it *right,* he would hear the grass, the leaves, the trees, all speaking to him. Straining his ears, he held his breath, listening. *Nothing.* What was wrong with him, that he couldn't do it?

He heard the soft crunch of a dry leaf under a paw and opened his eyes. Root had come out of the bracken and was watching him. "What're you doing?" he asked.

Tree felt hot with embarrassment. He hesitated uncomfortably, shifting his paws. "I'm . . . trying to talk to the grass," he mewed quietly. "As a tom, I'm supposed to be able to, and I never have."

Root came over and sat down next to him. "Does the grass really have a lot to say?" he asked. He wasn't laughing, but his whiskers twitched.

Tree glared at him. "Toms are the guardians of the land," he told him. "How am I supposed to do what I need to, if I can't even speak to the world around me?" He dropped his head onto his paws. "I keep *failing.*"

Root hesitated for a heartbeat, then brushed his tail gently over Tree's back. "Look," he mewed, his eyes warm with sympathy. "Not every cat believes what the Sisters believe. A tom doesn't *have* to look after the world. The world will keep on going."

"Moonlight told us—" Tree began.

"You don't live with Moonlight and the Sisters anymore,"

Root interrupted. "You don't have to live by their rules. You've changed your name, and you don't have to keep anything else they gave you either, unless you want to. Be who *you* want to be."

Who I want to be? Who is that cat? Tree didn't know, but he felt a little lighter. Maybe not wanting to wander and care for the land was okay. The Sisters had made him leave, but maybe he could *choose* to leave, too.

The idea was amazing . . . but very lonely.

"I wanted to try again to speak to the land," he told Root, "because I'll need some cat to talk to." Root looked puzzled, and Tree hurried to explain, his words falling over one another in a rush. "I appreciate everything you've done for me," he said. "If you hadn't let me stay with you, I'd probably be dead by now, or I would've given up and become some Twopaw's everkit. I haven't forgotten that you're a loner and that I can't just stay with you forever. Even a couple of moons has been great. But I know it has to end."

Root cocked one of his hind legs to scratch at his ear. "Um," he began slowly, looking up at the sky. "You're a good hunter now, but I still have a lot to teach you. You'll need to know how to set up a territory for yourself. Maybe we should stay together a little longer."

Confused, Tree opened his mouth to object—he'd lived in enough different territories with the Sisters that he was sure he could manage—and then closed it again. There was an embarrassed gleam in Root's eye.

He doesn't want me to go, Tree realized. *He'd miss me, too.* Maybe

Root wasn't as much of a loner as he'd thought he was.

Warmth filled Tree's chest, and he blinked at his father affectionately. *Root's right,* he thought. *I can be any cat I want to be now. And maybe who I want to be is Root's kin.*

"I thought you just wanted the prey to come to you," Tree meowed a few days later, following Root through the forest.

Root flicked his tail dismissively. "That's fine when you're hunting mice," he answered. "But I've got a taste for rabbit today, and rabbits are a two-cat job."

Tree waved his tail happily as they walked. There was a touch of chill in the air, but there were still a couple of moons to go before icetime really arrived. Prey would be tasty, still fat from the warmer weather. Tree's mouth watered at the thought of rabbit.

"Look," Root pointed out softly. They had come to the edge of a sunny clearing, where two rabbits nibbled at long stalks of grass, periodically rising up on their hind legs to check for predators.

"One for each of us," Tree breathed, but Root shook his head.

"If we go after both, we won't catch either. Let's go for the big one. Circle around and drive it toward me."

Tree dipped his head in acknowledgment and began to work his way silently around the edge of the clearing, a careful eye on the rabbits. The smaller one suddenly lifted its head high, ears twitching, and he froze as it sniffed the air. When it finally began to eat again, Tree headed straight toward the rabbits, crouching so low that his belly almost brushed the ground and he was completely hidden by the long grass.

It wasn't until he had almost reached the rabbits that they suddenly stiffened. With thumps of their big back paws, they took off, zigging away from each other, and Tree saw that Root had been right. If he hadn't already been sure which to chase, he would have lost both. Instead he launched himself after the larger one, a fat brown one with a white tail, leaping almost on its heels, driving it toward where he knew Root was crouched.

The rabbit was faster than he was, but it didn't matter: it had only pulled a few strides away when Root charged out of the grass ahead and brought it down. With a quick bite to its throat, the rabbit went still.

"Good work, Tree!" Root called happily, looking up with the rabbit's blood still spattered across his chest.

"Same to you," meowed Tree. The rabbit looked delicious. "Do you want to eat here or take it back to the tree?"

"I'd feel safer on our own territory," Root answered. "Here, help me carry it."

Carrying the rabbit between them, the two cats set off back into the forest. Tree enjoyed the weight of the prey in his mouth and its warm, fresh smell. His stomach rumbled, and he dropped the rabbit to say, "I'm *starving.* Maybe we should just eat it here."

Root dropped his end of the rabbit, too, and began to say something, purring with laughter, when he suddenly paused and sniffed the air. "Do you smell that?"

Tree tasted the air, too, trying to smell something above the insistent scent of rabbit. There *was* something. Something meaty and rank that made his pelt prickle. "What is it?" he asked.

"A fox. We'd better hurry," Root told him. He began to bend to pick up the rabbit again, then straightened, the fur along his spine rising. Tree followed his gaze just in time to see a thin red creature slink out of the woods and lope toward them, its teeth bared.

"Run!" Root yowled, but Tree snarled and pressed his side against his father's. He wasn't going to abandon Root.

And then the fox was upon them. Its teeth were sharper than a dog's, and it snapped at Tree as he dodged, its bite grazing his shoulder painfully. But Root had taught him how to fight. He dropped to the ground and slid beneath the fox, clawing at its belly, while Root leaped to one side, slashing the fox's shoulder with his claws as he went.

They fought together, Root attacking the fox's hindquarters while Tree jabbed at its nose, Tree sinking his teeth into the fox's leg while Root swiped at its side.

We're winning, Tree thought, feeling both jubilant and terrified, as the fox gave a strange high-pitched howl and twisted toward him. Tree dodged again, but his paw slipped in a muddy pile of leaves and he fell, his side hitting the ground hard, knocking the breath out of him.

I have to move, he realized, but he was frozen. All he could see was a flash of teeth as the fox came for him. Everything seemed to slow down, and Tree couldn't move. *Just like when the rogues attacked,* he thought dazedly, remembering Hawk.

And then there was a flash of yellow fur. Root threw himself between Tree and the fox's teeth, and everything sped up again. "Root!" Tree yowled. He scrambled to his paws just as Root snarled and sliced his claws across the fox's eyes. With a yelp of pain, the fox scrambled backward, then turned tail and ran.

"That was amazing!" Tree exclaimed breathlessly. He turned to Root, but Root was swaying on his paws, his eyes glassy. Just as he fell, Tree realized blood was streaming down the other cat's side.

"Root!" Tree gasped and hurried to him, nosing through his yellow fur to find the wound. There was a deep bite on his side, dark red blood gushing from it and pooling onto the ground beneath him.

After a terrified moment of silence, Tree started to think again. "Moonlight taught me how to bind wounds," he meowed quickly. "I'll get cobwebs to help the bleeding, and, um"—his head was spinning as he tried to remember—"comfrey will help soothe the injury." He started to get up, but before he could go, Root laid his tail across Tree's back.

"Don't go," he breathed weakly. "It won't do any good. I'm dying, and I don't want to be alone." He looked up at Tree, his gaze unfocused. "I want my son with me when I die. Please."

"Of course I'll stay," Tree meowed, and lay beside his father, his heart aching. Root was right: no cobweb could stop this rapid stream of blood. It ran across the ground and coated Tree's fur, too, quickly growing cold and sticky. Tree licked at Root's shoulder and back, trying to clean his father's fur. "I'm sorry," he added. "You had to save me again. I wish—I should have been a better fighter. Braver, like you. I wish we had known each other longer. Always."

Root's tail brushed over Tree's back again, comfortingly. He looked into Tree's eyes and tried to speak, but his mouth was full of blood. It ran down across his chin and over his chest, mixing with the rabbit's. His body spasmed once, and then again, and then he was still.

"Root?" Tree asked softly. But his father's eyes had closed, and Tree knew that he was dead.

Tree pressed his face against Root's fur. A wave of guilt and horror passed over him. *My fault.*

He lay there for a long time, his face against Root's cooling fur. Gradually, he became aware that it was growing cold and dark around them, that night had come.

The sun rose before he began to think again.

He had loved his father, and his father had loved him. But in the end, it had hurt them both.

Never again.

Root had been right: it was better not to count on any cat. Tree had learned his lesson. Maybe this was the lesson that Moonlight and the Sisters had meant to teach him all along.

I should wander alone.

CHAPTER 9

A warm breeze blew through Tree's fur as he crouched on the side of the silver boulder, gazing at the Twopaw trash inside. Spotting something tasty, he reached in and hooked the remains of a piece of Twopaw food with one claw. *Chicken,* he thought, sniffing. His mouth watered at its smell and his belly rumbled.

He jerked up his head as he caught another scent on the wind, above the heavy smells of the Twopaw trash, and Tree tensed. *A strange cat.* Since Root's death eight moons before, Tree had barely spoken to any other cats, except for being snarled at and driven off claimed territory a few times. Gripping the chicken tightly in his mouth, he let himself drop into the space between the silver boulder and the Twopaw nest behind it. With any luck, the other cat wouldn't even realize Tree was there.

Tree heard the padding of soft paws and then a stern meow. "I know you're there. Come out where I can see you."

Adjusting his grip on the chicken with a sigh, Tree sidled out from his hiding spot. Staying there would only leave him cornered.

There was a brown-speckled white she-cat standing between the boulders, watching him warily. Her sides were round with kits: from his time with the Sisters, Tree could guess that she was maybe half a moon from giving birth.

He wasn't afraid of a pregnant cat, but he knew she might have a mate or kin nearby, so he dropped the chicken and spoke respectfully. "Is this your territory? I'm only passing through. You can have the food if you want it."

The she-cat's whiskers went back in disgust. "I don't eat Twoleg trash," she said scathingly. "I'm a warrior. I can hunt my own food."

Tree shrugged, wondering what a warrior was. "Feel free," he told her. He hopped back up onto the silver boulder and watched with interest as the she-cat began to prowl around, scenting the air, her ears cocked for the sound of prey. After a little while, she stiffened, then dashed with surprising speed into a nearby tangle of bits and pieces from dead monsters. Tree leaned forward to watch.

A moment later, she popped out from behind a round black monster foot, a rat dangling from her mouth.

"That was amazing," Tree told her sincerely. "You're so fast, even carrying kits."

The she-cat's tail twitched with pride. "Thanks," she meowed, dropping the rat. After a moment, she offered, "Do you want to share it with me?"

Tree hesitated for a heartbeat. A fresh rat *would* taste good, better than the discarded Twopaw food. But the she-cat looked too thin, despite her rounded sides. "No," he told her. "Keep the rat. But do you want to eat together? I'd be glad to have some company."

The she-cat shrugged and sat, the rat in front of her. Tree leaped down from the silver boulder, carrying the chicken, and settled beside her. "I'm Tree," he meowed.

"My name's Pebbleshine," the she-cat told him, taking a bite of her prey. "Nice to meet you."

"Pebbleshine?" Tree asked curiously. "That's a strange name. Pretty, though," he added.

Pebbleshine raised her chin proudly. "All SkyClan warriors have names like that. We change them as we get older: I was Pebblekit when I was born, and then Pebblepaw when my mentor trained me. Our leader, Leafstar, gave me the name Pebbleshine when I was ready to become a full warrior."

Tree shifted uneasily. Had Leafstar been like Moonlight? Was that why Pebbleshine was here on her own when she was expecting kits? Maybe this SkyClan cast out she-cats and kept toms. "And that's when you had to leave?"

"What? No!" Pebbleshine meowed. "I was traveling with my Clan, and we got separated. I'd never leave them on purpose."

"Oh." Tree felt relieved that Pebbleshine wasn't on her own. Kits were a big responsibility. "What happened?"

Pebbleshine grimaced. "I climbed into the back of a monster after prey. And the monster took me. I got away, but now I'm far from SkyClan, and I need to find them again."

Tree blinked. *She climbed into a monster?* He wasn't sure what she meant, but he had a more pressing question. "What's Sky-Clan?"

"We're a Clan of warriors," Pebbleshine explained. "We take care of one another, and we follow the code StarClan gave us." She sighed. "We had to leave our territory, and we've been traveling to find a new one. The monster took me a long way, I think."

"So, you're a *warrior*?" Tree asked, trying to understand.

"Of course," Pebbleshine said. "And my kits will be Sky-Clan warriors, too." She hesitated, looking at him a little suspiciously. "Are you a rogue?"

Am I? Tree wondered. He thought of the pair of rogues who had attacked when he and Hawk were hunting, back with the Sisters. He wasn't like that—he wouldn't harm another cat unless he had to. "No," he decided. "I'm just a loner, I guess."

Pebbleshine settled herself more comfortably. "I didn't think you seemed like a rogue," she meowed, and Tree felt a little warmer under her approval. He took another bite of chicken, watching her out of the corner of his eye. She looked *very* close to having her kits, he thought. If she was going to find her way back to her Clan before the kits were born, she would have to hurry.

"How are you going to find them?" he asked. "You said they were traveling when you got taken by the monster. So you don't know where they are, and they don't know where you are." He hesitated. "I hate to say it, but I doubt you're going to find them, at least not before your kits are born."

Pebbleshine lifted her chin stubbornly. "StarClan will help

me find my Clan again, and my mate, Hawkwing. My kits are special, I can feel it. SkyClan needs them." Her eyes were shining. "They have a destiny. They *belong* in the Clan."

Something in her eyes reminded Tree of Moonlight, how sure she was when she talked about the Sisters' duty to speak to the stars, and toms' duty to guard the land. "If you find your Clan again, will the kits get to live there always?" he asked warily. "No matter what? Whether they're toms or she-cats, or even if they can't do everything a warrior is supposed to do?"

"Of course," Pebbleshine told him, surprised. "SkyClan would never drive out their warriors. We belong there. That's why I have to get back to them."

She was so *sure*. Tree felt warm with admiration. "I think you'll be a really good mother," he meowed, and her whiskers twitched with pleasure at the compliment.

Something was still bothering Tree. "I understand you want to get back there," he began. "But if you have a long way to travel before you find them, it'll be dangerous, especially since you're expecting kits. Maybe you should wait. Sometimes it's better to accept what's happened to you and just get on with living your life, even if it's not what you wanted." He stared down at his paws, hoping that Pebbleshine wouldn't be offended.

"That isn't how it is in a Clan," Pebbleshine told him firmly, and Tree looked up again. She didn't look offended, but she did look determined. "Hawkwing and the rest of SkyClan aren't going to stop looking for me. So I can't stop looking for them, either." She glanced up at Tree with a little shrug. "Eventually we'll find each other. It's the only way I want to live, especially now that I've seen what life is like as a loner."

Tree nodded. She was right: life as a loner was difficult, and not for every cat. "It'll be a hard wander," he told her. "I hope you find them." Looking back on his time with the Sisters, and how that had ended, and then Root's death, Tree couldn't help wondering if he'd always been fated to be a loner. The idea made him feel lonely and sad, even though Pebbleshine was right beside him.

Pebbleshine was staring at him. When he caught her eye, she bent her head and licked at her chest fur, embarrassed. "You know," she began after a moment, "you're right that it'll be hard. Maybe you'd want to come with me?" Tree's face must have shown his confusion, because she went on. "It doesn't seem like you have anything keeping you here. This isn't your territory or anything. If you helped me find SkyClan, I'm sure Leafstar would let you join us."

For a moment, Tree let himself picture it. A whole group of cats—like the Sisters, but toms and she-cats together—working and living as a group. Always some cat to hunt with, some cat's soft fur to curl up beside.

No.

Stream had died. The Sisters had cast him out. Root had died, saving Tree.

Getting attached to other cats just led to heartache. It was better not to care for any cat.

"Living in a Clan sounds nice," he admitted. "But I think I'm just a loner."

Pebbleshine flicked her tail dismissively. "You can't have been alone your whole life," she meowed. "Surely you lived with your mother and littermates when you were a kit."

Tree paused. He half wanted to tell her about Moonlight and the other Sisters. Surely a mother so determined that her kits would be welcomed and loved would see how terrible it was to drive out a kit just because he was a tom.

But, suddenly, he didn't want to go over that ground again. There wasn't any point to holding on to that old resentment. He was grown now, and he could look after himself.

Root had said Tree could be any cat he wanted to be. Why would he want to remember the Sisters? Why give them that power over him?

"I grew up almost alone," he lied. "Just my mother and my sister and me. But when I was very young, my mother left me." He thought of Ice and how sick she'd been, and added, "My sister was sick, and my mother thought a Twopaw might help her, but that the chances were better if it was just the two of them."

"That's awful!" Pebbleshine meowed indignantly "They *left* you?"

Tree fluffed out his fur, comforted by her outrage. "I guess I was lucky not to be eaten by badgers or something, but I was all right."

"It doesn't sound like a good start in life." Pebbleshine's

gaze was sympathetic. "You must be angry at your mother."

Tree shrugged. "I was," he told her. "But not anymore. This is just how things turned out. I'm used to being alone." It felt strangely true. He might never see Moonlight and the Sisters again, and he felt like maybe he could forgive them.

Pebbleshine laid her tail across his back. It had been a long time since another cat had touched him, Tree realized. It felt comforting. "I don't think you'll be alone forever," she meowed. "You're a good cat, Tree."

She sounded so sincere that Tree almost believed her. The idea of *not* being alone forever gave him a funny pain, like an empty space in his chest. It was so hard to imagine.

Licking her chops, Pebbleshine pushed away the remnants of the rat carcass and got to her paws. "I'll start searching for SkyClan again in the morning," she announced. "Do you know anywhere safe to spend the night?"

It was beginning to get dark, and there weren't any good climbing trees near the Twopaw trash place, so Tree led the way to a nearby thornbush that they could shelter beneath. It felt so familiar and comforting to have another cat beside him, their fur brushing. There was a continuous growl coming from a Thunderpath not far away, but he listened instead to Pebbleshine's steady breathing as he drifted into sleep.

When his eyes opened onto pitch darkness, he could tell that it was much later, long past moonhigh. Pebbleshine was still sleeping. Tree didn't know what had awakened him, and he blinked into the night, feeling confused and sleepy. Then a familiar voice spoke, close beside him.

"Tree! You have to wake up!"

Tree's breath caught in his throat, and, without thinking, he sprang to his paws. Thorns tore at his pelt, but he barely noticed. He knew that voice.

"Root?"

Chapter 10

His father was glowing ever so slightly, like the light of a faraway star, and he seemed not quite solid. But his face and his voice were the same, and he looked desperately worried.

"You have to get up," he meowed urgently. "You and this pregnant cat, you have to run."

Tree couldn't breathe. He couldn't *think*. "How . . . how am I seeing you?"

Root slashed his tail impatiently. "There's no time for that. Both of you need to get out of here. You're in danger."

Blinking, Tree forced himself into action. He wasn't going to let another cat get hurt if he could prevent it. Gently, he shook Pebbleshine awake. "We have to go—it's not safe here."

Groggily, Pebbleshine blinked up at him. "What's wrong?"

"We have to go," Tree repeated, more urgently. He couldn't answer her question, but Pebbleshine struggled to her paws anyway, her large belly making her awkward, and followed him out of the bush.

A light rain had begun to fall, misting their whiskers, and they both hunched their shoulders against it.

"Where should we go?" Pebbleshine asked, and Tree began

to answer—*out into the forest, maybe*—but then paused, the scents of the night rushing over him. Cutting through the smell of rain and of the Twopaw trash was a rank scent he recognized. He'd scented it for the first time the day his father had died.

Fox!

Tree's heart pounded. Suddenly his mouth was dry. He *couldn't* fight a fox. The last time a fox had attacked him, he had frozen, and Root had died. He couldn't let that happen to Pebbleshine. They had to get out of here.

"Come on," he meowed, glancing back at Pebbleshine. Her green eyes were wide with fear, their sleepiness gone; she had scented the fox now too. If they got to the forest on the other side of the Thunderpath, they could climb a tree.

He peered at the Thunderpath through the rain, which was coming down harder now. A lone monster, its eyes glowing, roared past. The hard black stuff the Thunderpath was made of would be slippery underfoot because of the rain. Would Pebbleshine be able to move fast enough?

The fox scent was getting stronger. With the rain falling all around them, he couldn't tell what direction it was coming from.

"Let's cross the Thunderpath," he decided. *It'll be safer than here.*

"Good idea," Pebbleshine meowed, and led the way, Tree close behind her.

As they walked, Tree kept scenting the air, all his senses on alert the way Root had shown him. *Root. I* saw *Root.* Emotion washed over him like a river.

I never thought I could do it. I never thought I'd see him, or anyone I lost, ever again. How? *Did he come back just to save us?*

Tree had thought that he was broken. But Root had come back. *Maybe the Sisters were right. Maybe none of the dead are ever lost,* he thought, and it comforted him for the first time since the terrible day when Stream had died.

A snarl came from his left as they approached the Thunderpath. Before he could do more than turn his head, the fox shot out of the bracken, coming straight toward them.

No, Tree thought. *Not again.*

Baring his teeth, he puffed out his tail and screeched, making himself as big and fierce as possible, then charged at the fox. "Go!" he yowled to Pebbleshine.

The fox slowed, then started forward again.

"I'm not leaving you to fight alone!" Pebbleshine yowled back. He could hear her coming behind him as he leaped to slash at the fox's eyes, just as Root had. The fox flinched backward, and Tree's swipe missed.

The ground was already muddy from the rain. Tree's paw slipped and he fell hard. *Did* the land still hate him? He had fallen when he and Root had been fighting for their lives, too. Looking up at the advancing fox, he was struck by a wave of memory. *This is how it happened.* He was going to freeze and the fox would kill them both.

No! he thought. Scrambling to his paws, he launched himself at the fox. He caught its nose with his claws this time, leaving a long scratch, and the fox yelped in pain. Pebbleshine came up beside him, faster than she looked despite her rounded belly, and slashed at the fox's ear.

As Tree swiped at the fox's eyes again, his claw catching near the edge of its eye, the fox had had enough. Shaking Pebbleshine off as she raked her claws along its side, it backed away, then turned and ran.

Panting, Tree and Pebbleshine looked at each other. "We'd better get across the Thunderpath while we can," she meowed, and Tree nodded. As they headed that way, he glanced back over his shoulder. There was no pale-star glimmer behind them, nothing that looked like it could be a ghost. Maybe his father had come just that once, to save them.

Thank you, Root.

By dawn, the rain had stopped. Tree leaped down from the low branch where they had slept, watching with concern as Pebbleshine awkwardly—but safely—sprang after him.

The grass was wet, raindrops glittering on its stalks. Only a few tail-lengths away, monsters streamed along the Thunderpath, so close that they were almost nose to tail. One screamed its harsh howl, and both cats winced.

"I didn't say it last night, but thank you," Pebbleshine told him. "If you hadn't woken me, and fought the fox with me, I could have been killed."

An embarrassed warmth spread through Tree at her praise. "It's okay," he replied. "I'm just glad I could help save you."

Pebbleshine purred. "You saved more than one cat," she meowed. Tree realized she was talking about her kits, and he felt warmer still. *We saved a family, Root.*

"Speaking of which," Pebbleshine added, "I'd better be going. I want to find my Clan before the kits are born. Are you sure you won't come with me? I think you'd make a wonderful SkyClan warrior."

"I don't think it's for me. But I'm grateful to be asked," Tree answered. Part of him yearned to live with other cats again. It had been good to share a den with Pebbleshine and to fight beside her. But were all cats meant to live in big groups like SkyClan or the Sisters? The happiest part of his life so far had been with just Root beside him.

Pebbleshine looked around, examining the sky and the Thunderpath as if making up her mind which way to go.

"How will you ever find them?" Tree asked, unable to stop himself. "Are you *sure* you wouldn't rather stay here?"

Pebbleshine flicked her tail. "I know I'll find SkyClan eventually. My kits . . ."

"Have a destiny," Tree chimed in. Who knew? Maybe they did. *That's SkyClan's business.*

Pebbleshine twined her tail with Tree's and stood beside him for a moment. "You'll always be welcome in SkyClan," she told him.

Tree watched her walk out of sight, her tail held straight up behind her. She looked determined, like she was setting out on an adventure, like she knew where she was going. *I hope she finds her Clan,* he thought. *But I guess I'll never know.*

Tree spent the day wandering through the woods. He caught a few mice and basked in the sunlight for a while, but he felt strangely unsettled. As if he was waiting for something.

He crossed beneath a beech tree, and a pale light up among the tree's branches caught his eye. Could it be? Was Root nearby?

With a leap, Tree began to climb the beech, his paws slipping on the still-wet bark. Halfway up, he found Root sitting on a branch, his tail dangling, a mischievous gleam in his eye.

"You're real," Tree meowed breathlessly, clambering onto the branch beside him.

"Of course I'm real," Root replied. "I've got to keep an eye on you, kit."

"Yeah." Tree worked his claws against the branch, suddenly feeling shy. "I'm so sorry," he blurted out at last. "You *died* saving me. I never wanted that to happen."

Root twitched his ear dismissively. "Don't worry about it," he meowed. "I wouldn't say I *wanted* it to happen, either, but it was definitely worth it. I don't want you feeling guilty or apologizing or any of that."

"But . . . ," Tree began.

Root sat up straighter and stared directly into Tree's eyes. When he spoke, his voice had lost its teasing edge. "I was so grateful for you," he told him. "I thought I was a happy loner, that doing whatever I wanted, wherever and whenever I wanted, was what it meant to have a good life. I was wrong. Dying to save you was the best thing I ever did."

"But we only had a couple of moons together," Tree argued, his voice shaking. "It was so short." *We lost so much time.*

Root leaned forward and pressed his cheek to Tree's for a

heartbeat. It felt like nothing, except for a faint coolness, but Tree was comforted. "I could be angry about that," his father told him softly, "but I'm just happy we got to know each other at all. You showed me I was more than just a loner. I want you to know how proud of you I am."

Tree's tail drooped. "Proud of what?" he asked. "I'm a loner, too. I saved Pebbleshine, but that was because of you."

"It was because of *you*," Root corrected him. "I only woke you. You saved her yourself." He looked away across the forest, his tail swinging steadily. The sky was still cloudy from the earlier rain, but patches of sun shone through. "If there's one piece of fatherly advice I can give you, it's this: a friendship you *choose* is sometimes stronger than kinship. You can find some cat to care for." He looked back at Tree, his eyes affectionate. "Don't spend your life alone, Tree. Even if you lose a cat you love, it's better than never having had them beside you."

"Maybe so," Tree meowed. He thought of Stream and of his sisters. Of Root himself, and of Pebbleshine, even though he had known her only for a day. Losing all of them had hurt, but they had been worth that pain.

Root was beginning to fade, his edges blurry and faint.

"Don't leave me!" Tree yowled, alarmed. Had Root returned only to leave again?

But the other cat purred, amused. "Don't worry about that," he meowed. "You might not be able to see me all the time, but we'll speak again. I'll wander with you from now on."

Gradually, Root faded, his form growing paler and paler until Tree was alone. He didn't feel lonely, though: he knew that Root would travel beside him.

Like Root had a few moments before, Tree gazed out over the trees. The sun was low on the horizon, shining a pale, clear violet through what remained of the storm clouds. Something about the beauty of the scene made Tree's heart lift in hope.

A friendship you choose is sometimes stronger than kinship, Root had said. Surely, somewhere there was another cat who could touch Tree's heart. Some cat who would make caring worth the risk.

For the first time since Root's death, Tree's heart began to fill with excitement. There was a whole future out there, toward the horizon, and he could go anywhere he liked.

And, someday, maybe another cat would walk beside him.

WARRIORS

MOTHWING'S SECRET

Special thanks to Clarissa Hutton

ALLEGIANCES

RIVERCLAN

LEADER LEOPARDSTAR—unusually spotted golden tabby she-cat

DEPUTY MISTYFOOT—gray she-cat with blue eyes

MEDICINE CAT MUDFUR—long-haired light brown tom

WARRIORS (toms and she-cats without kits)

BLACKCLAW—smoky black tom

HEAVYSTEP—thickset tabby tom

STORMFUR—dark gray tom with amber eyes

FEATHERTAIL—light gray she-cat with blue eyes

MOSSPELT—tortoiseshell-and-white she-cat
APPRENTICE, SWALLOWPAW—dark brown tabby she-cat with green eyes

HAWKFROST—broad-shouldered dark brown tom

MOTHWING—beautiful golden tabby she-cat with amber eyes

QUEENS (she-cats expecting or nursing kits)

DAWNFLOWER—pale gray she-cat

SKYHEART—pale brown tabby she-cat

ELDERS (former warriors and queens, now retired)

SHADEPELT—very dark gray she-cat

LOUDBELLY—dark brown tom

THUNDERCLAN

LEADER

FIRESTAR—ginger tom with a flame-colored pelt

DEPUTY

GRAYSTRIPE—long-haired gray tom

MEDICINE CAT

CINDERPELT—dark gray she-cat
APPRENTICE, LEAFPAW (light brown tabby she-cat)

WARRIORS

MOUSEFUR—small dusky brown she-cat
APPRENTICE, SPIDERPAW (black tom with amber eyes)

DUSTPELT—dark brown tabby tom
APPRENTICE, SQUIRRELPAW (dark ginger she-cat with green eyes)

SANDSTORM—pale ginger she-cat
APPRENTICE, SORRELPAW (tortoiseshell-and-white she-cat with amber eyes)

CLOUDTAIL—long-haired white tom

BRACKENFUR—golden-brown tabby tom
APPRENTICE, WHITEPAW (white she-cat with green eyes)

THORNCLAW—golden-brown tabby tom
APPRENTICE, SHREWPAW (small dark brown tom with amber eyes)

BRIGHTHEART—white she-cat with ginger patches

BRAMBLECLAW—dark brown tabby tom with amber eyes

ASHFUR—pale gray tom with dark blue eyes

RAINWHISKER—dark gray tom with blue eyes

SOOTFUR—lighter gray tom with amber eyes

QUEENS

GOLDENFLOWER—pale ginger she-cat with yellow eyes

FERNCLOUD—pale gray she-cat with green eyes

ELDERS

FROSTFUR—beautiful white she-cat with blue eyes

DAPPLETAIL—tortoiseshell she-cat, the oldest cat in ThunderClan

SPECKLETAIL—pale tabby she-cat

LONGTAIL—pale tabby tom with dark black stripes, retired early due to failing sight

SHADOWCLAN

LEADER

BLACKSTAR—large white tom with huge jet-black paws

DEPUTY

RUSSETFUR—dark ginger she-cat

MEDICINE CAT

LITTLECLOUD—very small tabby tom

WARRIORS

OAKFUR—small brown tom
APPRENTICE, SMOKEPAW (dark gray tom)

TAWNYPELT—tortoiseshell she-cat with green eyes

CEDARHEART—dark gray tom

ROWANCLAW—ginger tom
APPRENTICE, TALONPAW (pale gray tom)

TALLPOPPY—long-legged light brown tabby she-cat

ELDERS — **RUNNINGNOSE**—small gray-and-white tom, formerly the medicine cat

WINDCLAN

LEADER — **TALLSTAR**—elderly black-and-white tom with a very long tail

DEPUTY — **MUDCLAW**—mottled dark brown tom
APPRENTICE, CROWPAW (dark gray tom with blue eyes)

MEDICINE CAT — **BARKFACE**—short-tailed brown tom

WARRIORS — **ONEWHISKER**—brown tabby tom

WEBFOOT—dark gray tabby tom

TORNEAR—tabby tom

WHITETAIL—small white she-cat

ELDERS — **MORNINGFLOWER**—tortoiseshell she-cat

HIGHSTONES

BARLEY'S FARM

FOURTREES

WINDCLAN CAMP

FALLS

CAT VIEW

SUNNINGROCK

RIVER

RIVERCLAN CAMP

TREECUTPLACE

CARRIONPLACE

SHADOWCLAN CAMP

THUNDERPATH

OWLTREE

GREAT SYCAMORE

THUNDERCLAN CAMP

SNAKEROCKS

SANDY HOLLOW

TALLPINES

TWOLEGPLACE

KEY
To The
CLANS

THUNDERCLAN

RIVERCLAN

SHADOWCLAN

WINDCLAN

STARCLAN

NORTH

TWOLEG VIEW

DEVIL'S FINGERS
[disused mine]

NORTH ALLERTON ROAD

WINDOVER FARM

DRUID'S
HOLLOW

WINDOVER MOOR

DRUID'S
LEAP

RIVER CHELL

MORGAN'S FARM
CAMPSITE

MORGAN'S
FARM

MORGAN'S LANE

NORTH ALLERTON AMENITY TIP

WINDOVER ROAD

WHITE HART WOODS

CHELFORD FOREST

CHELFORD MILL

CHELFORD

KEY To The TERRAIN

DECIDUOUS WOODLAND

CONIFERS

MARSH

CLIFFS AND ROCKS

HIKING TRAILS

NORTH

Chapter 1

Mothwing rolled onto her back and stared up at the branches at the top of the warriors' den. In the darkness she could just make out the shapes of the feathers and sweet-smelling grasses that had been woven among them.

"I can't sleep," she whispered. Her tail twitched nervously.

Beside her, her brother Hawkfrost sighed. "Just shut your eyes," he said. "You'll fall asleep eventually."

"I feel . . ." *Bad,* Mothwing thought somberly. Before she could finish, a yowl came from the opposite side of the den.

"*None* of us will be able to sleep if you two don't settle down," Blackclaw said fiercely, and other warriors growled in agreement.

"You're warriors now," Mosspelt added firmly from her nest. "Be sensible and let the rest of the den sleep."

"Sorry," Mothwing said. She turned onto her belly again and tucked her tail tightly around herself. Closing her eyes, she thought, *I'm a warrior now, not an apprentice. I can look after myself.* Despite the soft fresh moss in her nest, she couldn't get comfortable, and she shifted onto her side. *I miss Sasha.*

When their mother had left RiverClan and returned to life as a rogue, she'd invited Mothpaw and Hawkpaw to come with her. Mothpaw had loved being a RiverClan apprentice—she'd learned to hunt and fight and, for the first time, trust cats who weren't her kin—but she loved her mother more. If it had been up to her, she would have left with Sasha.

But Hawkpaw had wanted to stay. He'd dug his claws into the dirt as if he could force them to stay in RiverClan by clinging to the camp.

So they had stayed. Mothpaw wouldn't go without Hawkpaw. He was her littermate, her only littermate now. They *belonged* with each other.

I made my choice, she thought. *I decided to become a RiverClan warrior.* She rolled onto her other side. *I just hope I can be a good one.*

Hawkfrost groaned. "Settle down!" he hissed softly. "I can't sleep if you're awake!"

"Sorry," Mothwing whispered. She squeezed her eyes tightly shut, resolving to stay still. Part of her wanted to explain to Hawkfrost why it was so hard to fall asleep. After all, he'd been there when it had happened. He'd understand why she never liked to sleep . . . why she was afraid to dream. But the effort it took to stay awake was exhausting.

Despite herself, her breaths grew deep and steady, and soon she drifted off. The dream always came, and the terrible thing always happened, just like it had in real life. She could never stop it.

* * *

"We'll never find Ken," Hawk complained, hurrying to keep up with Tadpole. "We don't know which Twoleg nest was his."

Tadpole flicked his tail dismissively. "Sasha told us lots about where she used to live. I'm sure we'll recognize it. She'll be so happy we found him." Sasha was always worried, but her sad eyes lit up when she told them about the long-ago days when she had been a kittypet and lived with an old Twoleg named Ken.

Moth walked closer to Hawk, her fur brushing his, and they exchanged a doubtful look. She didn't believe it would be that easy, no matter what Tadpole thought.

As they came to the edge of the Twolegplace, Moth's paws slowed in dismay. There were so many nests! She had never realized how big the Twolegplace was. Suddenly she wanted to run right back to their cozy den and curl up in a tiny ball. How could they ever find one Twoleg in such a huge, confusing place?

"Come on!" Tadpole called cheerfully. "We've never had such a big adventure!"

An adventure, *Moth thought, heartened, and took a step forward. She was with her littermates on their biggest adventure yet. They would take care of one another.*

The Twoleg path was strangely rough underfoot, and Moth placed her paws hesitantly, while Hawk sat down and licked his front paws, as if trying to wash away the sensation. A breeze ruffled Moth's fur. Somewhere among the Twoleg nests a dog barked, and all three kits flinched.

Moth spotted a tree up ahead with branches low enough to the ground that even a kit could climb them. "Doesn't that look like the tree Sasha told us about?" she asked, her tail lifting with excitement. "The one she climbed every day when she was a kittypet?"

Tadpole tilted his head and looked at the tree thoughtfully. "I bet you're right," he replied. "Good work, Moth!"

"Let's look over the fence." Hawk rushed forward, the other kits on his heels. It was easy to hop up onto the lowest branches of the tree, and Moth dug her claws into its rough gray bark and clambered up ahead of her brothers. Peering over the fence, she saw a Twoleg kit running through the grass outside its nest, kicking at a ball with its pale, furless legs.

"Did Ken have kits?" she asked.

Tadpole peered over her shoulder. "I don't think so," he mewed doubtfully. "He was an elder, wasn't he?"

At a sudden rapping noise, the kits looked up. There was an opening in the nest covered with clearstone, and a female Twoleg stood behind it, knocking on the clearstone and glaring at them.

"She looks angry!" Hawk yowled.

"We'd better get out of here," Tadpole added.

Moth nodded, backing up on the branch. "That's not Ken."

Safely on the ground again, the kits searched the area. A pair of Twolegs, their heads close together in conversation, was coming down the path, and Moth crouched instinctively, her belly fur brushing the earth. Don't notice me! *With a loud whirring noise, another Twoleg approached, riding on the back of a skinny monster that had two narrow round paws, one behind the other. As it sped past, the Twoleg turned its head to look at the kits, and Moth panicked.*

"Run!" she screeched, and raced down the path, heading for a narrow opening between the Twoleg nests. She could hear her brothers running after her.

By the time she stopped, her breath ragged and her heart pounding, they had traveled a long way.

"How will we get back home now?" Hawk panted, looking around.

Tadpole's ears twitched. "We just ran in a straight line," he told Hawk. "If we go back, we'll get to the nest that wasn't Ken's again. And then we can find our way home from there."

"Sasha will be mad if we're not there when she gets back from hunting," Moth mewed in a small voice. "I don't want to get in trouble."

"We won't be in trouble," Tadpole told her. "We're doing something nice for Sasha. We're finding Ken." Hawk and Moth exchanged a glance, and Moth saw her own doubt reflected in her brother's blue eyes.

"Maybe we should—" Hawk began, but another, harsher voice interrupted.

"What do you kits think you're doing?" A big gray cat, his ears notched with scars, padded out of the shadows. "Strangers aren't welcome here."

Tadpole stepped in front of his littermates. "We're not doing anything wrong."

The stranger sniffed and wrinkled his nose. "Is that the forest I smell on you? Three little scraps, straight out of the woods. You'd better tell me why you're sneaking around here."

Another tom, black-and-white and just as large as the first, slunk out of the shadows behind him, followed by a third, a tabby even bigger than the others.

"Um, we were just . . ." Tadpole was getting rattled. The gray cat narrowed his eyes as the other two cats circled around, coming up behind the kits. Hawk and Moth crowded closer to Tadpole. Moth could feel both her brothers trembling. Were these really the kind of cats who lived in a Twolegplace?

From what Sasha had said, cats who lived with Twolegs should be nicer.

"Little cat skins, just walking around," the black-and-white cat growled. "They think they belong here."

"Let's show them what we do to outsiders," the tabby sneered, baring her claws.

Moth's nerve broke. "Run!" she yowled, and took off, barreling past the gray cat. He let her go, purring with laughter, and her brothers raced after her.

They dashed down the path and cut across a patch of grass beside a Two-leg nest, then, dropping to their bellies, wiggled under a fence. A dog lunged at them, barking, and, with a squeak of terror, Moth scrambled over another fence. Everything was a blur: her heart pounded as she ran first one way and then another, crossing Twoleg paths and leaping over ditches.

At last, out of breath, they halted at the base of a tree.

"I think we lost them," Tadpole panted.

Moth glanced back with a shiver.

"We'd better hide for a while," Tadpole decided.

"Where?" Hawk asked. The three kits looked up at the Twoleg nest ahead of them. It didn't look neat and solid like the other nests they'd seen, but lifeless and run-down. There were holes in the walls, and its colored skin was peeling off in long strips.

Moth shifted her paws. "I think it's empty."

"Look!" Tadpole yowled, gesturing with his tail toward an opening in the nest's wall. "We can hide in there!"

Moth hesitated.

In RiverClan, older and dreaming, Mothwing half woke and murmured, "No. Don't." But she couldn't change the dream, couldn't change what her younger self had done.

"Okay," she mewed finally. "Do you think it's safe?"

"It'll be an adventure," Hawk answered cheerfully, and the three kits slunk through the overgrown grass. The hole was supposed to have clearstone over it, Moth saw, like the one the Twoleg had glared at them through, but the clearstone was propped open, a stick holding it up.

There was a drop below the opening, and they clambered down a pile of Twoleg stuff into a cold, gray place where objects rose around them like a strange forest. As Hawk passed through the hole, he knocked the stick away, and the clearstone closed with a heavy thud behind them.

"Uh-oh," he meowed, looking up at it.

"Don't worry—we'll figure out how to escape when we're ready," Tadpole told him confidently. Big drops of rain had begun to spatter on the clearstone, and he added, "It's raining out there, and we're safe and dry in here."

The kits explored. Sniffing, Moth smelled dry dust and the faint scent of mouse. There were tiny scratching noises coming from the corner, and she crouched, narrowing her eyes like Sasha did when she hunted.

Hawk gave a mrrow *of laughter. "Your tail's too high! You'll lose your balance!" Moth glanced back, then guiltily lowered it.*

Tadpole dashed past them both, and the scratching noises got louder and then abruptly stopped. He padded back to them. "Sorry. It got away."

"If you'd just let me—" Moth began, irritated, but a loud gurgling interrupted.

All three kits whipped around to stare at the tall silver tube, like a branchless tree, that ran up the corner of the room from the floor to the ceiling. It had been silent and uninteresting, but now it was making terrible watery noises, as if a whole river were running through it.

"What's that?" Hawk asked. All three kits backed away.

"It can't hurt us," Tadpole mewed uneasily.

The gurgling intensified. Then, with a sharp crack, the tube broke open. Water poured out, rushing across the floor. In moments, the kits were knee-deep. It was freezing.

"We have to get out of here!" Hawk yowled. Dashing to the pile of Twoleg junk beneath the clearstone, he began to scramble up.

"That's closed, remember?" Moth wailed, but she followed him. A dusty round wooden thing slipped beneath her paw, and she fell a tail-length, landing in a tangle of soft pelts with a grunt. "Help me!" she yelped, struggling as the Twoleg stuff wrapped around her. Water lapped at her belly.

"Hold still, Moth!" Tadpole helped her untangle herself. "Come on!"

Together they began to scale the Twoleg junk again. Moth's claws caught on another pelt, and she slipped with a squeal of terror.

"You can do it, Moth!" Tadpole called out. With his shoulder he pushed her forward, and she began to clamber up again. The water was rising fast. A wave lapped at her hind paws, and she looked back to see it washing over Tadpole's shoulders.

"Hurry!" she meowed.

Hawk had climbed onto the narrow ledge where they had first come in. "I—can't—get it—open," he gasped, pounding his paws against the clearstone.

Moth was panting. Suddenly the ledge seemed so far away. Her paws slowed.

"Come on!" Tadpole yowled, and shoved at Moth's hindquarters. Hawk leaned down, gently biting the scruff of Moth's neck and tugging, urging her to rise. With a heave, she grabbed hold of the ledge and scrambled up beside Hawk. A familiar tawny form appeared outside the clearstone, looking in at them with frantic blue eyes.

"Sasha!" Moth cried, relief surging through her.

She turned to stretch out a paw for her littermate, just in time to see the rising water wash Tadpole away.

Mothwing woke from the familiar dream with a gasp, still reaching out for her lost littermate. One paw brushed against Hawkfrost, who woke with a grunt. "Stop," he muttered, and then, more quietly, asked, "Are you okay?"

"I'm fine," Mothwing told him. She could see his eyes glittering in the darkness of the den, watching her, so she rolled over and turned her back to him. She didn't want to talk about what she'd seen, even though Hawkfrost was the only one who would understand.

The dream was over, but the rest of the memory played out in her mind. Sasha managing to open the window, and Hawk and Moth tumbling out into the freedom of the grass. Their mother howling Tadpole's name. Peering past her, Moth had seen Tadpole surface, his paws outstretched toward Sasha, then sink again.

The rain had beaten down on Moth's head as she strained toward the ledge, expecting at any moment to see Tadpole's small, determined black face, but he hadn't appeared again. Tadpole had been the strongest of them, the bravest. She couldn't believe he wouldn't survive, not when she and Hawk had. But Tadpole had drowned.

Moth hadn't been able to stop shivering. Hawk had clawed at their mother, trying to jump into the water and pull Tadpole out, but Sasha had held him back. Her eyes shining with grief, she had said it was too late. Hawk had collapsed onto the ground, wailing, and Moth had lain down next to him, pressing her side to his, shaking hard.

One thought had cut through her sorrow like a claw: from that point on, she and Hawk would have to stick together. Without Tadpole, they would need each other more than ever.

At last, Sasha had shepherded them back to their den in the woods and dried them with short, rough licks, then curled up and fallen asleep without a word. Hawk had slept, too, an uneasy, whimpering sleep. But Moth had stayed awake, her eyes on her brother's tabby form.

"We'll both be as brave and strong as he was," she'd whispered. "I'll never leave you, I promise."

Now Mothwing rolled over and looked at her brother again. Dawn light, chilly and clear, had begun to spread through the den. "We'll stay together," she whispered, her chest aching with love and sorrow. Whether she belonged in RiverClan or not didn't matter. Her home would *always* be where Hawkfrost was.

They belonged with each other. Without Tadpole, without Sasha, that was all they had.

Later that morning, Mothwing brought up the rear of a fishing patrol as they returned to camp, a minnow dangling from her mouth. Her paws felt heavy and her eyelids were drooping—the little sleep she had gotten hadn't been restful.

"Hi," Hawkfrost greeted her, coming up to her as she

dropped the minnow onto the fresh-kill pile. "Did you catch that?"

Mothwing yawned. "No, it's Stormfur's. I was helping him carry some of his catch."

Hawkfrost's tail twitched. "He's good," he admitted. "But you should be better."

"I *am* good at fishing," Mothwing argued, offended. "I'm just tired today."

"I know." Hawkfrost glanced around and then led her toward the edge of camp, where they couldn't be overheard. "Listen," he mewed urgently. "We have to do our best all the time. Not every cat wants us here."

Mothwing sighed. She knew. Because they hadn't been born in the Clan, because their mother had been a rogue, some cats would always see them as outsiders. *And if they ever find out that Tigerstar, who almost destroyed the Clans, was our father, things will be much worse.* "But what can we do?" she asked, helpless.

Hawkfrost crowded closer, his pale eyes intent on hers. "*Some* cats don't want us. But I heard Leopardstar telling Mistyfoot what strong cats we are and what good additions we are to the Clan. Our leader and deputy believe in us."

"That's good." Warmth curled through Mothwing. Mistyfoot had been her mentor, and Leopardstar had startled the whole Clan by taking Hawkfrost as her apprentice. The leaders of RiverClan *wanted* them to belong.

"If we both do our best, all the time," Hawkfrost told her, his ears pricked with excitement, "every single one of the RiverClan cats will have to accept us. Maybe *we'll* be the leader and the deputy one day."

"Maybe," Mothwing mewed. She couldn't see herself leading RiverClan. But she could be a good warrior. And maybe Hawkfrost would rise to be leader, someday. *If he's determined to be the best warrior he can, I'll be right by his side.*

CHAPTER 2

A few days later, Mothwing picked her way over the muddy ground at the edge of the river, her tail drooping. *I can't wait to get back to camp and rest,* she thought. Her dreams of Tadpole's death had been more frequent lately, keeping her awake in her nest until it got so late that sleep pulled her under despite her racing thoughts.

Ahead of her, Hawkfrost sniffed eagerly at a small, limp-leaved plant. "Is this it?" he asked.

Mistyfoot circled back around to look, Mosspelt and Swallowpaw close behind. "No," she told him. "Didn't Mudfur tell you all what watermint looks like? The leaves are lighter-colored and more oval."

Mosspelt flicked her ears. "*I* knew that."

Swallowpaw peered at the plant. "Those are sort of oval," she mewed. "Are you sure this isn't right?"

Mothwing yawned. Her eyelids felt so heavy. Mistyfoot's blue eyes passed over her, then looked around the circle of cats.

"We don't really need so many cats on a patrol like this," she decided. "Mothwing and Hawkfrost, why don't you head back to camp? Mothwing looks like she could use some sleep."

Mothwing ducked her head and licked at her chest hot with embarrassment. "I'm okay," she insisted, but Mistyfoot waved her off.

"The three of us can handle it," the deputy told her.

Hawkfrost dipped his head and replied, "Yes, Mistyfoot," while shooting Mothwing a threatening glance. He swept past her, and she followed him back toward camp, eyes fixed on his brown tabby tail.

When they were out of sight and hearing of the patrol, Hawkfrost whipped around to face Mothwing. "Moth, we need to do well on patrols. We have to be the best. You know that."

Mothwing stiffened. "It's Mothwing now. *You* know *that*."

"Exactly." Hawkfrost relaxed a little and brushed his tail over hers. "It's okay. We can practice some fighting moves when we get back to camp. That's more important than looking for herbs anyway."

Mistyfoot told me to get some rest, not to play-fight. Mothwing's pelt prickled with irritation, but she didn't say anything. She'd rather practice battle moves with her littermate than argue with him.

Pushing her way through the reeds at the entrance to camp, Mothwing sniffed, picking up a strange smell. The mustiness of oak leaves mixed with the familiar scents of the RiverClan camp. "What's that?" she asked.

Hawkfrost gestured with his tail toward the medicine den. "The ThunderClan medicine cat," he said. "She must have come to talk to Mudfur."

Mothwing looked at the strange cat curiously. She had never seen her before—Leopardstar hadn't taken her and Hawkfrost to a Gathering yet—but the dark gray she-cat must be Cinderpelt. She looked small next to the broad-shouldered RiverClan medicine cat, whose light brown fur was speckled with gray. Mudfur had been a warrior before he became a medicine cat, and he still looked as powerful as any RiverClan warrior.

The two were deep in discussion. Mothwing pricked up her ears, intrigued. There was something fascinating about medicine cats. They knew so much! This past newleaf, Mothwing—she had still been Mothpaw then—had been bothered by pains in her belly, and Mudfur had been so kind, and so confident, as he fed her herbs to make her feel better, and he had reassured an anxious Sasha that Mothpaw was in no danger.

"My stock of chamomile is low, too," Mudfur was saying. "I can't spare any. But have you tried burnet?"

Cinderpelt blinked thoughtfully. "You know, there should be some growing near the Twolegplace now. Maybe all the medicine cats could . . ."

Mothwing crept closer, intrigued. Medicine cats worked together sometimes, no matter what Clan they were from. No other warriors did that. Cinderpelt looked up as Mothwing moved closer, and Mothwing froze. Would the medicine cats be angry that she was eavesdropping?

But Cinderpelt only gave a small nod of greeting. Relaxing, Mothwing nodded back.

And then something slammed into her side, knocking her across the clearing.

"I'm a ShadowClan warrior," Hawkfrost snarled playfully. "Sneak attack!"

Mothwing struggled beneath her brother's paws, trying to throw him off. "Stop it!" *What will Cinderpelt think of us? Behaving like kits!* She couldn't get away. Purring with laughter, Hawkfrost pushed down harder, pinning her beneath him.

"Surrender!" he yowled. "Or I'll drag you off to my boggy forest!"

"I don't want to play," Mothwing told him flatly. She stopped struggling and lay still, glaring up at her brother.

"Come on," Hawkfrost pleaded. He let his claws slip out and pricked her lightly on the shoulder. "What kind of RiverClan warrior doesn't fight back?"

"A tired one," Mothwing retorted, not moving a muscle.

"You're no fun," Hawkfrost told her. Letting her go, he strolled off toward the warriors' den. Mothwing got to her feet and shook out her pelt, her shoulder aching. *Why can't I fight as well as he does?* Hawkfrost was bigger than her, but he was faster, too, and he seemed to learn fighting moves the moment they were shown to him. *Maybe he inherited that from Tigerstar.*

Mothwing shook her pelt again, shaking off the thought. They needed to forget that Tigerstar was their father: Sasha had made it clear that if the Clan cats found out, they would never trust them, never let them stay.

The medicine cats were still discussing herbs. Mothwing

glanced tentatively at them, but Cinderpelt wasn't looking at her now.

"Are you all right? Skyheart came over from where she had been watching her kits play at the edge of camp, her green eyes wide. "Hawkfrost was pretty rough."

"I'm fine," Mothwing mewed, standing straighter. "I'm used to my brother's games."

"Hmm." Skyheart eyed her skeptically. "You were moving kind of slowly."

Mothwing stiffened. *Is she worried about me, or is she wondering whether I'm good enough to be in RiverClan?* Maybe Hawkfrost was right that they needed to prove themselves. "I'm fine," she repeated. "A little tired from patrolling with Mistyfoot, I guess."

Before Skyheart could respond, there was a commotion at the entrance to camp. All the cats looked up as Heavystep burst through the reeds. "Blackclaw's stuck in the mud," he panted. "We can't pull him out."

Horror shot through Mothwing. The mud at the edge of the river was a worse threat than the water itself. Every RiverClan cat could swim. But the lack of rain the past moon had made the river run low. The thick, sucking black mud at the water's edge could trap a cat and drag them down.

She raced toward the entrance, other cats on her heels. Heavystep led them to a steep part of the river bank. "We were coming back from hunting," he explained, "and he slipped off a stone."

Below, two voles lay abandoned, half sunk into the mud, while Blackclaw strained toward the shore, already up to his knees in muck.

"The bank's too steep here for me to reach him alone," Heavystep added, obviously distressed.

Mothwing stepped forward to the edge of the bank. *Maybe I'm light enough to get across the mud to him.* Blackclaw looked up at her and struggled forward a few steps, but he only sank deeper. Mud splattered his chest, and he slipped face-first into it, floundering for several heartbeats before he pulled himself back up to his paws. The crowd of cats on the bank gasped.

No! Mothwing recoiled. She remembered another black tom's face, staring up at her with the same desperation. *He's going to sink like Tadpole,* she thought, dizzy with fear. *He's going to drown. I can't save him.*

"Hold my legs," Leopardstar told Heavystep. The broad-shouldered tom lay across her hind legs, holding their golden-furred leader as she wriggled forward on her belly, her front paws reaching for Blackclaw. The black tom struggled forward a few more paces, sinking deeper into the mud with every step, until Leopardstar's claws caught in his fur. As she dragged Blackclaw forward, other paws reached out to help, and finally, with a sucking sound, Blackclaw burst out of the mud and collapsed on the riverbank.

Mothwing let out her breath in relief. Blackclaw was covered in muck, and he looked exhausted, but he was whole and safe.

But instead of getting to his paws, Blackclaw let out a

strange, strangled sound and flailed his legs, his claws scraping at the grass.

"He can't breathe!" Leopardstar yowled, crouching to paw at Blackclaw's face. The black tom opened his mouth, gagging, and Mothwing saw that it was full of thick mud. His eyes rolled back in his head and he made a horrible choking sound.

He's going to die! They pulled him out of the mud, but he's still drowning! Mothwing couldn't move.

"Let us through!" Cinderpelt, the ThunderClan medicine cat, wormed her way between the gathered cats, Mudfur close behind her. The gray she-cat hurried to Blackclaw and, without pausing, pushed at his side, rolling him onto his back. Mudfur held Blackclaw's jaws open and began to scoop mud from his mouth as Cinderpelt reared back on her hind paws and drove her front paws into Blackclaw's stomach. As the RiverClan cats watched in stunned silence, she threw her weight against Blackclaw again and again.

It's too late. They can't help him. Mothwing remembered Tadpole's limp body when Sasha had finally managed to get him out of the Twoleg nest, after the rain had stopped. He hadn't been breathing, and there had been no way to bring him back. Her shoulders sank and her tail drooped as she watched Blackclaw's limp body jerking under Cinderpelt's repeated blows.

Then, suddenly, he coughed. Cinderpelt pulled back, and Blackclaw rolled onto his side, retching weakly, a steady stream of mud and saliva coming from his mouth.

Mothwing watched in amazement as Cinderpelt gently helped Blackclaw to his paws. Leaning on Mudfur, he began to head slowly back toward camp.

They saved him. He hadn't sunk like Tadpole. He hadn't died. The medicine cats had been able to save Blackclaw when no other cats could.

While the sun began its slow descent beneath the tree line, Mothwing hovered near the medicine den, peeking through the reeds that shielded its entrance. The mud had been carefully cleaned from Blackclaw's fur, and now he was sleeping in a nest in the corner of the medicine den, his breathing hoarse but steady.

Mudfur was sorting through some dried leaves, his back to the entrance, but he cocked a brown ear back toward her. "Do you need something, Mothwing?" he asked. "Feeling sick?"

"No, I'm okay," Mothwing told him, leaning in to look more closely at the medicine den. There were little caves dug in the earth at the sides of the den where Mudfur stored herbs, and three more nests, empty now, soft with fresh moss.

Mudfur looked over his shoulder, fixing a bright golden eye on her. "Then why are you here?"

"Oh," Mothwing meowed, embarrassed heat spreading through her. "I just . . . I'm just interested. In how you're taking care of Blackclaw."

"Blackclaw will be fine," Mudfur replied calmly. "But taking care of him is medicine-cat business. I'm sure you have some warrior tasks you should be doing."

"I guess." Mothwing shuffled her paws. She took a few steps away from the den, then stopped.

I feel like I belong in this medicine den.

When Mudfur and Cinderpelt had saved Blackclaw, Mothwing had felt something she'd never felt when she'd learned to hunt, or to fight. She wanted to be able to save sick and hurt cats, not just fight for them.

Maybe I feel like I belong here because this is what I should *be doing.*

She turned back to the medicine den. "What if I trained to be a medicine cat?" she blurted out, then held her breath.

Mudfur turned then and gave her a long, searching look. "You'd better come in."

Inside the medicine den, Mothwing sniffed the air eagerly. It smelled mysterious and rich, full of the scents of so many different herbs. Mudfur watched her for a moment, his golden gaze thoughtful, then asked, "Why do you want to be a medicine cat?"

Mothwing shuffled her paws nervously. "When Hawkfrost and I were kits, our littermate drowned," she began. "I saw how you and the other medicine cats saved Blackclaw today, and I thought . . . maybe he didn't have to. I want to save other cats from dying if I can."

Mudfur gave a short, pleased purr at her answer. "Usually, a medicine cat starts their training as an apprentice," he told her. "You're already a warrior. You've served one apprenticeship. But I was a warrior before I trained to be a medicine cat, too."

Mothwing's chest felt tight with excitement. Mudfur had been a warrior for a long time; he had even mated and fathered a litter. He was Leopardstar's father. Maybe her idea wasn't so crazy. "You'd train me?" she asked.

Mudfur shook his head. "Don't get excited just yet. I'd have to talk to Leopardstar and Mistyfoot first. It's not like we've had a sign from StarClan about you."

"StarClan?" Mothwing cocked her head, confused. She'd *heard* of StarClan, of course. RiverClan thanked them every time they caught a piece of prey, and she'd heard the elders tell kits that StarClan was watching over them. But she'd always thought it was just something they said to honor their ancestors. It was a surprise to hear that the medicine cats actually consulted with StarClan before making major decisions. "I'm right here, willing to do the work to help my Clan. Why would we need a sign from StarClan?"

Mudfur blinked. "Of course, you weren't born in the Clans," he muttered. "Listen, Mothwing, StarClan guides the Clan's paws. Medicine cats don't just take care of their sick Clanmates. Medicine cats also advise Clan leaders as they make their decisions. And for that, we have to speak to StarClan. We tell the rest of our Clan what our ancestors see in our future and what they want us to do."

Mothwing felt her eyes widening. "You *talk* to StarClan?" she asked, nearly squeaking in surprise. She could accept that her Clanmates had been showing respect for their ancestors when they talked about StarClan. But she found it harder to believe that the ancestors spoke back. "They tell you what to do?"

Mudfur nodded, his golden eyes fixed on hers. "A medicine cat must have a special connection to StarClan," he told her solemnly. "It's the most important part of our duties."

Mothwing sat back on her haunches, feeling breathless. Mudfur could talk to the spirits of dead cats? And Cinderpelt could, and the other Clans' medicine cats? If she became a medicine cat, maybe someday she would, too. She remembered how much she would have given to be able to talk to Tadpole after he died. Her pelt prickled with excitement. *I hope StarClan believes I can do it.*

Mothwing hurried across the camp toward the medicine den. It had been days since she'd spoken to Mudfur, and he didn't let her sleep there yet—he was still waiting for a sign from StarClan. But Leopardstar had agreed that she could start helping Mudfur to care for their Clanmates.

"Off to play healer?" Mistyfoot was in the clearing, the remains of a fish at her paws.

"I—" Mothwing didn't know what to say. Was her former mentor angry with her? "I like healing," she meowed softly.

"It's all right, Mothwing." Mistyfoot's gaze softened. "I think you were a good warrior, and I spent a lot of time training you. But if StarClan decides you can be a medicine cat, it'll be useful. Mudfur isn't getting any younger. It's time he took an apprentice," she added, licking a front paw, "but try not to be too disappointed if it can't be you."

"Why *wouldn't* it be me?" Mothwing wondered aloud after Mistyfoot walked away.

"You'd better hope it is you," growled Hawkfrost. "Or else we're ruined."

Mothwing spun around in alarm. She hadn't seen her brother lurking among the reeds outside the medicine den. "What do you mean?" she mewed.

Hawkfrost sat on his haunches, his eyes glinting with anger. "We finally became real RiverClan warriors. We have a place here, a purpose. Then you go and decide you want to be a medicine cat. If you fail, how do you think that will look for us?"

Mothwing hesitated. She hadn't thought about how the Clan might see her change of course. She'd only wanted to follow what she believed to be her calling. When she didn't respond, Hawkfrost continued.

"It will look like you couldn't commit to being a warrior and weren't good enough to be a medicine cat. They might decide that means you shouldn't be part of RiverClan, and I shouldn't either."

Mothwing shook her head. "No, they wouldn't do that," she insisted.

"It's not only up to them," Hawkfrost reminded her. "It's like Mistyfoot said—StarClan decides if you have what it takes."

Hawkfrost was right. So much had been left up to ancestors Mothwing didn't even know. But she had to believe that her skills would count just as much as StarClan's wishes. "This is our home now," she stated firmly, trying to feel as confident as her words. "I'll work hard. I'll prove to them that I can be a great medicine cat."

Hawkfrost rose to his paws and started to walk away,

stopping after a few steps to peer over his shoulder at Mothwing. "You'd better," he growled. "For both our sakes."

As she watched her brother disappear into the reeds, her confidence faltered. Surely StarClan wouldn't tell Mudfur *not* to let her be a medicine cat? She didn't know a lot about StarClan, but she knew they acted for the good of the Clans—how could having another medicine cat *not* be good for RiverClan? It wasn't like any other cat was asking Mudfur to train them.

Inside the medicine den, Blackclaw was coughing, a hoarse, painful sound. Mudfur was rubbing his back with one firm paw and talking to him soothingly: "You breathed in too much of that river mud. Go ahead and get it out. You're getting better all the time."

Eager to help, Mothwing hurried over to the little caves full of Mudfur's collection of herbs. *What does he use to help Blackclaw breathe?* She found some purple juniper berries and began to mash them, then pulled a few coltsfoot leaves from another cave and chewed them to a pulp.

"Nicely done," Mudfur meowed. Startled, Mothwing looked up from mixing the coltsfoot and berries together and saw him regarding her with approval. "You seem to have a real talent," the medicine cat added. "Maybe StarClan is guiding your paws."

Mothwing hesitated. *No cat is guiding my paws. I just remembered what herbs you used yesterday!* "Th-thanks," she stammered.

Mudfur blinked at her, his eyes warm. "You know, any doubts I had about making you my apprentice are disappearing.

You've been working hard, Mothwing."

A thrill shot up Mothwing's spine. Whether she quite understood about StarClan or not, she valued Mudfur's opinion of her. *I'm already becoming a medicine cat!*

A few days later, a full moon glowed above the forest as RiverClan left the Gathering. Mothwing couldn't stop shaking. The Clans had been so *angry*.

Leopardstar had introduced her and Hawkfrost to the Clans, and for a moment, Mothwing had been proud: in front of cats of all four Clans, while the full moon shone overhead and the shadows of Fourtrees fell over them, Leopardstar had called out Mothwing and Hawkfrost's names.

And they hated us!

"Rogues!" some cat had yowled, and even a few RiverClan cats had growled at Mothwing and Hawkfrost in disapproval. But Leopardstar had stood up for them, pointing out that there were former rogues in ShadowClan, too, and that ThunderClan's leader, Firestar, had once himself been a kittypet. As the gathered cats settled, Mothwing and Hawkfrost had exchanged a look of half-frightened relief.

And then Leopardstar had announced that Mothwing had begun training to be a medicine cat. The cats had *howled* in protest.

"What do rogues know of StarClan?" Blackstar, the ShadowClan leader, had growled, outraged, and a chorus of snarls had echoed him. Surrounded by glaring eyes and unsheathed claws, Mothwing had been afraid. What if they attacked her? Mudfur sat beside her, silent. Would he protect her? Could he?

Hawkfrost, among the warriors, had been quivering with rage, digging his claws into the dirt.

At last, Mudfur had gotten to his feet, and the other cats had quieted—no matter how angry they were, they would listen when a medicine cat spoke. He had said that Mothwing was talented, and pride had warmed her, protecting her from the cold sneers of the warriors. And then he had said that, because she was not Clanborn, he was waiting for a sign before making her his apprentice.

This wasn't the first time that Mudfur had said that he wanted a sign from StarClan about her. But it hadn't really struck her that if he didn't get one, there was no chance of becoming Mudfur's apprentice. No matter how hard she worked.

As she followed Leopardstar toward RiverClan territory, Mothwing's paws felt heavy and cold.

Mudfur laid his tail across her back, and she looked up at him. "I'm sure you will be a medicine cat, Mothwing," he meowed comfortingly. "You'll prove them all wrong."

"What if StarClan doesn't give you a sign?" she asked, her voice sounding small and afraid to her own ears. "What happens then?" Maybe there was a way around this.

"I'm sure they'll give me a sign," Mudfur told her briskly. As they reached camp, he dropped his tail from her back. "I'll see you bright and early in the medicine den. We'll make a sore-throat poultice."

As she watched him disappear into the medicine den, Mothwing's heart sank. Mudfur seemed so confident, but what if that sign from StarClan never came? *What if StarClan doesn't even exist?* Quickly, Mothwing shook off the idea, glancing around as if some cat could have heard her thoughts.

If StarClan was real, she needed to be careful not to make them angry. *I need to become a medicine cat. I can't let my Clan down. And Mudfur stood up for me. I can't let* him *down either.*

Chapter 3

Before long, Mothwing managed to push her worries away. Surely, if she worked hard enough, StarClan would decide she should be a medicine cat.

And she *loved* working in the medicine den. Happily, she inhaled the mixture of scents, many of which she could identify now: marigold, ragweed, borage, tansy, feverfew. Each plant had its own smell, appearance, and use, and Mothwing was proud at how quickly she was learning them. *Tansy for cough, marigold for infection,* she thought, sorting them into their places.

There were no sick cats in the medicine den now that Blackclaw had recovered, but Mudfur had told her that, in quiet times like these, it was the medicine cats' job to prepare for the patients who would inevitably come. So Mothwing packed mixtures of herbs into beech leaves so that they would have the perfect amounts of catmint and tansy ready if greencough broke out in camp. She put fresh moss into the nests each day and laid herbs out in the sun to dry for storage. She foraged around the territory, looking for strong cobwebs to slow the bleeding of wounds. She listened as Mudfur told her how best to take a thorn out of a kitten's paw or strap reeds to a broken bone to keep it in place.

Mudfur moved around the medicine den with confidence: he never forgot the name of an herb and could put his paw on any one of them with instant accuracy. He seemed to know everything, and Mothwing could not wait to become just like him.

As Mothwing sorted the herbs, he curled beside her, his eyes half-closed and his voice content. "Now, helping a queen birth kits is one of the most important jobs a medicine cat does, and it can also be the happiest—or the saddest. You need to be sure to have a good supply of chervil on hand, and raspberry leaves if you can get them. The first sign . . ." A cloud must have swept across the sun, because the medicine den went dark for a moment, and Mudfur stopped talking.

I hope it rains, Mothwing thought. The drought had gone on too long. RiverClan had the river, but water sources were drying up in the other Clans—WindClan had even gotten permission from Leopardstar to come to the river to drink.

Mudfur was still silent, and Mothwing looked up from the herbs to find him thoughtfully staring out the door of the den at the sky.

"Are you okay?" she asked.

Mudfur blinked at her as if she was a long way away. "I have to ask you to leave the den," he told her after a moment. "I think this darkness may have been a sign from StarClan, and I need to be alone to interpret it."

"But it was just a cloud," Mothwing protested, and then, at Mudfur's look, hunched her shoulders in embarrassment. *I don't sound very much like a medicine cat.* "Sorry. I'll go."

She hurried out of the medicine den, almost tripping over her own paws. By the time she reached the fresh-kill pile, she had gotten over her embarrassment. But when she thought of Mudfur, trying to decide the meaning of a cloud, she still felt uncomfortable, as if she had earth stuck between her paw pads.

Hawkfrost was picking through the prey, just back from a patrol, and he looked up at her in surprise. "What's up?"

Mothwing told him, glancing around first to make sure that no cat could overhear them. "It just seems so stupid to me," she confessed. "And Mudfur's the smartest cat I know. It was just a cloud passing over the sun. That happens every *day*! It can't always mean that StarClan has something to tell us!"

Hawkfrost shook his head, his eyes narrowing. "Mothwing, you can't talk like this."

Mothwing's pelt prickled with annoyance. "Well, what do *you* think? Is StarClan in charge of everything that happens?"

"It doesn't matter what I think," Hawkfrost mewed firmly. "I don't know if StarClan is real, but if I have to pretend to believe in them to be part of RiverClan, I will."

"You will?" Mothwing felt as if the breath had been knocked out of her. She had never considered *lying* about believing in StarClan. Reflexively, she flinched and glanced at the sky—what if even talking about this made StarClan angry?

"And you will, too." Hawkfrost stepped closer to her, lowering his voice to a dangerous whisper. "It was mouse-brained of you to become an apprentice again after you'd already been made a warrior. But we can still make this work. Every cat respects a medicine cat. If Mudfur decides to make you his apprentice, they'll all forget we weren't born in the Clans." His blue eyes met hers. "We'll belong. If you're a medicine cat, we can stay here forever. We can be important. You don't want to be thrown out to be a rogue again, do you?"

Mothwing shook her head slowly. The threat beneath his words was unmistakable. She didn't want to deceive any cat, yet what Hawkfrost said was true. Their place in the Clan depended on her now. She'd chosen this path, and she had no choice but to see it through—and there was only one way forward that would satisfy her brother without forcing her to lie. Hawkfrost was right. *I have to believe in StarClan.*

"Okay," she said, the weight of responsibility falling on her shoulders.

"I'm not sure how much this will help, Loudbelly," Mudfur said sadly. "The most we can do is ease your pain a little."

It had been two days since the cloud had passed over the sun, and if Mudfur had decided it was a sign from StarClan, he hadn't told Mothwing what it meant. Now Mudfur was carefully feeling along Loudbelly's legs and hips, purring sympathetically as the dark brown elder groaned.

"I'm not expecting to jump like a kit again," Loudbelly grumbled. "But anything that lets me walk across camp without falling over will be much appreciated."

Mothwing gnawed at the comfrey root, trying not to swallow its bitterness. Finally, she spat out the chewed bits and pounded them into a poultice. "Should I put it on?" she asked shyly, but Mudfur shook his head.

"Not until you're my apprentice," he meowed. Mothwing backed away obediently as Mudfur began to smear the poultice in long, even strokes across Loudbelly's hips. "This will ease your joints," he told the elder.

As Mothwing stood beside Mudfur and watched him work, worry curled in her belly. Mudfur let her clean the medicine den and sort herbs, but he wouldn't let her touch a patient. Not until StarClan gave him a sign.

What will happen if he never gets a sign? Would she grow old putting fresh moss in nests and chewing up herbs and never actually being a medicine cat, or even a medicine-cat apprentice? Or would he send her back to being a warrior? Would the rest of RiverClan even *want* her as a warrior, knowing her heart was in the medicine den?

The next morning, Mothwing huddled outside the warriors' den, watching the sun rise. It was going to be another hot greenleaf day, but she felt cold. She hadn't slept well, and when she'd finally dozed off, Hawkfrost had accidentally woken her as he came back from the dirtplace. She yawned, her mouth dry.

Would Mudfur even notice if I spent the whole day in my nest? Well, he'd notice, of course, but would it matter? The other warriors were starting to talk about her to one another in low voices—she'd felt their eyes on her when they didn't think she was looking. They thought StarClan didn't want her. It had been more than a moon. *Maybe I should leave RiverClan,* she thought grimly. *If I'm not a medicine cat, I don't belong here.* Listening to the familiar, soothing rustle of the reeds outside camp, she felt hollow. *I don't want to go.*

Looking up, she saw Mudfur outside the medicine den, his body taut with something—surprise? Expectation? He stared directly at her for a moment, and Mothwing lifted her chin in greeting, but he didn't respond. Bending, he picked up something small from the ground in front of his paws and hurried over to Leopardstar's den. Mistyfoot and Shadepelt, sitting near the fresh-kill pile, raised their heads in surprise as he passed.

A soft murmur of voices came from Leopardstar's den, and then the leader poked her head out—she still looked sleepy, as if Mudfur had woken her—and called to Mistyfoot to join them.

Mothwing's eyes met Shadepelt's. The dark-furred elder looked just as confused as Mothwing was.

After a few moments, Leopardstar stepped out of her den and strode to the center of the clearing, Mistyfoot and Mudfur padding beside and a little behind her. "RiverClan!" she called. "All cats old enough to catch their own prey, gather to hear my words!"

A confused cacophony of voices came from the warriors' den.

"What's going on?" yowled Heavystep.

"It's so early!" Mosspelt mewed.

"Is something wrong?" Blackclaw cried, and, one by one, the cats, stretching and blinking sleepily, streamed out of the den. Skyheart and Dawnflower poked their heads out of the nursery, Skyheart's kits crowding around her legs curiously, while Swallowpaw hurried out of the apprentices' den.

As Hawkfrost came out of the warriors' den, Mothwing followed him, and they joined the others in a wide circle around Leopardstar. "Do you know what's going on?" he asked, and she shook her head.

RiverClan quieted, looking at their leader expectantly. When the clearing was silent except for the rustling of the reeds and a jay crying overhead, Leopardstar spoke.

"StarClan has given Mudfur a sign."

She gestured with her tail, and the medicine cat stepped forward. "I've been sure for a while that Mothwing is suited to become a medicine cat, even though she isn't Clanborn. But we decided to wait for a sign from StarClan, so that no cat could argue against her. We've been waiting for more than a moon." He paused, and Mothwing held her breath, excitement swelling inside her. Had it finally happened?

"This morning," Mudfur went on, the sun giving a glow to his pale brown fur, "I discovered a moth's wing outside my den. An unmistakable sign that StarClan approves of Mothwing becoming a medicine-cat apprentice." He blinked proudly at Mothwing, and she dipped her head to him. Her heart was beating hard. *At last . . .*

A chorus of excited congratulations broke out as Mothwing's Clanmates crowded around her, nuzzling her cheeks and purring. Hawkfrost knocked his side against hers. "See?" he meowed cheerfully. "You were worried about nothing."

Mothwing was so full of joy that she felt for a moment as if she might lift right off the ground. StarClan had chosen her. And her Clanmates were glad! A sense of belonging rushed through her. Closing her eyes for a moment, she sent a quick thought to StarClan. *Thank you. I'm so sorry I doubted you.*

The half-moon sailed high overhead, shining a pale light through the trees of the forest as Mothwing and Mudfur walked side by side back toward the RiverClan camp.

"So," Mudfur asked, after a companionable silence, "how do you feel?"

"That was *amazing,*" Mothwing burst out. "I feel really good. Excited." Words weren't enough to express what her first medicine-cat meeting had been like, but Mudfur gave a brief purr, as if he understood.

They'd risen at dawn and left camp without even a glance at the fresh-kill pile: you couldn't eat if you wanted to share tongues with StarClan. It had been a long, hungry walk to Highstones—Mothwing would have sworn the scent of prey in the distance had never been more tantalizing—and the sun was sinking by the time they and the other medicine cats stopped at the bottom of the steep, bare slope that led to the dark cavern that was Mothermouth.

Mothwing had been that far before, accompanying Leopardstar on one of the leader's trips to the Moonstone. But she'd never been inside.

This time, she'd gotten to enter. At first she'd felt a little disappointed. It had been cold and damp, darker than the darkest night. She hadn't been able to see even a tail-length in front of her as she walked with the other medicine cats through the twisting passages of Mothermouth. And then they had stepped through into a vast cavern where stars twinkled high above smooth walls of stone. There was a huge stone in the middle of the cave, and the other cats had made her sit before it for what seemed like moons. They'd waited in silence, in the dark, and Mothwing had thought: *Is this all?*

And then the moon had appeared above the cavern, and the Moonstone had burst into brilliant, shimmering light.

Her heart had pounded as if it would break out of her chest as Mudfur led her to the Moonstone and presented her to StarClan. He had told her to lie down and press her nose against it, and, one by one, the other medicine cats had joined her, their eyes closed, their bodies tense with expectation. With them, she had waited for the cats of StarClan to reveal themselves.

As they crossed the river back to their camp, a flicker of doubt entered Mothwing's mind. StarClan *had* spoken to her, hadn't they? They had sent her a vision of her Clanmates? She'd pictured RiverClan's future in her mind and felt happy and accepted. She'd seen—or imagined?—Hawkfrost, brave and strong, leading a patrol. Dawnflower's kits growing, healthy and strong. A fine catch of fish on the fresh-kill pile.

Was there supposed to be *more*? From the way Mudfur talked, it seemed like there should have been something like a conversation.

As they passed Mosspelt, who was guarding the camp and

greeted them with a nod, Mothwing shook her pelt as if she could also shake off her worries. *I just didn't understand until it happened.*

The camp was quiet, most of the cats asleep. Soon the sun would rise again.

"I'm going straight to my nest," Mudfur told her, "but if you're hungry, have some prey."

"I will," Mothwing replied, her mouth watering. She'd walked a lot today, and the small vole she'd caught on their way back from Mothermouth hadn't satisfied her.

Mudfur flicked his tail across her back affectionately. "You did well today, Mothwing," he mewed. "I'm proud of you. But try not to wake me when you come in."

"Sleep well," Mothwing told him. Maybe she would sleep better in the medicine-cat den now that she was a full, StarClan-approved apprentice. Mudfur had given her a nest there as soon as he'd gotten the sign from StarClan, but she'd missed the scents and sounds of the warriors' den. She'd missed Hawkfrost sleeping next to her. This was the first time in their whole lives that they hadn't shared a den.

As she approached the fresh-kill pile, she smelled his familiar scent before she saw him, a dark shape huddled near the prey. "What are you doing awake?" Mothwing asked, surprised and pleased.

Hawkfrost stretched and purred, his eyes shining in the gray of the early dawn. "I wanted to see you," he meowed. "How was it? Did StarClan accept you?"

"I think so," Mothwing answered proudly. "I'm an official

medicine-cat apprentice now. All the medicine cats were so nice to me. Especially Leafpaw, the ThunderClan apprentice. We're the only two apprentices."

"And now we really belong," Hawkfrost added. There was something smug in his voice, and a little warning tickle began between Mothwing's shoulder blades. That was the way Hawkfrost had sounded when they were kits and he'd gotten an extra piece of prey without Sasha noticing, or won a game of moss-ball by tricking Tadpole.

"Of course we do," she mewed uneasily. "Hawkfrost, what's going on?"

Hawkfrost hesitated for a moment and then, as if he couldn't stop the words bursting out of him, announced, "*I* put the moth wing outside Mudfur's den."

Mothwing stiffened. She couldn't breathe. She couldn't think for a few heartbeats, and then she croaked, *"What?"*

"Shh," Hawkfrost shushed her. "You were *meant* to be a medicine cat. Any cat could see it. But just because we weren't born in the Clan, Mudfur insisted on waiting for some kind of sign. You already proved yourself, so why should we wait for something that might never happen?"

"But . . ." Mothwing felt sick. Had her vision just been her imagination after all? "StarClan didn't approve of me? I should tell Mudfur."

Hawkfrost moved closer and dropped his voice. "StarClan let it happen." His breath was hot on her cheek. "If StarClan is real, they must think it's okay. Maybe they don't care. Or maybe they don't exist."

"Maybe." Mothwing felt like she was breaking into pieces. Maybe StarClan was just a story after all, and what she'd seen at the Moonstone had just been a dream.

Surely they wouldn't have let Hawkfrost do something so sneaky, if they were real? If StarClan was *true*, surely they wouldn't have tortured her by making her wait so long—they would have told Mudfur yes or no themselves.

"I should tell Mudfur," she meowed again, feeling less sure.

"But you won't." The clearing was lit by gray dawn light now, and Hawkfrost was watching her through pale, half-slitted eyes. "You know RiverClan will be better off with you as a medicine cat."

Mothwing took a deep breath. Hawkfrost was right. And if she told Mudfur, she'd lose everything. RiverClan would probably kick her and Hawkfrost both out for tricking them. She swallowed hard. Where would they go? All she wanted was to be a RiverClan medicine cat. Was that bad? Even if StarClan hadn't picked her? *Whether StarClan exists or not,* she promised silently, *I'll be the best medicine cat I can.*

Chapter 4

"Sixteen, seventeen, eighteen . . . ," Mothwing murmured, carefully separating dock leaves with one claw.

"Twenty-four," Mudfur interrupted irritably, his voice weak. "You've counted every herb in this den five times."

"You're the one who taught me to be thorough," Mothwing told him. A cold breeze blew through the medicine den and she shivered. This leaf-fall had been bitterly cold, and it had been a while since she had been able to find any fresh herbs.

"I didn't teach you to do the same thing over and over," Mudfur grumbled, more faintly than before. Mothwing ran a worried eye over him. The older medicine cat's eyes were bleary and his meow was hoarse. Touching his side gently with one paw, she felt that his thin body was radiating heat.

Mudfur's sickness had come at exactly the wrong time. Terrible things were happening in the Clans' territories. Twolegs had invaded the forest. They'd chopped down Fourtrees and brought monsters to dig up the earth. Prey had fled. The other Clans were talking about leaving the forest. *What if we have to leave? How will Mudfur manage the journey?*

Young warriors from each Clan had disappeared and come

back, including Stormfur from RiverClan, although his sister, Feathertail, had been killed on their journey. They said that StarClan had given them a prophecy: that a sign would tell the Clans where to go, when to leave. But the sign hadn't come yet.

RiverClan, protected by the river, had been safe from the Twolegs so far. Leopardstar had said they would stay where they were unless the Twolegs came onto RiverClan territory. But the river grew shallower by the day—more so than it had been during the terrible drought that summer, even though rain fell regularly—and no cat knew why. *We might have to leave.*

Mudfur groaned and laid his head down on the side of his nest as if he was too tired to hold it up. His frail frame shook.

"Is the pain very bad?" Mothwing asked. Mudfur moaned again, and she quickly mixed some poppy seeds with honey and feverfew leaves. The poppy seeds would help with the pain and the honey with the infection, while the feverfew leaves should cool him. "Try to eat this," she mewed, lifting the mixture to his mouth, and Mudfur licked weakly at her paw.

Mothwing watched as her mentor began to doze restlessly, his thin sides moving in shallow breaths. *Please get better,* she thought. *I can't do this on my own.*

She had only been an official medicine-cat apprentice for a few moons. She had memorized the uses of herbs and she had helped Mudfur care for injured paws and sick kits. She knew a lot already, but she didn't know everything a medicine cat should.

Maybe if StarClan had really chosen her . . .

That's ridiculous, she scolded herself. *StarClan must be only a dream. If they were real, they never would have let Hawkfrost trick Mudfur.*

There wasn't anything she cared about more than keeping her Clanmates strong and healthy. If that didn't make her a true medicine cat, what would? But she wasn't ready to do it alone.

As night began to fall, Hawkfrost stuck his head into the medicine den. "I brought you a mouse," he announced, with a nervous glance at dozing Mudfur.

"Thanks," Mothwing meowed. "I don't want to leave him."

Hawkfrost dropped the mouse in front of her and then hesitated, shifting from one powerful paw to the other. "I was talking to Sasha at the edge of our territory," he told her slowly.

"Oh, good," Mothwing replied. A few moons before, Sasha had been captured by Twolegs along with several Clan cats, including Mistyfoot. Some ThunderClan cats had gotten them all free, and Mistyfoot had invited Sasha to visit whenever she wanted. It had been wonderful to see their mother again, even though she wouldn't stay. *Couldn't* stay, not if she wanted to keep the secret that Tigerstar was their father. Too many ShadowClan cats knew that she and Tigerstar had been mates. If ShadowClan knew that Sasha was Mothwing and Hawkfrost's mother, they might figure out their secret. But it was good to know Sasha was nearby. "Was she okay?"

"Yeah . . . ," Hawkfrost began, then looked down. "But Firestar and a couple of other ThunderClan cats saw us. They were coming onto RiverClan territory to talk to Leopardstar.

Firestar asked if we were Tigerstar's kits, and Sasha said yes."

"What?" Mothwing went cold. "Why would she admit it?"

Hawkfrost hunched his shoulders. "The way he said it . . . he already knew. I look like Tigerstar, I guess. At least, I look like Brambleclaw. And every cat knows he's Tigerstar's son, but he was born in the Clans, so no cat worries about *him*."

"They would have found out eventually, I suppose," Mothwing mewed dully. Hawkfrost and Brambleclaw *did* look a lot alike. "Do we have to leave?"

RiverClan wouldn't want Tigerstar's kits, she was sure of it. They still talked about the cats he'd killed, the terrible things he'd done as he rose to power. They used his name to frighten naughty kits, as if he were a monster or a fox.

"Maybe not." Hawkfrost came closer and touched his nose to her cheek, gently. "I don't think Firestar will tell any cat or let the cats he was with tell anyone. I think he's known for a long time."

Mothwing's belly was heavy with dread. "But if they do . . ."

Hawkfrost extended his long claws, digging them into the ground. "I'm RiverClan's strongest warrior," he insisted. "If anyone tries to turn against us, they'll be sorry." Mudfur shifted restlessly in his sleep, and Hawkfrost glanced at him again. "I'd better go."

Mothwing nodded, distracted, as he left the medicine den. Everything was falling apart.

A small sound came from Mudfur's nest, and Mothwing looked up to see his eyes open and fixed on her. *What if he heard?* she thought, dismayed. Would he still want her as his apprentice, if he knew she was Tigerstar's kit?

"Mudfur?" she asked. The brown tom made a strange wheezing noise and tried to climb to his paws. He looked worried, not angry. He made it halfway up and then fell back into his nest, gasping.

"Mudfur!" Mothwing forgot about Hawkfrost and Tigerstar and ran to her mentor's side. His eyes were fixed on hers, and he seemed to be struggling to speak, but only a thick gargling noise came out. "Where does it hurt?" she asked. "What do you need?"

Mudfur gagged. A string of bile ran from the corner of his mouth and he panted, gasping for breath. Mothwing pressed her paw against his side, feeling how shallow his breathing was. "Help!" she called. "Help!"

After what seemed like an endless moment, a pounding of paws came from outside, and Blackclaw and Swallowtail dashed into the medicine den. Blackclaw's apprentice, Volepaw, was close on their tails. "Get Leopardstar!" Mothwing snapped at them, and Volepaw doubled back out of the entrance, running hard.

A few heartbeats later, Leopardstar pushed her way between the warriors and stared down at Mudfur, horror in her amber eyes. "What's wrong with him?"

Mudfur gagged again, his thin body trembling uncontrollably.

"I don't know," Mothwing wailed. "He . . . he's been ill and he just fell and can't seem to catch his breath or talk. I've been giving him poppy seeds and feverfew and—"

Leopardstar cut her off. "Will he recover?" Her meow was calm, but something in it reminded Mothwing that Mudfur was not only Leopardstar's medicine cat, but her father. If Mudfur died, it would be a terrible blow to their leader.

"I don't know," Mothwing repeated, feeling helpless. "I've been doing all I can, but . . . I might need advice from a more experienced medicine cat." She felt ashamed. "Can I ask Cinderpelt for help?"

Leopardstar nodded. "ThunderClan's camp is at Sunningrocks now. Go as fast as you can. I will stay with Mudfur."

Outside, there was enough moonlight to guide Mothwing's paws as she raced out of camp and toward the river's edge. *I'll find Leafpaw first,* she decided. *She likes me, and she's Firestar's daughter. She'll get him to let Cinderpelt come.*

She waded into the shallow river, heading for Sunningrocks on the other side. In the moonlight, she could see ThunderClan cats curled on the bare surface of the rocks, sleeping. They would be leaving the forest soon: their camp had been destroyed. There was nothing left for them here.

What if Mudfur dies? Mothwing felt cold with dread and grief. Mudfur was old and sick; he might not survive. If the RiverClan medicine cat died, and the other Clans left, she would have to take care of RiverClan alone. *I'm not ready.*

If she had been chosen by StarClan, maybe she *would* be ready by now. Maybe she would automatically know what to do. Mothwing splashed her paws a little more firmly through the water. She had been working hard. No cat would know more than she did after so little training. But the lingering thought remained, no matter how she tried to shake it away: *If they're real, StarClan is punishing me.* But even if that was true, she couldn't let Mudfur down. He'd had faith in her abilities and had suffered the Clan's anger because of it. That was reason enough for her to stay and become the medicine cat Mudfur seemed so sure she could be. She would start by using everything he'd taught her to take care of him. Come what may, Mothwing resolved to make her mentor proud.

Mudfur lay in the center of the medicine clearing, his sides barely moving with slow, shallow breaths. Rain ran through the branches above onto his flank, but he didn't flinch or try to move away. Mothwing had tried to move him to his nest when the rain started, but he had whimpered like a hurt kit, and she hadn't had the heart to keep trying.

For a few sunrises after Cinderpelt and Leafpaw's visit, Mudfur had rallied, getting back on his paws and moving slowly around the medicine den as Mothwing had fed him herbs to ease his pain and stave off infection.

At the same time, things had been going from bad to worse in the territory outside their medicine den. WindClan was almost starving. The river had gotten lower and lower; the cats had discovered that the Twolegs had diverted the water away. When ShadowClan's camp had been destroyed in front of the Clans' eyes, Leopardstar had decided that it was too dangerous for even RiverClan to remain. All four Clans would leave together to find a new home.

Or at least that had been the plan. But now Mudfur was

dying. There was no way he could travel. *We can't leave him to die alone,* Mothwing thought, stroking his side with her tail.

Leopardstar came through the reeds and looked down at her father, her eyes clouded with grief. "How long?" she asked.

"I don't know," Mothwing told her. "Not long."

Leopardstar nodded. "I'll tell the Clan. We'll wait until the end. He's served RiverClan well, and we should honor him."

As she left, Shadepelt came into the medicine clearing. "I wanted to say good-bye," the dark gray elder meowed sadly. "Mudfur and I were kits together." Sighing, she sat beside Mudfur and pressed her nose against his cheek.

They sat together in silence, Mothwing comforted by Shadepelt's steady presence. Mudfur's breathing grew slower and slower. Mothwing had given him a last dose of poppy seeds at dawn, but now he was too far gone to swallow any more. It was just a matter of time.

A little later, Runningnose, the ShadowClan medicine cat, came through the reeds into the clearing, Cinderpelt and Leafpaw trailing behind him.

"Firestar is here," Leafpaw told Mothwing. "And he's brought Frostfur and Speckletail, our elders. They want to care for Mudfur when RiverClan leaves."

Mothwing shook her head. "They won't need to. There's nothing more any cat can do." She looked down at Mudfur's still form, her shoulders sinking. "At least he's not in pain. I've made sure of that."

Runningnose stepped forward and pressed his muzzle to Mudfur's shoulder. "Go swiftly to StarClan, my friend. We will look after your Clanmates." Cinderpelt and Leafpaw buried their noses in Mudfur's fur, their eyes closed.

With one last shuddering gasp, Mudfur grew still. As the other cats pulled back, their faces full of grief, Mothwing closed Mudfur's golden eyes for the last time with a gentle paw. "He's with StarClan now," she announced sadly, hoping it was true. He had believed he would be.

She gasped as the thought of StarClan brought a new wave of panic. How could she take care of her Clan, if she didn't even know if StarClan was real?

Mothwing was confident that she could care for the health of her Clan, but Mudfur had been RiverClan's connection to StarClan. Now the Clan would be turning to Mothwing to interpret StarClan's wishes. How could she do any of this—her whole *life*—without her wise mentor? "How will I manage without him?" she asked. Her meow sounded harsh and frantic to her own ears.

Cinderpelt nuzzled her. "You'll be fine. And there will be time to grieve, but not now."

Mothwing looked around at the medicine cats, taking comfort in their sad, calm gazes—*they* believed Mudfur was in StarClan—and took a deep breath before padding back out to tell RiverClan that Mudfur was dead.

As the cats wailed in grief and then began, one by one, to stream through the tunnel to pay their respects to Mudfur for the last time, Mothwing felt numb. She heard what was going on, but it was as if she were at a great distance from her Clanmates. Cold rain trickled through her fur, and Mothwing stared up at the gray morning sky. Was StarClan up there somewhere? Was Mudfur among them?

Mothwing couldn't make herself believe that Mudfur's spirit had traveled anywhere. He was dead. Whatever was left of him was lying in the medicine den's clearing. The elders would watch over all that remained of Mudfur.

Hawkfrost, with Stormfur beside him, came over to Mothwing. Hawkfrost's gaze was softer than Mothwing had seen in a long time, and he rested his muzzle on her head, giving her silent support. Mothwing closed her eyes, pressed her face into his fur, and breathed Hawkfrost's familiar scent. *He's all I have left,* she thought.

Leafpaw came and spoke to her, but Mothwing barely heard her friend. When she lifted her head, she found Leafpaw and Cinderpelt gathering the remaining stores of herbs in the den, making sure nothing was left behind. "I can do that," Mothwing offered weakly. "I want to help."

After all, even in the midst of their grief, every cat was doing their part to prepare for their journey—cleaning out dens and bundling up the remains of the prey. She needed to prepare too. But Cinderpelt and Leafpaw returned her gaze with sympathy in their eyes. "You've already done so much," Cinderpelt mewed. "Let us help."

After a long moment, Mothwing nodded gratefully. She realized then that she was wrong. Hawkfrost was not all she had left. No cat would ever replace Mudfur, but she could turn to these medicine cats—they were from different Clans, but they were all healers, and that was more important. She felt the weight on her lighten with relief.

Soon, every cat assembled in what had been the center of their camp while Leopardstar addressed them. She announced that Loudbelly and Shadepelt, as well as the ThunderClan elders, had decided to stay behind rather than travel to find an unknown territory. They would sit vigil over Mudfur while RiverClan left with the other Clans.

At least he won't be alone, thought Mothwing. Then, glancing from her brother to her fellow medicine cats, she added silently, *And neither will I.*

"Are we ready?" Leopardstar asked the Clan. Mothwing opened her eyes and got to her paws. All around her, RiverClan was preparing, their tails high and their eyes determined, ready to go. She saw among them so many that Mudfur had treated and restored to health. But Mudfur was gone, and they would need Mothwing to take care of them through injury and illness on their journey and in their new home. *I'm responsible for RiverClan now.*

"I have traveling herbs for us all, Leopardstar," she said, her meow calm, and turned toward the medicine den.

Hawkfrost stuck close to Mothwing, padding beside her as they left RiverClan's territory for the last time. ThunderClan and ShadowClan were waiting for them at the edge of the forest. WindClan would meet them on the moor before they all left Clan territory entirely.

What's left of it, Mothwing thought, looking out across what had been ThunderClan's camp. The huge yellow Twoleg monsters had dug deep gouges in the earth and slaughtered many trees, leaving shockingly bare patches. Beyond where she could see, she knew that Fourtrees was gone and the Great Rock had been torn from the earth.

Her fur brushed Hawkfrost's, and she glanced at him to see him looking back at RiverClan's camp, an expression of longing on his face. This had been the first place they had been safe. The place where a Clan had taken them in and taught them how to not be rogues. To depend on cats other than themselves. *Wherever we go, I'll never forget this home,* she promised herself.

As they crossed through what remained of the forest, she spotted a flash of tawny fur between the trees. A moment later, Sasha slipped out and stood in the Clans' path, her tail held high. Mothwing's heart lifted for the first time since Mudfur had died. *We couldn't have left without saying good-bye,* she realized. She raced toward Sasha and rubbed against her legs, rolling on the ground like a kit. Hawkfrost followed her more slowly and looked at Sasha, his ears twitching.

"I'm glad to see you," he mewed quietly. "RiverClan is leaving, I don't know if we'll find each other again."

Sasha's blue eyes were troubled. "Don't go with them," she pleaded.

Mothwing stilled, then climbed to her paws to look their mother in the eye. "But this is our Clan," she argued. "You brought us to them so we could become warriors."

Sasha shook her head. "I brought you here so you'd be safe," she protested. "It's not safe now. I've seen what happened here.

Come with me and we'll be together again."

Pain shot through Mothwing. She didn't want to lose Sasha. But . . . she belonged in RiverClan.

Hawkfrost drew back. "I'm a RiverClan cat now," he meowed. "One day I'll be leader."

Sasha's bright eyes dimmed. "No," she insisted. "You won't." Brushing past him, she padded toward the watching cats. Hawkfrost and Mothwing followed, Mothwing's belly churning uneasily.

There was hostility in the eyes of the ShadowClan and ThunderClan cats, and several of them hissed softly as Sasha got closer. But Leopardstar dipped her head in greeting. "I didn't think we'd see you again," she meowed.

"Nor I you," Sasha replied calmly. "I have come to ask Hawkfrost and Mothwing to leave RiverClan and come with me." Leopardstar bristled, but Sasha went on. "I've seen what the Twolegs are doing to your homes. It is no longer safe for them to stay with you."

Mothwing's heart beat faster. Leopardstar wouldn't just let them go, would she? But it was Leafpaw, her fellow medicine-cat apprentice, who pushed out of the crowd toward Mothwing, her gaze outraged. "You wouldn't really go, would you?" she asked.

Mothwing blinked. Sasha had turned to face her, and she could see pain in her mother's eyes. "I—I don't know," Mothwing mewed.

"Your Clan *needs* you," Leafpaw hissed. She turned to Hawkfrost. "You wouldn't abandon your Clanmates, would you?"

Hawkfrost's eyes narrowed; he didn't like being questioned by a ThunderClan cat. Before he could answer, Firestar spoke up, cutting off Leafpaw's anger. "The choice is theirs. But I agree they should remain with their Clan."

Sasha's ears flattened, and Mothwing knew what she was going to say. "You want them to stay?" she snarled. "In spite of the fact that Tigerstar was their father?"

There was a moment of silence from the gathered cats. The RiverClan cats were staring at Mothwing and Hawkfrost, their eyes wide. All Mothwing could hear was the steady beat of the rain. She braced herself. Would the other cats rip them to pieces? Or just chase them out of the Clans?

Firestar answered, his voice calm. "I want them to stay *because* Tigerstar was their father," he meowed, and Mothwing's pelt prickled in surprise. Beside her, Hawkwing flexed his long claws, distrustful. "Tigerstar was a great warrior," the ThunderClan leader went on, "and these cats have proved they have inherited his courage."

He was looking at Brambleclaw, Mothwing realized, and remembered that the ThunderClan warrior, the cat every cat thought would be Firestar's next deputy, was Tigerstar's son too. And Tawnypelt, Tigerstar's daughter, was a respected ShadowClan warrior. *Of course, they were born in the Clans,* she thought. *Their mother was a ThunderClan cat. Things are different for them.*

"Their Clan needs them more than ever," Firestar continued. "Tigerstar's kits have earned their place in the Clans many times over."

Brambleclaw's eyes were wide. Mothwing knew Firestar wasn't talking about her and Hawkfrost, not really, but she warmed a little with hope—maybe the fact of their parentage wouldn't turn the Clans against them after all. She looked up at the faces of her Clanmates, hoping for their approval.

Leopardstar held her gaze. "RiverClan needs all our warriors," she meowed. "And we certainly need our medicine cat."

"But they're Tigerstar's kits!" Dawnflower hissed. Her pale gray tail was bushed in horror. Mothwing lifted her chin and stared the she-cat down. *I gave you catmint for your cough,* she thought. *When Minnowkit had an infected cut on her paw, I healed it.*

"Hawkfrost is one of our best warriors," Stormfur countered, the fur along his back bristling. He looked to the rest of RiverClan. "Have any of you ever doubted his loyalty?"

"Never," Mistyfoot replied firmly, and other warriors nodded their agreement.

"Will you stay?" Leopardstar asked, looking at Mothwing and Hawkfrost.

"Of course," Hawkfrost told her. He didn't even look at Sasha.

Mothwing did. Tail drooping, rain plastering her fur to her sides, Sasha looked sad and utterly alone. "I have to stay with my Clan, too," Mothwing explained. "I'm their medicine cat now. They need me." She gazed at her mother pleadingly. *Please understand. Forgive me.*

Sasha nodded once, then lifted her tail high. "Very well," she answered. "Firestar is right. I see your father in both of you." Dawnflower growled, and Sasha glared at her sharply.

"Tigerstar never knew about these kits," she went on, "but he would have been proud of them." She looked around at the rest of RiverClan. "You're lucky to have them." She turned and padded over to Mothwing and Hawkfrost.

Mothwing tensed. Was Sasha going to walk away without a word? Or would she give them some last bit of motherly wisdom? Sasha's blue eyes met hers steadily, but she only brushed her pelt against them, first Mothwing, then Hawkfrost.

"I wish you well on your journey," she told them, then padded away into the forest.

Mothwing stared after her, her mouth dry and her heart heavy. *I'll never see her again,* she thought. *We don't even know where we're going.*

"Let's go," Firestar mewed quietly, and the Clans began to pad forward once more. Mothwing looked up at Hawkfrost, but he was staring straight ahead, his eyes narrowed.

"We made the right choice, didn't we?" she asked.

He nodded. "RiverClan is our home."

Hawkfrost was right. But Mothwing shivered, looking at the land stretching out in front of them. They were part of RiverClan, and she had to trust that they were going where they belonged.

CHAPTER 5

Mothwing curled up more tightly in her mossy nest, and pushed her nose between her paws, letting the sound of the stream nearby soothe her aching heart. Heavystep, who had become an elder at the end of their journey to the Clans' new territory, had died yesterday. *I wish I could have saved him.*

Mothwing had known how to treat him. Greencough was a disease every medicine cat dreaded, because it could spread through a Clan as fast as a river overflowing its banks and was often fatal. If she had given Heavystep catmint in time, he would have recovered. She'd searched the territory around the lake. She'd gotten Leopardstar to send out patrols. But none of them had been able to find catmint. And Heavystep had suffered the consequences.

At least she had been able to stop the disease from spreading throughout RiverClan. At the first sign that Heavystep's mild whitecough was developing into greencough, she had isolated him in the elders' den. Not one other cat was showing symptoms.

But that didn't make losing a cat she *could* have saved any easier.

Willowpaw, Mothwing's new apprentice, hesitated at the entrance to the medicine den. "Should I . . . " She trailed off.

Mothwing sat up and twitched her ears at the small gray cat, trying to look reassuring. Willowpaw was just starting to learn the ways of a medicine cat. Mothwing had to guide her, no matter how she was feeling. "I'd like you to try to find some cobwebs for us," she told the younger cat, as cheerfully as she could. "If we have them here in the den, we'll be ready if any cat is injured. You don't even have to leave camp—there are probably some webs between the reeds behind the warriors' den."

"Okay," Willowpaw replied.

"After that, I'll teach you some more herbs," Mothwing told her, and the apprentice nodded eagerly.

"Yes, please," she meowed. She started out of the den, then turned back. "It wasn't your fault," she added quietly. "I saw how hard you worked to save Heavystep."

Startled, Mothwing hesitated, then dipped her head to Willowpaw. "Thank you," she told her. *I feel like it was my fault, though,* she added silently as Willowpaw slipped out of the medicine den.

Willowpaw herself was another worry for Mothwing. The small gray apprentice was eager to help her Clanmates and quick to learn the herbs and techniques she would use to heal their illnesses and injuries. Mothwing was confident that she could train Willowpaw well in all of that.

But there was another part of being a medicine cat, one that Mothwing had failed at over and over again.

I can't believe in StarClan. I just can't.

She had tried. Mothwing had never seen StarClan in a dream, had never had a vision. But that didn't mean StarClan didn't exist. Hawkfrost had cheated the Clan into accepting Mothwing as a medicine cat; maybe StarClan didn't want to share tongues with her.

The other medicine cats believed. They saw visions, they dreamed dreams where they spoke to the dead cats of their Clans, and they saw signs everywhere around them. Mothwing didn't doubt their sincerity: it shone in every word they said. But it wasn't *real.* It couldn't be. When they dreamed their dreams, she thought that their minds must be remembering small things they hadn't noticed, making connections they hadn't thought of, then using memories of cats they had known to explain these things to themselves.

Mothwing couldn't do it. And if she couldn't teach Willowpaw to do it, her apprentice would never be a true medicine cat either.

Mothwing sighed, her tail drooping. She was a good medicine cat in a lot of ways—she *knew* she was. But lately, she felt like she was failing.

The grass and thorny vines that protected the medicine den rustled, and she looked up to see Hawkfrost pushing his way into the den.

"Oof." He shook out his pelt. "Those thorns pull at my fur."

"You're almost too big to fit," Mothwing meowed, eyeing her brother. Hawkfrost seemed to grow broader and more powerfully muscled every day. He had become the most formidable warrior in RiverClan. And right now, his gaze seemed too intent for this to be a casual visit. "What do you need?" she asked.

"I wanted to talk to you," Hawkfrost told her. "As River-Clan's medicine cat, not just my sister."

Mothwing looked at him again. His fur was as thick and shiny as ever, but his eyes were tired, and there was a long scratch across his chest. "Are you feeling all right? Does that scratch need treating?"

"I'm fine." Hawkfrost licked at the scratch quickly. "It's nothing, just a scrape."

"It looks like it was made by claws," Mothwing meowed, worried. Surely, she would have heard if Hawkfrost had been fighting.

"Maybe I got it during battle practice," Hawkfrost answered dismissively. He lowered his voice. "I'm worried about River-Clan, not about myself."

"What's wrong?" Prey was running well, and they'd had little conflict on their shared border with ShadowClan lately. "Have Twolegs been coming onto our territory?" Now that full greenleaf was here, Twolegs had been riding their strange water monsters across the lake, but they rarely came onto the reedy, muddy banks that surrounded RiverClan's camp.

"It's not Twolegs." Hawkfrost tucked his tail more tightly around himself. "I don't like Stormfur and Brook being here."

"Stormfur and Brook?" Mothwing asked, puzzled. The dark gray tom had left RiverClan during their journey and joined the Tribe of Rushing Water in the mountains, but he—and his Tribe mate, Brook Where Small Fish Swim—had recently rejoined the Clan, with little explanation. "They're fitting in, aren't they? They hunt and patrol and all that? Every cat seems to like them."

"Every cat likes them too much," Hawkfrost growled. "I don't trust them."

"Stormfur was one of the cats who went to the sun-drown-place and found the way to our new territory," Mothwing protested. The fur at the back of her neck was prickling uncomfortably. What was Hawkfrost getting at? "He's always been a loyal warrior."

"No, he hasn't!" Hawkfrost jumped to his paws. "He *left* RiverClan. He's a traitor!"

A traitor? Mothwing wondered dubiously. Stormfur had left the Clan, but it was because he had been in love. She didn't think of him as a traitor. All of RiverClan had missed him.

"And Brook! She's not even one of us. RiverClan's just supposed to let her join?"

"They let *us* join," Mothwing reminded him.

Hawkfrost glared at her. "That's not the same thing. RiverClan took us as apprentices. We had to work to be accepted, and we've proved ourselves over and over again. Brook just walked in and she pretends to be a warrior! She can't even fight!" The fur between his shoulders bristled with anger.

"Well, in the Tribe, she was a prey-hunter. She never had to fight," Mothwing shot back, wishing her brother would be reasonable. "Why does it matter, anyway? If Leopardstar is okay with them being here, it's her decision, isn't it?"

"I don't know why she lets them stay." Hawkfrost began to pace, his tail slashing back and forth. "I don't like it."

"Why do you care?" Mothwing asked, puzzled. "Even if they are still loyal to the Tribe, they're no danger to River-Clan. We can always use more hunters."

Hawkfrost stopped pacing and stared at her, his ice-pale blue eyes narrowing. "Leopardstar is the oldest Clan leader now," he meowed. "Before many seasons pass, Mistyfoot will become RiverClan's leader."

"Leopardstar is perfectly healthy," Mothwing replied defensively. She didn't like to think about Leopardstar dying, even though she knew their leader was getting old.

"I want to be RiverClan's next deputy," Hawkfrost told her flatly. "I deserve to be. I'm the strongest warrior in the Clan, and I've always been loyal."

"You're the clear choice to be deputy," Mothwing agreed. "Leopardstar already made you temporary deputy once, when Mistyfoot was missing."

"Yes, but Mistyfoot likes Stormfur better than me!" Hawk-frost hissed. "I don't know who she'd choose."

Mothwing cocked her head, considering. "Do you really think she'd choose Stormfur? You're right about one thing—he did leave the Clan."

Hawkfrost's ears twitched. "Maybe she wouldn't choose him now, but in a few moons? When the Clan's memory of his desertion isn't so fresh? Tigerstar kept both Mistyfoot and Stormfur as prisoners because they were half-Clan cats. He planned to kill them! Don't you think when Mistyfoot becomes leader, she would prefer Stormfur as her deputy, instead of Tigerstar's son?"

Mothwing blinked at him. "Mistyfoot's always accepted us. I'm sure she wouldn't hold what Tigerstar did against you."

"I can't take that chance." Hawkwing's eyes narrowed.

"What do you mean?" Mothwing asked. The prickle of unease was getting stronger. Hawkwing had gotten angrier, *colder,* since they'd traveled to the lake. He'd always wanted to be the best of the RiverClan warriors, but now he seemed to resent any cat who might have an advantage over him.

"I can't risk Mistyfoot choosing Stormfur," Hawkfrost explained. "And I can't do anything about it, but you can."

"*I* can?" Mothwing replied. "It doesn't have anything to do with me."

"You're the medicine cat," Hawkfrost told her. "If *you* told Leopardstar and Mistyfoot that Stormfur and Brook don't belong in RiverClan, they'd have to listen to you."

"Why should I say that?" Mothwing felt her eyes stretch wide. "They're doing well here."

Hawkfrost glanced back over his shoulder, then stepped closer, until his breath was hot on her cheek. "Don't you agree I'd be a good deputy?" he asked softly. "Don't you want to help me? After all we've done for RiverClan, we deserve to lead it. No cat respects the warrior code and what being part of a Clan means more than we do."

Mothwing swallowed. Would Hawkfrost be a good leader? *I'm not sure.* Before they'd come to the lake, she would have said yes. But lately he'd been restless, and she wasn't sure she liked the brooding look in his eyes. She'd seen the same look in the eyes of their ThunderClan half brother, Brambleclaw. The two toms were more alike than she'd thought.

"I can't just tell Leopardstar to get rid of Stormfur," she argued. "Not without a reason."

"Have a reason, then," Hawkfrost answered, even more quietly. "Tell her you had a vision." His tail was sweeping slowly back and forth, as if he scented prey.

Mothwing gasped. "I can't!" she protested. "I couldn't lie about that. Being a medicine cat means I have to be trustworthy." She willed her brother to understand. "The way that it happened—that you tricked Mudfur into thinking he'd gotten a sign about me from StarClan—I've always been ashamed of that. I've been afraid of any cat finding out I'm not a proper medicine cat. It's like heavy paws pushing me down sometimes, knowing that the whole Clan would turn on me if they knew. I *can't* lie again. Being a medicine cat is the most important thing in my life."

Hawkfrost looked at her calmly, his eyes cold. He'd never looked at her quite that way before, and suddenly Mothwing was sure that Tigerstar, the father she'd never met, had looked at cats with that same clear, considering gaze, before he'd done the awful things he did. "Sometimes it takes a lie to keep another lie secret," he meowed softly.

Mothwing jerked back in shock. "You wouldn't tell them, would you?"

There was a long, silent pause. Then, without acknowledging her question, Hawkfrost asked, "What if StarClan sent you a dream? A dream about Stormfur and Brook."

As he outlined his plan, his long claws unsheathed and digging at the dirt of the medicine den's floor, Mothwing couldn't speak. She could only stare at him silently, her heart pounding. She felt scared, and terribly sad. What had happened to her littermate? When had he changed?

"I hope you're proud of yourself," Mothwing muttered. She licked angrily at the long scratches dug into Hawkfrost's belly.

"Ouch!" Hawkfrost protested, jerking away. "You're supposed to be on my side. We belong with each other, remember?"

"I am on your side," Mothwing replied automatically, then stilled for a moment in her treatment of his wounds. Were she and Hawkfrost really allied now? Would he have threatened to expose her if they were? "I'm on RiverClan's side," she amended. "What good does it do the Clan for you to taunt Stormfur into attacking you? When Leopardstar made him and Brook leave, we lost good Clanmates."

"We got rid of a threat," Hawkfrost corrected her. "And I couldn't have done it without you. When you told the Gathering about that dream you made up—two pebbles out of place, stopping the river from flowing smoothly—it began to turn the Clan against them. If our Clanmates weren't already wary of him, they might have seen my fight with Stormfur differently."

"I'm *ashamed* I made up that dream," Mothwing hissed. "I wish I'd never done it."

"Is that why you didn't back me up this time?" Hawkfrost

asked, his voice chilling. "'Sometimes a dream is just a dream,'" he mimicked in a squeaky meow. "You're forgetting where your loyalties lie."

"My loyalties lie with RiverClan," Mothwing told him. "And so should yours."

"They do." Hawkfrost looked down at her with wide, startled eyes. "When I'm the leader of RiverClan, we'll be the strongest Clan of all." He began to purr. "You'll be at my side as medicine cat. We'll take over ShadowClan one day, too. And our brother Brambleclaw will be the leader of ThunderClan, and they'll take over WindClan. All the cats of the forest, safe in our kin's paws."

A cold shudder ran through Mothwing. "That's not right," she meowed. "There have to be four Clans." Taking over the other Clans—wasn't that what Tigerstar had wanted? Was her brother—along with her half brother; she knew Brambleclaw must be part of this plan—following in their father's footsteps?

"There *have* to be?" Hawkfrost asked, still purring. "Who says? StarClan? I thought you didn't believe in them."

"No." Mothwing's tail drooped sadly. "I wish I did. But it's still not right. Isn't RiverClan enough?"

Hawkfrost's ears twitched. "Just keep your mouth shut and stick to giving out herbs," he snapped. He leaned down and pressed his muzzle to hers. "I'll take care of you. And you'll see, RiverClan will thank us in the end. Our home will always be safe."

Hawkfrost's wounds were clean. Instinctively, Mothwing

reached for the marigold, to keep away infection. Who would be treating Stormfur's wounds? She felt suddenly exhausted, the secrets and lies she was carrying weighing her down, pushing her into the mud of the stream banks. Her mouth was sour with guilt.

Maybe RiverClan would be safer with Hawkfrost in the lead, the way he claimed. But she didn't feel safe.

Chapter 6

"It was scary, but it was beautiful, too," Willowpaw gushed, as she and Mothwing walked side by side up the path that led out of the Moonpool's hollow. Mothwing glanced down affectionately at her young apprentice, whose green eyes were shining brightly with excitement.

"You did very well," she meowed. "How does it feel to be an official medicine-cat apprentice?" Mothwing had worried that somehow her secret would come out as she presented Willowpaw to StarClan for the first time. How was she going to guide her apprentice into having the right sort of dreams when she didn't herself?

But it seemed like everything had gone perfectly. Willowpaw had dreamed of StarClan, and if she thought it had been more than a dream, Mothwing wasn't going to discourage her. And Leafpool had offered to guide the apprentice in all the parts of her training where Mothwing couldn't: interpreting the dreams and signs the other medicine cats believed were sent by StarClan.

Mothwing's pelt prickled uneasily as she looked ahead to where she could see Leafpool's silhouette leading them up the path. Had she been right to tell Leafpool the truth? She'd told her everything, from the false sign Hawkfrost had planted to how Hawkfrost had made her lie to turn the Clan against Stormfur. Guilt and horror churned inside her whenever she thought about it, and she'd half expected Leafpool to expose her to the other medicine cats and encourage RiverClan to drive her and Hawkfrost away.

But Leafpool had been so kind. Mothwing wanted to trust her.

Still, Mothwing was nervous. If Hawkfrost, Mothwing's own littermate, could turn on her and use her secrets against her, so could any cat.

As they reached the top of the path, Mothwing breathed in deep and let the cool night air caress and calm her until one thought became clear: *What's done is done.*

Leafpool had pointed out to her that Hawkfrost wouldn't risk telling any cat that he had planted the moth-wing sign. No leader would make him deputy if they knew how he'd lied and cheated. He was as vulnerable as Mothwing was. But the thought wasn't as comforting to Mothwing as it should have been. She wanted them both to be safe.

A shadow fell across the hollow, and Mothwing looked up to see a cloud slipping across the moon. *A proper medicine cat would read a message in that shadow,* she thought, and shivered as a cold breeze blew through her pelt.

Flipping her tail in farewell to Leafpool, and to Barkface and Littlecloud, who were already hurrying in the directions of their own territories, Mothwing turned her attention back to her apprentice as the half-moon reemerged from behind the cloud and they headed toward RiverClan's camp.

"I couldn't tell you about my dream in front of the others, because Leafpool said we don't tell other medicine cats about our dreams unless their Clans are involved," Willowpaw mewed seriously, her green eyes lit by the moonlight.

"What did you dream?" Mothwing asked. It was just a dream, no matter what Willowpaw and Leafpool believed, but even she could admit that the medicine cats' dreams of StarClan often carried truths the medicine cats' waking minds didn't see. Maybe Willowpaw had seen something her mind hadn't realized she'd noticed.

"I was by the Moonpool, just like when I was awake," Willowpaw explained. "But it was only me and Leafpool and this StarClan cat from ThunderClan, Spottedleaf. You and Barkface and Littlecloud weren't there. I was looking into the Moonpool, and at first it just reflected the stars. But then storm clouds started gathering in the pool. And a cold wind blew so hard it almost blew me away." Willowpaw shuddered, her thin shoulders hunching against the remembered storm, then looked up at Mothwing again. "What do you think it means?"

I think it just means you're worried about something. But that wasn't what a medicine cat would say to her own apprentice. "Well," she mewed slowly, brushing her tail across Willowpaw's back, "what do *you* think it means?"

"Maybe trouble is coming?" Willowpaw offered hesitantly. "And because only Leafpool and I saw it, it's coming to

ThunderClan and RiverClan, not to all the Clans?"

"Could be," Mothwing answered. They padded together around the lake toward RiverClan's territory. As they went, Mothwing kept thinking about Hawkfrost. It felt good to have told Leafpool the truth about what was happening, but that hadn't helped her decide what she could do about her brother. *He's changed. He wants power now, not just to be a loyal warrior.* That kind of thirst was bad for the Clan, she was sure of it. It was cooperation, cats working for the Clan instead of themselves, that made RiverClan strong.

Hawkfrost used to know that. What had changed him? What was he going to do?

As they reached the stream that marked the edge of RiverClan's camp, the moonlight was quenched again, blotted out by another, larger cloud overhead. Its shadow fell across RiverClan's camp, throwing it into darkness.

Mothwing's fur brushed Willowpaw's, and she could feel her apprentice shiver.

"Do you think it's a sign?" Willowpaw asked.

"I don't know," Mothwing answered slowly. *I don't need a sign to know that trouble is coming.*

The next day, Mothwing drilled Willowpaw on the uses of herbs. "What's this?" she asked, shoving a fragrant leaf under the apprentice's nose. She enjoyed teaching Willowpaw, passing on the skills that Mudfur had taught her. *I can't give her everything a medicine cat needs, but I'll give her everything I know.*

Willowpaw sniffed. "Borage?" she guessed tentatively.

"Very good," Mothwing praised. "And what's it for?"

"We give it to new mothers to help bring their milk supply," Willowpaw replied, more confidently.

"And?"

"Um." Willowpaw nosed at the leaves again, thinking hard. "It can help bring down fevers," she added at last.

"Great!" Mothwing meowed. "Now what else—" She broke off at a commotion outside the thorny tunnel into the medicine den.

"Quick! Voletooth got stung by bees!" Blackclaw was supporting the small brown tom as they crossed into the den. Voletooth had clearly been stung badly; his face was already swelling up in several places, and one of his eyes was swollen shut. The tom whimpered softly.

"Don't worry, Voletooth, we'll take care of you," Mothwing reassured him. She lapped at the stings, hoping to sooth the pain a little, then looked at Willowpaw. "What do we need to do?" she asked, testing her apprentice's memory.

"What?" The apprentice froze for a moment, then answered hesitantly, "Blackberry leaves? Yes, blackberry leaves! We make a poultice and it'll help the swelling and pain from the stings."

"Well done," Mothwing told her, and returned to licking Voletooth's stings.

Voletooth grimaced. "I must have angered StarClan," he groaned, staring plaintively at Mothwing. "Why else would so many bees come after me at once?"

"I'm sure there's a perfectly good—" Mothwing started.

But Voletooth cut her off, his voice desperate.

"Could you please tell them whatever it is I did to deserve this, I'm sorry?"

Mothwing held his gaze. "That's the pain talking. You're being silly. And anyway, you can always tell them yourself, the same way you'd thank them after a good hunt."

Voletooth yowled. "Yes, but it would make me feel better if a cat who talks to StarClan directly could pass along my message. *Please?*"

Mothwing suddenly felt like an uncertain apprentice again being put on the spot. She didn't want to promise this injured cat she'd do anything that she couldn't actually do. But neither did she wish to deny his request—even if it was silly.

"I—I . . . ," she began uncertainly. She looked up and found Willowpaw staring at her with wide eyes. She saw realization dawning there. *She's figured it out,* thought Mothwing. *She knows I can't talk to StarClan.*

For a long moment, Mothwing worried that Willowpaw would reveal her secret out loud. But instead the young apprentice quickly approached Voletooth, licked at his stings once more, then whispered, "I'm sure StarClan isn't angry with you, but I will tell them what you've said. Don't worry. All will be well." Once again, she glanced up at Mothwing, who could only nod gratefully.

"Hurry now," Mothwing urged, eager to move past the talk of StarClan. "The leaves."

Willowpaw did as she was told and rushed to find the leaves in their stores.

"Oh, no!" she yelped after a moment, her meow edged with panic. "Mothwing, we're almost out of blackberry leaves."

There were blackberries growing at the edge of the horseplace, Mothwing remembered. "I can get some more," she meowed. "Blackclaw, come with me?" She could use the tom's help to help her carry the leaves, and to warn off the cats from the horseplace if they came too close. Blackclaw nodded and helped Voletooth lie down in one of the medicine den's nests.

Willowpaw's eyes widened, and she looked from Mothwing to Voletooth, whose whimpering was getting louder. "I could go instead?" she mewed, clearly reluctant to be left alone with the injured tom.

"No," Mothwing nudged Willowpaw reassuringly. "I know exactly where I can find the leaves. You take care of Voletooth."

Still looking nervous, Willowpaw dipped her head in acknowledgment and went to Voletooth, holding his head steady with one gentle paw. "We'll have you feeling better soon," she murmured, and began to lap at the stings.

She'll be fine, Mothwing thought. Willowpaw was a natural medicine cat, and her instincts were sharp. She knew when she had to offer something Mothwing could not, and she was kind enough to keep that to herself. All she lacked was confidence. It would be good for her to take care of Voletooth on her own. *Maybe I'll have her put the poultice on as well.*

"Let's go." She hurried toward the camp entrance, Blackclaw behind her, wondering how many leaves they'd be able to carry back with them. It would be good to have a store of them on hand—in greenleaf, there were a lot of bees buzzing around the lakeshore.

Hawkfrost was sitting in front of the thicket that concealed the warriors' den, his gaze passing thoughtfully over the cats in camp—the kits playing in front of the nursery, the warriors sharing prey, the apprentices gossiping at the edge of the clearing. They'd barely spoken since Mothwing had told him she would never lie for him again.

Her paws slowed as she passed him, and she jerked her head into a quick dip of greeting. Hawkfrost merely looked at her, his icy blue gaze watchful. Once, she would have been able to tell what he was thinking.

I don't know what's going on in Hawkfrost's head anymore. . . . The thought scared her, and she shivered. But there would be time enough to worry about that later. She pushed Hawkfrost's inscrutable look to the back of her mind and hurried off to gather the leaves she needed. She had a job to do.

Chapter 7

"It's nothing to worry about," Mothwing told Swallowtail a moon later. "The cut is healing, but it's bound to sting a bit if you exert yourself too much."

"Well, I wasn't going to let that trout get away just because my leg hurt a little," Swallowtail purred. "Thanks, Mothwing, I was afraid I'd made it worse."

Before Mothwing could answer, she heard a cat rushing through the tunnel into the medicine den and scented Willowpaw. "What's wrong?" she started to ask as her apprentice emerged, thinking about what herbs they had on hand if some cat was seriously injured.

Then she saw Willowpaw's face. The meow faded before she could speak. Willowpaw looked frightened, and more than that, she looked like she felt intensely sorry for Mothwing. Mothwing stared at her apprentice, her heart pounding, and her mouth grew dry. She couldn't speak.

"Mothwing?" the small gray apprentice said tentatively, and Mothwing broke into sudden motion, pushing past Willowpaw and out into the camp. Something was terribly wrong.

The first cat she saw was Leafpool, and she relaxed a little at the sight of her friend. Maybe things weren't as bad as she thought. Leafpool's clear amber gaze was serious, but she seemed calm. Then Mothwing saw Firestar, the ThunderClan leader, speaking with Leopardstar. Behind him were Brambleclaw and Squirrelflight. Between them, the two warriors were carrying a limp cat, a huge one with dark brown tabby fur, draped across their backs.

Mothwing froze. And then she gasped in horror. *Hawkfrost.*

Her brother was dead.

Every strand of fur on her pelt stiffened, and she walked forward, one slow step at a time, toward her littermate's body. Squirrelflight and Brambleclaw lowered Hawkfrost to the ground and stepped back, respectfully giving her room.

He's not breathing. Mothwing reached out one tentative paw and found that her brother was cold. His chest fur was thick with sticky clumps of drying blood. There was a deep, round wound in his throat.

She turned to look at the ThunderClan cats and realized that her Clanmates were staring at them, too, their pelts bristling with shock and hostility. Leafpool and Squirrelflight looked uninjured, though shaken, but Firestar's neck was badly scratched, and Brambleclaw had claw marks on his throat and side.

"What *happened?*" Mothwing asked at last, her voice thin. Distrust welled up inside her: Brambleclaw and Hawkfrost had planned to rule the territories together one day. Had their plan fallen apart? Or had Brambleclaw decided to eliminate his rival for power instead of working with him?

As she stared at Brambleclaw, the tabby tom's shoulders slumped and he gazed past her, his eyes dark with horror. *No,* Mothwing decided. Whatever had happened, the ThunderClan tom did not look like a triumphant victor.

"I think we'd all like to know what happened," Leopardstar growled, her dappled tail slashing from side to side. "Why are ThunderClan cats bringing me the dead body of one of RiverClan's best warriors? We need an explanation, Firestar!"

Firestar blinked solemnly. "Hawkfrost was killed by a fox trap," he began. "It was a terrible accident. I'm so sorry." He gazed around at the assembled RiverClan cats, who stared back at him with a mixture of hostility and grief. "I know that many cats, both in and out of RiverClan, will mourn him."

Suspicion ran through Mothwing, and she unsheathed her claws, digging at the earth of the clearing. Hawkfrost was *dead.* Surely RiverClan would rise up against these ThunderClan cats who had brought his body here. Mothwing trembled, her body shaking with grief and rage.

But Leopardstar bowed her head solemnly. "He was a great warrior and a loyal RiverClan cat," she meowed. "Thank you for bringing Hawkfrost home, but I ask you to leave now so that we can sit vigil for him."

"Of course." Firestar glanced at his Clanmates. In response, Squirrelflight and Bramblestar moved toward the camp entrance, but Leafpool stayed where she was.

"I need to speak to Mothwing," she announced.

Leopardstar's eyes widened in surprise, but she only replied, "That's Mothwing's choice." Mothwing walked toward the medicine den, gesturing with her tail for Leafpool to follow. Her paws felt as heavy as stones. She was aware of Willowpaw hurrying behind them.

When they were safely inside the medicine den, she rounded on Leafpool. "What *happened*?" she growled again. The ThunderClan cat hesitated, and Mothwing went on, desperately, "Please don't lie to me, Leafpool. My brother was a dangerous cat. But I have to know the truth."

Leafpool swallowed hard. Then she glanced at Willowpaw.

"You can speak freely in front of Willowpaw," Mothwing told her. She trusted her apprentice.

Willowpaw nodded solemnly. "I would never betray one of Mothwing's secrets," she said. Mothwing knew that to be true. Willowpaw had guessed Mothwing's greatest secret—that she didn't speak to StarClan. But instead of revealing what she knew, her apprentice had simply stepped up and taken care of that aspect of a medicine cat's duties herself.

Leafpool hesitated, then finally spoke, her voice almost a whisper. "Hawkfrost tried to kill Firestar," she mewed, and Mothwing froze, horrified.

"He wouldn't," she protested hoarsely, but something inside her insisted: *He would.*

"He led him into a fox trap and told Brambleclaw to kill him so that Brambleclaw could become leader of ThunderClan," Leafpool went on. "But Brambleclaw wouldn't do it. He saved Firestar instead. Hawkfrost attacked Brambleclaw, and Brambleclaw put the stick at the end of the fox trap through Hawkfrost's throat." She looked miserable. "Brambleclaw was just defending himself. And Firestar."

Mothwing squeezed her eyes shut. It was *true*, she knew it. She remembered Hawkfrost's voice, saying that one day he and Brambleclaw would lead the Clans together. He hadn't been willing to wait. She felt sick.

Leafpool's tail brushed across her back. "I'm so sorry, Mothwing," she continued. "Only a few of us know, and we'll keep how Hawkfrost died a secret. There's no reason to hurt RiverClan that way."

Willowpaw came close on her other side, her pelt touching Mothwing's, reassuring her. "He wasn't all bad," she meowed softly. "RiverClan knows there was more to Hawkfrost than ambition."

Was there? Mothwing thought bleakly. She remembered the eager kit her brother had been, and how devastated he had been at Tadpole's death. She and Hawkpaw had clung to each other when they were apprentices, abandoned by their mother, with no other cat to depend on. But Hawkfrost had changed.

He had decided they would stay in RiverClan when Sasha left. *He* had faked the sign that made sure Mothwing was chosen to become a medicine cat. He had lied and schemed, grasping at power.

Mothwing moaned and collapsed to the floor, pushing her face between her paws. Was that a tiny thread of *relief* running through her? Now she didn't have to worry about what Hawkfrost would do, or what terrible thing he would try to make her do. And now she knew that no cat would ever reveal her secret: that she had never been chosen by StarClan, that she couldn't even bring herself to believe in them. Only Leafpool and Willowpaw knew, and she trusted them utterly.

At this realization, that she trusted the other medicine cats more than she'd been able to trust her own littermate—the cat who'd belonged to her, and who she'd belonged to, the only one—Mothwing began to wail with misery. Leafpool and Willowpaw pressed closer, trying to comfort her.

I loved him. I did *love him, Hawk, my littermate, despite everything. How can I never see him again?* But they had lost each other somewhere along the way.

Moons had passed since Hawkfrost had died. Mistystar was the leader of RiverClan now, and Willowpaw had become a full medicine cat alongside Mothwing. The Clans had gone on. But there was always a small hurt spot deep inside Mothwing where she held on to the memory of him. *My brother.*

And yet the work of a medicine cat went on. It was something she could rely on.

"Okay," she told Duskfur, pushing thoughts of Hawkfrost away. "I'll keep giving Podkit comfrey for a few more days, but his cough should be gone soon. He'll be fine."

The gray-and-white kit bristled. "Yuck! These leaves taste horrible!"

"They'll make you strong, though," Mothwing stroked the kit's back with her tail. "Be as brave as a grown warrior and eat them up."

Duskfur purred. "Thank you, Mothwing."

"You're welcome," Mothwing replied. "Now, you've heard

what Mistystar said. Be careful, and if any trouble starts, stay in the nursery where your Clanmates can protect you and your kits."

Duskfur stopped purring. "Do you really think something's going to happen?" she asked. "Is the Dark Forest coming?"

"I don't know," Mothwing told her. "But we should take precautions, just in case."

As Duskfur and Podkit left the medicine den, Mothwing exchanged a worried look with Willowshine.

"I've been making the bundles," Willowshine meowed, nodding at a neat pile of leaf-wrapped herbs at her feet. "Each one has all the right herbs to treat a cat's wounds, plus cobwebs. We'll be prepared."

Mothwing sniffed at the herb bundles, smelling the sharp scents of marigold and nettle. "Good thinking," she told her Clanmate, then burst out, "Do *you* really think the Dark Forest is coming?"

Willowshine held her gaze, her green eyes steady. "I'm sure of it."

The Dark Forest was where Clan cats believed that their wicked Clanmates went when they died. Cats who broke the warrior code so badly that they didn't deserve to go to StarClan ended up in the Dark Forest. Mothwing had always assumed that, like StarClan, the Dark Forest was only a story.

But strange things had been happening. The medicine cats of each Clan—including Willowshine—had told their Clanmates that StarClan wanted them to enforce their borders and keep away from the other Clans. Even the medicine cats had stopped meeting at the Moonpool. Before, Mothwing had just shaken her head. Why did intelligent cats let the imagined mumblings of the dead control their actions?

Then some of her Clanmates had begun acting strangely: Turning up in the medicine den with battle injuries at dawn when they had headed into their dens uninjured the night before. Seeming exhausted after a long night's sleep. Sneaking off to scheme with cats from other Clans, who they seemed to know better than they should.

Jayfeather, the young blind medicine cat from ThunderClan, had come to Mothwing and told her that these cats, and cats from every Clan, were being trained in the Dark Forest by the most vicious cats from every Clan: Tigerstar, Darktail, Brokenstar, Mapleshade . . . cats who had died before she was born, but whose names were remembered with a shudder. And Hawkfrost.

Now, prompted by their medicine cats, the Clans were uniting to prepare for an invasion by the Dark Forest cats.

It can't *be true,* Mothwing thought. The dead were dead and gone.

But this wasn't like the other medicine cats' dreams and signs, which were so easy for Mothwing to explain away. Cats she trusted claimed to have seen the Dark Forest cats. Beetlewhisker, a young warrior, had disappeared from his nest one night, leaving no trace behind. The scents of strange cats had started turning up deep inside every Clan's territory. All the Clans were getting ready for an invasion.

It can't be true, Mothwing thought again. But it was her

responsibility to protect her Clan. So she would prepare as if it were.

She nodded to Willowshine. "I'll get some moss so we can bring water to the wounded." *It won't hurt to have it. Just in case.*

Mothwing pushed her way through the tunnel and came out into the clearing at the center of RiverClan's camp. The air was thick with tension, and every cat seemed to be in motion. Mistystar was calling out orders, her deputy Reedwhisker beside her, assigning cats to guard duty and extra patrols. Graymist and Mallownose were squaring off against Pebblefoot and Grasspelt, practicing battle moves. Icewing and Minnowtail were reinforcing the brambled sides of the elders' den and the nursery, making sure that no cat could easily break through. Mosspelt, her fur bristling, was pacing in front of the nursery entrance. Even the elders, Dapplenose and Pouncetail, looked fierce and alert.

Nine RiverClan warriors were missing, gone to fight for the other Clans, and ShadowClan and WindClan cats who had come to fight for RiverClan wove their way between Mothwing's Clanmates, their scents dry and distinct among the familiar fishy smells of RiverClan.

"Where are the ThunderClan cats?" she asked Dapplenose, and the mottled gray she-cat flicked her ears.

"Late," she spat. "Even though trading warriors was all Firestar's idea. Who knows if they'll come at all."

Paws pounded through the reeds outside of camp, and Mothwing cocked her ears. "Maybe this is them now," she said. A moment later, Foxleap burst through into the clearing, his reddish-brown sides heaving. Toadstep and Rosepetal were close behind, their eyes wide and shining with panic.

"They're coming," Foxleap yowled. "The Dark Forest is attacking!"

CHAPTER 8

"Breathe slowly," Mothwing advised, trying to ignore the screeches and yowls of battle outside the medicine den.

Mosspelt groaned, her eyes shut, and Mothwing wrapped cobwebs around the gaping wound on her leg, pressing hard to stop the bleeding. "I have to . . . protect the kits," the tortoiseshell warrior insisted weakly.

"They're fine," Mothwing reassured her, hoping desperately that it was still true. "Every RiverClan cat will protect them with their lives." Mosspelt didn't answer, and Mothwing saw that she had lost consciousness. Her breathing was steady, though, and, once Mothwing had finished bandaging her wound, she picked up another bundle of herbs and headed out into camp.

As she hurried through the tunnel, the sounds of battle became deafening. In the clearing, so many cats were fighting that Mothwing had trouble picking out her individual Clanmates. It all seemed to be a mass of fur and blood and rage.

Mistystar, blood running down her chest from multiple wounds, was grappling with a long-legged dark tabby Mothwing didn't recognize—*a Dark Forest cat? Or a rogue?* Mothwing wondered. Dapplenose, Pouncetail, and Duskfur were tightly bunched in front of the nursery entrance, facing off against a wild-eyed cat with patches of black, white, and brown fur covering his pelt. Willowshine was at the far side of the clearing, wrapping cobwebs around a wound on Troutpaw's leg. Rosepetal, one of the ThunderClan warriors, stood over them, fending off attackers as Willowshine worked.

The strange cats were fighting like warriors, only even more fiercely. As Mothwing watched, the calico landed a mighty blow on Duskfur's neck, sending her to her knees. *That's a warrior's blow.* Were these cats really from the Dark Forest?

And if they were, where was StarClan?

If the other medicine cats were right all along, why isn't StarClan protecting us?

A moan of pain made Mothwing refocus. Whether the dead walked the Clan territories or not, she was still a medicine cat, and she had to help her Clanmates. Minnowtail was lying near the warriors' den, her face a mask of blood, and Mothwing made her way toward her, dodging battling cats.

"It's all right," she mewed soothingly, dropping her bundle of leaves next to Minnowtail. The warrior's injuries didn't look so bad, now that she was close to them. A long, shallow cut across her forehead was producing most of the blood.

"Mothwing," Minnowtail whimpered. "I have to tell you the truth. I didn't know what I was doing."

"Don't worry," Mothwing told her automatically. She cleaned Minnowtail's face, relieved to see that the she-cat's eyes were undamaged.

"You don't understand!" Minnowtail yowled, pushing Mothwing's paws away. "I trained in the Dark Forest. I gave away our battle secrets. They said they were training me to be a better warrior for my Clan."

Mothwing stared at her, feeling cold.

"They said they'd kill me," Minnowtail croaked. "But I would never have betrayed RiverClan." Her amber eyes stared into Mothwing's, pleading.

"Traitor!" The yowl was almost a roar, and Mothwing turned to see a gray Dark Forest cat swipe a heavy paw at Minnowtail. Instinctively, she crouched, shifting her body to protect the injured cat. Before the blow fell, Mallownose barreled at their attacker with a snarl, knocking him to the ground. Trying to shut out their struggle, Mothwing quickly staunched the flow of blood from Minnowtail's wound and chewed up some marigold to stop the infection.

Her mind was spinning. The Dark Forest was *here*—dead cats who lived on after death. That meant StarClan must exist as well. But where were they? Didn't they care? How had they let things get this far? Hot anger blossomed in her chest.

As she raised her head from Minnowtail's wound, another familiar cat rushed through the tunnel.

Hawkfrost. Mothwing rose to her feet and stared at him, her mouth dry and her heart pounding.

It was undoubtedly her littermate. He looked as powerfully muscled as ever, but he was no longer the sleek young cat who had died all those seasons ago. His coat was dull and matted, the shape of his ribs clear beneath his fur. Blood ran from his cheek, and one of his eyes was swollen shut. And the other eye was lit with fury and hot hate, different from the cold ambition of the living Hawkfrost. He looked *insane*.

This new Hawkfrost stood in the clearing for a moment, his good eye darting from one tangle of battling cats to another. Then, in one swift move, he turned toward the nursery.

Duskfur and the elders, bleeding but still standing, snarled at him, bunching more closely together. Hawkfrost, hissing, swung one huge paw, his claws extended, and slashed Dapplenose across the throat.

Blood streamed down her chest and the old she-cat collapsed, her eyes already glazing with death. Pouncetail and Duskfur yowled in horror.

"Hawkfrost!" Mothwing screeched.

Her brother jerked back and stared at her, his blue eyes lingering on hers for a long heartbeat.

"Don't," she pleaded. "Please."

Hawkfrost's face was unreadable. Was the sweet, brave kit she remembered still in there somewhere? After a long moment, he turned away and took a step toward the nursery.

"No!" Mothwing yowled. She leaped over the still-moaning Minnowtail and started toward him.

Then she stopped in confusion. Cats had begun to stream through the rushes that fringed the RiverClan camp. Some of them were familiar but changed, stars shining in their fur.

Leopardstar, her face grim. Dawnflower, her gray tail bushed. Voletooth, Blackclaw, Heavystep, and others, cats who must be from before Mothwing's time with the Clans.

At their advance, Hawkfrost fell back. Leopardstar, her ears pulled back in fury, prowled toward him, flanked on either side by starry-furred warriors.

Hawkfrost snarled, but then his nerve broke. He turned and fled, the other Dark Forest warriors following, rushing out of camp after him.

Mothwing felt as hollow as a dry husk. *Did we win?*

Her mind was spinning. She had always thought that the dead were gone forever. But today they had come back. *Hawkfrost,* the brother she had loved, had returned. But he had brought an army to fight the living, had tried to destroy the Clan he had once protected so fiercely.

All around her, her Clanmates were moving forward to greet their old friends in StarClan. Mistystar ran forward, purring despite her wounds, and pressed her muzzle to Leopardstar's. Stonestream bowed his head to Heavystep, who had once been his mentor. Even Minnowtail struggled to her paws, the blood beginning to stream down her face again, and twined her tail with her mother Dawnflower's. Everywhere Mothwing looked, the dead and the living greeted one another joyfully.

But around them, injured cats lay, some groaning, some quiet and still. Their blood soaked into the earth of the clearing. Dapplenose's body lay across the nursery entrance, her empty blue eyes staring at nothing. Mothwing bent to pick up her bundle of herbs.

"Mothwing."

Jerking up her head, she saw Mudfur standing before her.

His fur, thick with stars, was a rich brown now instead of flecked with gray, his golden eyes warm. For a moment, affection surged through her, and she stepped forward to press her nose against his shoulder, breathing in his familiar, comforting scent. "I've missed you," she whispered.

"You've done very well," Mudfur told her. "I'm proud of you."

Mothwing pulled back, her anger returning as she saw again the dead and wounded on the ground. "Where *were* you? Where was StarClan?"

Mudfur cocked his head to one side. "What do you mean?"

Gesturing with her tail at the injured cats, Mothwing said, "When the Dark Forest attacked us! Or earlier, when they were planning to invade! If StarClan exists, why didn't you stop all this from happening?" She thought of Hawkfrost, wild-eyed and furious. It would have been better for him, too, never to have come back to RiverClan. "You told the medicine cats to keep the Clans apart, when what we needed was to band together!"

Mudfur bowed his head. "We cannot always see the future," he told her. "And when we do, sometimes we can't act. StarClan could help in this battle, but it was the living Clans that had to come together to defeat the Dark Forest. What happened today will determine the Clans' future, their unity and harmony, for many moons."

"Cats had to die for unity and harmony?" Mothwing bristled. "All I see is StarClan's numbers growing."

"No cat ever *has* to die for things to get better," Mudfur

replied sadly. "But sometimes it seems to be the only way for the Clans to truly see their path."

With a growl of frustration, Mothwing turned her back on him. But she could still hear Mudfur's voice.

"After all this time not being able to reach StarClan, you'll turn away from us now?"

Mothwing whipped back around, her tail bushed in anger. "You know the worst thing for any medicine cat is to see so many of her Clanmates suffering. Why can't StarClan settle the battles between Clans without all this bloodshed? It's like everything I do is *useless*."

Mudfur brushed his tail along her back. "Don't think that way. You're a fine medicine cat."

Mothwing scoffed. "I shouldn't even be a medicine cat!" She aimed her words like claws at Mudfur and the other cats of StarClan. "Hawkfrost tricked you. He planted the moth's wing outside your den." Mudfur gazed at her, his calm expression unchanged. "Doesn't that bother you? You made a mistake. I wasn't the apprentice you wanted."

Mudfur's gaze softened. "I might have been deceived then, but StarClan wasn't," he assured her. "If I had to be tricked into taking you as an apprentice, I'm glad of it. You've done your duty for your Clan. StarClan makes no mistakes."

Stepping away from her, Mudfur began to fade. Leopardstar, her pelt shimmering, led the rest of the StarClan cats out of camp. From Dapplenose's body, a pale form—Dapplenose, young again—rose and followed.

As the cats around her burst into wondering chatter,

Mothwing looked again at the injured lying on the ground. *StarClan makes no mistakes?* All the cats who had died—drowned kits like Tadpole, sick elders, cats who had died on the journey to their new territory or during the long drought, all the cats who had died in accidents or battle—was that *meant* to happen?

In the past, she had wondered how the other cats could believe in StarClan. Now she saw that life after death was real. But StarClan wasn't the all-seeing force for good the other medicine cats seemed to think it was.

We can't rely on our ancestors. We can only rely on one another. That was what she had learned today. Bending to pick up her bundle of herbs again, Mothwing was filled with a new sense of resolution. StarClan didn't matter. She had Clanmates to care for.

CHAPTER 9

Mothwing padded beside the edge of the lake, her ears twitching as she took in the sounds of Twolegs playing in their water monsters and of black-headed gulls calling overhead. In her mouth she carried a fresh stock of catmint, picked from near the Twolegplace, and the sun warmed the fur of her back pleasantly. It was a good day.

Newleaf had come again, and, except for a few minor skirmishes over borders, the Clans had been at peace since their great battle with the Dark Forest. Maybe they would stay that way now that they had been allies in such a desperate struggle for survival. But Mothwing doubted it. Warriors loved to fight, and the Clans' rivalry with one another tied Clanmates more securely together. Still, she would enjoy the peace while she could.

Hawkfrost had not been seen in Clan territory again, nor had any of the other Dark Forest cats. She had to assume that they had returned to the Dark Forest and that they wouldn't be back.

The sun was beginning to journey down the sky when she crossed the stream that protected RiverClan's camp.

"Quick! Get her inside!" A desperate yowl broke the calm, and Mothwing pricked up her ears in alarm. The voice—and a babble of softer, worried voices, she heard now—came from the entrance to RiverClan's camp.

She dropped the catmint and began to run.

A patrol was bunched at the center of camp, their voices high with panic.

"It came out of nowhere!"

"Be *careful* with her."

"We need a medicine cat. Where's Mothwing? Where's Willowshine?"

"Let me pass." Mothwing pushed her way through the knot of warriors. Across the clearing, she saw Willowshine hurrying out of the medicine den. In the center of the group, supported between Icewing and Mallownose, Petalfur hung limply, her fur streaming with blood.

"Put her down," Mothwing mewed. There was no time to take Petalfur into the medicine den; they had to treat her now. She had so *many* wounds. Some were little more than scratches, but dark red blood welled from worryingly deep punctures—bite marks—on her belly.

"It was a dog." Mallownose's voice shook as he gently lowered his mate to the ground. "It came out of *nowhere*. We all fought it off, but it grabbed Petalfur in its mouth. . . ." His voice trailed off, his eyes clouded with fear. "You have to save her."

"She'll be all right," Mothwing reassured him, trying to assess which of Petalfur's wounds were most serious. The she-cat's eyes were open but dazed, and she didn't seem to be hearing what was said around her. "Willowshine, bring me some cobwebs."

Willowshine was quick, and the two medicine cats worked together, pressing the webs on the bites. The most important thing was to staunch the bleeding. But as she pressed down, more blood gushed out of Petalfur's wounds, warm and thick, soaking Mothwing's paws. Petalfur began to gasp—choking, panicked noises—and struggled, trying to rise.

"Mallownose, hold her down," Mothwing ordered. Petalfur was in too much pain to understand that they were trying to help her.

"StarClan is watching over you," Willowshine whispered comfortingly into Petalfur's ear. "They'll guide our paws, and we will keep you safe."

Mothwing sighed to herself—why would StarClan help now, when they let so many cats die every season?—but Petalfur stilled as if Willowshine's words had comforted her.

If believing that StarClan will help us makes Willowshine and Petalfur feel better, that's fine, Mothwing thought. *But I know we're on our own.*

It was hard to believe one small she-cat had so much blood in her. The cobwebs were soaked, and the pressure they were applying didn't seem to be helping at all. Willowshine looked at Mothwing, her green eyes desperate. "She's losing too much blood," she mewed.

Mothwing's heart was fluttering like a trapped bird in her chest, but she took a deep breath. *I've been a medicine cat for a long time. Mudfur trained me well, and I've treated many cats since then.* All those moons ago, she had begged to become a medicine cat, and she had never regretted it. This was her purpose.

"Let's try horsetail," she decided. "Run and get as much as we have. We've got to stop this bleeding."

She concentrated on trying to hold the edges of Petalfur's injuries together, hoping to slow the gushing blood, until Willowshine returned. Then she began to chew the bristly stemmed plant into a poultice as Willowshine cleared the cobwebs away from the bites.

She put the poultice on thickly, smearing it across the wounds until they were completely covered with the thick green paste. Slowly, the bleeding became a trickle. "Now the cobwebs," she added, and she and Willowshine carefully wrapped them over the poultice.

Petalfur was still now, and she blinked her eyes, trying to focus on the worried faces around her. "What's happening?" she asked, her voice faint. "Mallownose?"

"I'm here," her mate meowed quickly.

"Let's get her into the medicine den," Willowshine ordered. "If you help me, Mallownose, we can take her there without reopening her wounds." Mothwing watched as they lifted the wounded warrior gently to her paws and started toward the medicine den.

The circle of cats around them breathed in relief at last. "Thanks be to StarClan," Mistystar mewed softly.

Mothwing stopped herself from flicking her tail in irritation. StarClan hadn't guided her paws, or told her what herb to use. It was Mothwing and Willowshine's training and skill that had saved Petalfur. For a moment, resentment snagged like a claw on her heart.

Then she shook out her pelt and let her anger go. Whether StarClan had helped them or not, Petalfur would be healed, and that was what mattered. Calmly, she followed her patient toward the medicine den.

It had been the right decision to stay with Hawkfrost in RiverClan, all those moons ago. It had brought her the unity of a Clan. And it had been the right choice to ask Mudfur to train her.

This is exactly where I should be. I belong in the medicine den, and I belong in RiverClan.

Mothwing had a Clan, and she would save every cat she could.

KEEP READING FOR A SNEAK PEEK AT A NEW WARRIORS ADVENTURE!

WARRIORS

As a bitter leaf-bare season descends on the lake territories, the five warrior cat Clans face moons of cold and darkness—and far worse, the voices of their ancestors in StarClan have grown dim and silent. Only one medicine cat apprentice still hears them, in a strange vision that warns of a looming shadow within their borders. One that may threaten the warrior code itself.

Chapter 1

Shadowpaw craned his neck over his back, straining to groom the hard-to-reach spot at the base of his tail. He had just managed to give his fur a few vigorous licks when he heard paw steps approaching. He looked up to see his father, Tigerstar, and his mother, Dovewing, their pelts brushing as they gazed down at him with pride and joy shining in their eyes.

"What is it?" he asked, sitting up and giving his pelt a shake.

"We just came to see you off," Tigerstar responded, while Dovewing gave her son's ears a quick, affectionate lick.

Shadowpaw's fur prickled with embarrassment. *Like I haven't been to the Moonpool before,* he thought. *They're still treating me as if I'm a kit in the nursery!*

He was sure that his parents hadn't made such a fuss when his littermates, Pouncestep and Lightleap, had been warrior apprentices. *I guess it's because I'm going to be a medicine cat. . . .* Or maybe because of the seizures he'd had since he was a kit. He knew his parents still worried about him, even though it had been a while since his last upsetting vision. *They're probably hoping that with some training from the other medicine cats, I'll learn to control my visions once and for all . . . and I can be normal.*

Shadowpaw wanted that, too.

"The snow must be really deep up on the moors," Dovewing mewed. "Make sure you watch where you're putting your paws."

Shadowpaw wriggled his shoulders, praying that none of his Clanmates were listening. "I will," he promised, glancing toward the medicine cats' den in the hope of seeing his mentor, Puddleshine, emerge. But there was no sign of him yet.

To his relief, Tigerstar gave Dovewing a nudge and they both moved off toward the Clan leader's den. Shadowpaw rubbed one paw hastily across his face and bounded across the camp to see what was keeping Puddleshine.

Intent on finding his mentor, Shadowpaw barely noticed the patrol trekking toward the fresh-kill pile, prey dangling from their jaws. He skidded to a halt just in time to avoid colliding with Cloverfoot, the Clan deputy.

"Shadowpaw!" she exclaimed around the shrew she was carrying. "You nearly knocked me off my paws."

"Sorry, Cloverfoot," Shadowpaw meowed, dipping his head respectfully.

Cloverfoot let out a snort, half annoyed, half amused. "Apprentices!"

Shadowpaw tried to hide his irritation. He was an apprentice, yes, but an old one—medicine cat apprentices' training lasted longer than warriors'. His littermates were full warriors already. But he knew his parents would want him to respect the deputy.

Cloverfoot padded on, followed by Strikestone, Yarrowleaf,

and Blazefire. Though they were all carrying prey, they had only one or two pieces each, and what little they had managed to catch was undersized and scrawny.

"I can't remember a leaf-bare as cold as this," Yarrowleaf complained as she dropped a blackbird on the fresh-kill pile.

Strikestone nodded, shivering as he fluffed out his brown tabby pelt. "No wonder there's no prey. They're all hiding down their holes, and I can't blame them."

As Shadowpaw moved on, out of earshot, he couldn't help noticing how pitifully small the fresh-kill pile was, and he tried to ignore his own growling belly. He could hardly remember his first leaf-bare, when he'd been a tiny kit, so he didn't know if the older cats were right and the weather was unusually cold.

I only know I don't like it, he grumbled to himself as he picked his way through the icy slush that covered the ground of the camp. *My paws are so cold I think they'll drop off. I can't wait for newleaf!*

Puddleshine ducked out of the entrance to the medicine cats' den as Shadowpaw approached. "Good, you're ready," he meowed. "We'd better hurry, or we'll be late." As he led the way toward the camp entrance, he added, "I've been checking our herb stores, and they're getting dangerously low."

"We could search for more on the way back," Shadowpaw suggested, his medicine-cat duties driving out his thoughts of cold and hunger. He always enjoyed working with Puddleshine to find, sort, and store the herbs. Treating cats with herbs made him feel calm and in control . . . the opposite of how he felt during his seizures and the accompanying visions.

"We can try," Puddleshine sighed. "But what isn't frostbitten will be covered with snow." He glanced over his shoulder at Shadowpaw as the two cats headed out into the forest. "This is turning out to be a really bad leaf-bare. And it isn't over yet, not by a long way."

Excitement tingled through Shadowpaw from ears to tail-tip as he scrambled up the rocky slope toward the line of bushes that surrounded the Moonpool hollow. His worries over his seizures and the bitter leaf-bare faded; every hair on his pelt was bristling with anticipation of his meeting with the other medicine cats, and most of all with StarClan.

He might not be a full medicine cat yet, and he might not be fully in control of his visions . . . but he would still get to meet with his warrior ancestors. And from the rest of the medicine cats he would find out what was going on in the other Clans.

Standing at the top of the slope, waiting for Puddleshine to push his way through the bushes, Shadowpaw reflected on the last few moons. Things had been tense in ShadowClan as every cat settled into their new boundaries and grew used to sharing a border with SkyClan. Not long ago, SkyClan had lived separately from the other Clans, in a far-flung territory in a gorge. But StarClan had called SkyClan back to join the other Clans by the lake, because the Clans were stronger when all five were united. Still, SkyClan had needed its own territory, which had meant new borders for everyone, and it had taken time for the other Clans to accept them. Shadowpaw was relieved that things seemed more peaceful now; the brutally cold leaf-bare had given all the Clans more to worry about than quarreling with one another. They were even beginning to rely on one another, especially in sharing herbs when the cold weather had damaged so many of the plants they needed. Shadowpaw felt proud that they were all getting along, instead of battling one another for every piece of prey.

That wasn't a great start to Tigerstar's leadership. . . . I'm glad it's over now!

"Are you going to stand out there all night?"

At the sound of Puddleshine's voice from the other side of the bushes, Shadowpaw dived in among the branches, wincing as sharp twigs scraped along his pelt, and thrust himself out onto the ledge above the Moonpool. Opposite him, halfway up the rocky wall of the hollow, a trickle of water bubbled out from between two moss-covered boulders. The water fell down into the pool below, with a fitful glimmer as if the stars themselves were trapped inside it. The rippling surface of the pool shone silver with reflected moonlight.

Shadowpaw wanted to leap into the air with excitement at being back at the Moonpool, but he fought to hold on to some self-control, and padded down the spiral path to the water's edge with all the dignity expected of a medicine cat. Awe welled up inside him as he felt his paws slip into the hollows made by cats countless seasons before.

Who were they? Where did they go? he wondered.

The two ThunderClan medicine cats were already sitting beside the pool. Shadowpaw guessed it was too cold to wait outside for everyone to arrive, as the medicine cats usually did.

Alderheart was thoughtfully grooming his chest fur, while Jayfeather's tail-tip twitched back and forth in irritation. He turned his blind blue gaze on Puddleshine and Shadowpaw as they reached the bottom of the hollow.

"You took your time," he snapped. "We're wasting moonlight."

Shadowpaw realized that Kestrelflight of WindClan and Mothwing and Willowshine, the two RiverClan medicine cats, were sitting just beyond the two from ThunderClan. The shadow of a rock had hidden them from him until now.

"Nice to see you, too, Jayfeather," Puddleshine responded mildly. "I'm sorry if we're late, but I don't see Frecklewish or Fidgetflake, either."

Jayfeather gave a disdainful sniff. "If they're not here soon, we'll start without them."

Would Jayfeather really do that? Shadowpaw was still staring at the ThunderClan medicine cat, wondering, when a rustling from the top of the slope put him on alert. Looking up, he saw Frecklewish pushing her way through the bushes, followed closely by Fidgetflake.

"At last!" Jayfeather hissed.

He's in a mood, Shadowpaw thought, then added to himself with a flicker of amusement, *Nothing new there, then.*

As the two SkyClan medicine cats padded down the slope, Shadowpaw noticed how thin and weary they both looked. For a heartbeat he wondered if there was anything wrong in SkyClan. Then he realized that he and the rest of the medicine cats looked just as skinny, just as worn out by the trials of leaf-bare.

Frecklewish dipped her head to her fellow medicine cats as she joined them beside the pool. "Greetings," she mewed, her fatigue clear in her voice. "How is the prey running in your Clans?"

For a moment no cat replied, and Shadowpaw could sense their uneasiness. *None of them wants to admit that their Clan is having problems.*

Shadowpaw was surprised when Puddleshine, who was normally so pensive, was the first to speak up. Maybe the cold had banished his mentor's reserve and enabled him to be honest.

"The hunting is very poor in ShadowClan," he replied; Shadowpaw felt a twinge of alarm at how discouraged his mentor sounded. "If this freezing cold goes on much longer, I don't know what we'll do."

The remaining medicine cats exchanged glances of relief, as if they were glad to learn their Clan wasn't the only one suffering.

Willowshine nodded in agreement. "Many RiverClan cats are getting sick because it's so cold."

"In ThunderClan too," Alderheart murmured.

"We're running out of herbs," Fidgetflake added with a twitch of his whiskers. "And the few we have left are shriveled and useless."

Frecklewish gave her Clanmate a sympathetic glance. "I've

heard some of the younger warriors joking about running off to be kittypets," she meowed.

"No cat had better say that in my hearing." Jayfeather drew his lips back in the beginning of a snarl. "Or they'll wish they hadn't."

"Keep your fur on, Jayfeather," Frecklewish responded. "It was only a joke. All SkyClan cats are loyal to their Clan."

Jayfeather's only reply was an irritated flick of his ears.

"I don't suppose any of you have spare supplies of catmint?" Kestrelflight asked hesitantly. "The clumps that grow in WindClan are all blackened by frost. We won't have any more until newleaf."

Most of the cats shook their heads, except for Willowshine, who rested her tail encouragingly on Kestrelflight's shoulder. "RiverClan can help," she promised. "There's catmint growing in the Twoleg gardens near our border. It's more sheltered there."

"Thanks, Willowshine." Kestrelflight's voice was unsteady. "There's whitecough in the WindClan camp, and without catmint I'm terrified it will turn to greencough."

"Meet me by the border tomorrow at sunhigh," Willowshine mewed. "I'll show you where the catmint grows."

"This is all well and good," Jayfeather snorted, "every cat getting along, but let's not forget why we're here. I'm much more interested in what StarClan has to say. Shall we begin?" He paced to the edge of the Moonpool and stretched out one forepaw to touch the surface, only to draw his paw back with a gasp of surprise.

"What's wrong?" Puddleshine asked. One by one, the medicine cats cautiously approached the Moonpool's surface. Shadowpaw sniffed the Moonpool curiously, then reached out a tentative paw. He was stunned when he hit something solid. *What in the stars . . . ?* Instead of water, he had touched ice, so thin that it gave way under the pressure of his pad, the splinters bobbing at the water's edge.

"The Moonpool is beginning to freeze," Kestrelflight meowed, while Shadowpaw licked the icy water from his paw. *That felt really weird!*

"Well, that proves it: the cold is worse than usual," Jayfeather grumbled.

"Has it never happened before?" Fidgetflake asked, his eyes wide.

"I can't recall it happening before," Mothwing replied in an even voice. "There has been ice in the Moonpool from time to time, but I don't remember it freezing all the way through."

"Well, never mind—it's time to share dreams with StarClan," Jayfeather announced abruptly. "Maybe they can tell us how long we have to suffer this bitter cold."

"And maybe we'll be able to speak with Leafpool," Willowshine added, her voice soft with grief.

Shadowpaw had hardly known the ThunderClan medicine cat, but he had heard stories about her and knew how much every cat in the forest admired her. Even though ThunderClan had two other medicine cats, they must be feeling the loss of Leafpool as if a badger had torn away one of their limbs. He noticed that Jayfeather had closed his eyes, as if he was struggling with desperate pain, and he remembered that Leafpool had been Jayfeather's mother as well as his mentor.

Suddenly Shadowpaw could forgive all Jayfeather's earlier gruffness. *Dovewing can be really embarrassing at times, treating me like I'm still a kit, but I can't imagine how much it would hurt to lose her.*

Alderheart drew closer to his Clanmate. "She still watches over us from StarClan," he murmured.

"I know." Shadowpaw could hardly hear Jayfeather's low-voiced response. "But even for medicine cats, it's not the same."

Huddling together for warmth, the nine medicine cats stretched their necks out over the Moonpool and lowered their heads to touch their noses to the surface. Shadowpaw's breathing grew rapid from excitement. Within a couple of heartbeats, he knew, he would find himself transported into StarClan; either that, or the StarClan warriors would leave their territory and come to meet with the living cats at the Moonpool.

Instead there was only silence. Then, as the moments crawled by, Shadowpaw heard a confused clamor of cats' voices, faint as if coming from an immense distance. He couldn't make out what the cats were trying to say, or even if there were coherent words in their cries. Alarmed, Shadowpaw looked up to find cloudy images in the sky, like scraps of softly glowing mist. For a few heartbeats, each of the scraps would almost solidify into the form of a cat, then fade and dissolve again into a shapeless blur.

Icy fear flooded over Shadowpaw, and he pressed himself closer to Puddleshine's side. Fighting back panic, he tried to tell himself that he was being stupid. *I haven't been to the Moonpool as many times as the others,* he told himself. *Maybe this isn't unusual.*

But as the misty images faded, Shadowpaw saw that the other medicine cats were staring at one another, shocked and unnerved. "Has this happened before?" he asked, striving to stop his voice from squeaking like a terrified kit.

Kestrelflight shook his head. "I've never seen anything like that before," he replied. "I've never even heard of it, not from any cat."

The other medicine cats murmured agreement.

"What does it mean?" Shadowpaw asked. "It can't be good . . . right?"

"I wouldn't worry about it." Puddleshine pressed his muzzle briefly into Shadowpaw's shoulder, a comforting gesture. "Maybe it's because the Moonpool is freezing over. Once it thaws, the StarClan cats will be stronger presences again."

Shadowpaw wished he could believe his mentor, but the other medicine cats were exchanging doubtful looks, and he wasn't sure that even Puddleshine believed what he had just said. However, no cat spoke to contradict him. None of them seemed ready to talk about what had happened—they just headed back up the slope and out of the hollow, then said their farewells.

Padding at Puddleshine's side on the way back to ShadowClan, Shadowpaw still felt a worried tingle in his fur. *If this has never happened before, why is it happening now? What does it mean?* Turning to Puddleshine, he opened his jaws and began, "What do you—"

But Puddleshine's expression had grown somehow remote, as if he was turned in on himself in thought. Shadowpaw didn't know why, but he got the sense that this wasn't the time to bother his mentor with an apprentice's questions.

Remembering the cloudy shapes and the distant voices, Shadowpaw felt a dark cloud hovering over him and all the Clans, as if a devastating storm were about to unleash itself. Once again he tried to tell himself that he was anxious because he didn't have the others' experience. He just needed more time to get used to it.

Surely that's all it is . . . right?

WARRIORS

How many have you read?

Dawn of the Clans
- ❍ #1: The Sun Trail
- ❍ #2: Thunder Rising
- ❍ #3: The First Battle
- ❍ #4: The Blazing Star
- ❍ #5: A Forest Divided
- ❍ #6: Path of Stars

The Prophecies Begin
- ❍ #1: Into the Wild
- ❍ #2: Fire and Ice
- ❍ #3: Forest of Secrets
- ❍ #4: Rising Storm
- ❍ #5: A Dangerous Path
- ❍ #6: The Darkest Hour

The New Prophecy
- ❍ #1: Midnight
- ❍ #2: Moonrise
- ❍ #3: Dawn
- ❍ #4: Starlight
- ❍ #5: Twilight
- ❍ #6: Sunset

Power of Three
- ❍ #1: The Sight
- ❍ #2: Dark River
- ❍ #3: Outcast
- ❍ #4: Eclipse
- ❍ #5: Long Shadows
- ❍ #6: Sunrise

Omen of the Stars
- ❍ #1: The Fourth Apprentice
- ❍ #2: Fading Echoes
- ❍ #3: Night Whispers
- ❍ #4: Sign of the Moon
- ❍ #5: The Forgotten Warrior
- ❍ #6: The Last Hope

A Vision of Shadows
- ❍ #1: The Apprentice's Quest
- ❍ #2: Thunder and Shadow
- ❍ #3: Shattered Sky
- ❍ #4: Darkest Night
- ❍ #5: River of Fire
- ❍ #6: The Raging Storm

Select titles also available as audiobooks!

HARPER
An Imprint of HarperCollinsPublishers

www.warriorcats.com • www.shelfstuff.com

SUPER EDITIONS

- ❍ Firestar's Quest
- ❍ Bluestar's Prophecy
- ❍ SkyClan's Destiny
- ❍ Crookedstar's Promise
- ❍ Yellowfang's Secret
- ❍ Tallstar's Revenge
- ❍ Bramblestar's Storm
- ❍ Moth Flight's Vision
- ❍ Hawkwing's Journey
- ❍ Tigerheart's Shadow
- ❍ Crowfeather's Trial
- ❍ Squirrelflight's Hope

GUIDES

- ❍ Secrets of the Clans
- ❍ Cats of the Clans
- ❍ Code of the Clans
- ❍ Battles of the Clans
- ❍ Enter the Clans
- ❍ The Ultimate Guide

FULL-COLOR MANGA

- ❍ Graystripe's Adventure
- ❍ Ravenpaw's Path
- ❍ SkyClan and the Stranger

EBOOKS AND NOVELLAS

The Untold Stories
- ❍ Hollyleaf's Story
- ❍ Mistystar's Omen
- ❍ Cloudstar's Journey

Tales from the Clans
- ❍ Tigerclaw's Fury
- ❍ Leafpool's Wish
- ❍ Dovewing's Silence

Shadows of the Clans
- ❍ Mapleshade's Vengeance
- ❍ Goosefeather's Curse
- ❍ Ravenpaw's Farewell

Legends of the Clans
- ❍ Spottedleaf's Heart
- ❍ Pinestar's Choice
- ❍ Thunderstar's Echo

Path of a Warrior
- ❍ Redtail's Debt
- ❍ Tawnypelt's Clan
- ❍ Shadowstar's Life

A Warrior's Spirit
- ❍ Pebbleshine's Kits
- ❍ Tree's Roots
- ❍ Mothwing's Secret

HARPER
An Imprint of HarperCollins Publishers

www.warriorcats.com • www.shelfstuff.com

Don't miss these other Erin Hunter series!

SURVIVORS

Survivors
- ❍ #1: The Empty City
- ❍ #2: A Hidden Enemy
- ❍ #3: Darkness Falls
- ❍ #4: The Broken Path
- ❍ #5: The Endless Lake
- ❍ #6: Storm of Dogs

Survivors: The Gathering Darkness
- ❍ #1: A Pack Divided
- ❍ #2: Dead of Night
- ❍ #3: Into the Shadows
- ❍ #4: Red Moon Rising
- ❍ #5: The Exile's Journey
- ❍ #6: The Final Battle

SEEKERS

Seekers
- ❍ #1: The Quest Begins
- ❍ #2: Great Bear Lake
- ❍ #3: Smoke Mountain
- ❍ #4: The Last Wilderness
- ❍ #5: Fire in the Sky
- ❍ #6: Spirits in the Stars

Seekers: Return to the Wild
- ❍ #1: Island of Shadows
- ❍ #2: The Melting Sea
- ❍ #3: River of Lost Bears
- ❍ #4: Forest of Wolves
- ❍ #5: The Burning Horizon
- ❍ #6: The Longest Day

HARPER
An Imprint of HarperCollinsPublishers

www.shelfstuff.com

www.warriorcats.com/survivors • www.warriorcats.com/seekers